Son
of
INTERFLUX

Also by Gordon Korman

Born to Rock

Son of the Mob

Son of the Mob 2: Hollywood Hustle

Jake, Reinvented

The On the Run series

The Everest trilogy

The Dive trilogy

The Island trilogy

Son
of
INTERFLUX

Gordon Korman

Scholastic Canada Ltd.

Toronto New York London Auckland Sydney
Mexico City New Delhi Hong Kong Buenos Aires

Scholastic Canada Ltd.
604 King Street West, Toronto, Ontario M5V 1E1, Canada

Scholastic Inc.
557 Broadway, New York, NY 10012, USA

Scholastic Australia Pty Limited
PO Box 579, Gosford, NSW 2250, Australia

Scholastic New Zealand Limited
Private Bag 94407, Greenmount, Auckland, New Zealand

Scholastic Children's Books
Euston House, 24 Eversholt Street,
London NW1 1DB, UK

Library and Archives Canada Cataloguing in Publication

Korman, Gordon
Son of Interflux / Gordon Korman.

First published: New York : Scholastic, 1986.
ISBN 0-439-93873-2

I. Title
PS8571.O78S66 2006   jC813'.5   C2006-901215-6

6 5 4 3 2 1   Printed in Canada   06 07 08 09 10

For the 1986 All-Wall Street Team,
Nick Parcharidis
and
Sotirios "Sam" Panageas,
and
Sheldon "Shank" Paradis,
the class of '86 MVP

NEWSTIME MAGAZINE

Interflux Now World's Largest Corporation

According to a poll recently published by a London consulting firm, the international manufacturing giant, Interflux, is now the largest and richest corporation on the planet. There are virtually no Americans who have not heard the name Interflux. Most, in fact, have not only heard the name, but have in some way experienced the awesome power wielded by this company. Surprisingly few, however, can name a single product manufactured by the largest corporation in the world. And this is for good reason, since Interflux does not manufacture things, but rather parts of things.

The company was founded on one principle: for every two useful things in the world, there is a need for a third thing, useless by itself, to make the useful things even more useful together.

Interflux got its start in 1807 with the development of the toilet seat. There was the seat, and there was the toilet. An unnamed young inventor, sponsored by the Montrose family, designed the device that connected the two, and an empire was born.

The new enterprise quickly expanded to include a new generation of buggy whips, making neither the handle nor the whip, but the little thing that held the two together.

Interflux was fortunate enough to hold ninety-nine-year worldwide exclusive patents on these two items so that, by the time the patents ran out, the company had the financial resources to go into useless trivia in a big way. With the invention of the automobile, Interflux began to manufacture twelve distinct mechanical parts, not one of which was considered significant enough ever to make a schematic diagram published by any auto company, but without which no car could operate. Similarly, Interflux soon acquired seventy-five percent of the world's ballpoint pen business, making not one pen, but turning out billions of tiny balls for the ball points.

The list grew by leaps and bounds, and mammoth manufacturing plants sprang up like mushrooms all over the globe. Interflux, a company which had still yet to make an item complete, slowly and steadily made itself absolutely indispensable to the smooth running of modern society.

It now manufactures the central pin that attaches hands to all clocks and watches, the fuzz that makes Velcro stick, parts of light-bulb filaments, the right-click button (but only the right one) on a computer mouse, seven tiny parts of a machine used exclusively for stitching baseballs, and more than fifteen thousand other varieties of vital non-essentials. Perhaps most insignificant and profitable on this impressive tally is the sole product of the large Interflux installation in Greenbush, N.Y. — zipper teeth. In fact, Interflux controls a staggering ninety-four and four-tenths percent of the world's zipper teeth market, boasting that for every hamburger served by McDonald's, the Greenbush plant alone produces more than twenty thousand zipper teeth.

This Long Island zipper teeth Mecca is soon to become Interflux's new Head Office in a massive expansion program which will bring many of the company's top brass to the area. Perhaps from this new nerve center, Interflux will take its next great step and produce an actual finished item.

4

One

The black-and-red Mustang GT coupe had been a gift from his parents for his sixteenth birthday. It tooled down the highway at just under fifty, whitewall radials singing on the wet pavement. Through the late afternoon drizzle, his eyes made out a road sign which read:

> GREENBUSH, NEW YORK
> HOME OF INTERFLUX
> A GOOD NEIGHBOR

Simon Irving winced. Interflux. Every place he'd lived had had that same sign. The part about the good neighbor had been his father's idea. After all, who had more right? He was the senior executive vice-president of Interflux International, the world's largest and most useless corporation.

He turned off at Schuyler Avenue and drove through a massive housing development of identical little boxes which stretched as far as the eye could see, each finished in Long Island modern and carefully placed in the center of its own little patch of crabgrass. Beyond that was the large Interflux installation, soon to be a whole lot larger. That was what the Irvings were doing there — not living in Greenbush, but in adjacent Fosterville, which looked exactly the same. Past Interflux, the land was, for the most part, undeveloped, with the exception of small clusters of older established homes. It formed an attractive setting for the Nassau County High School for Visual, Literary, and Performing Arts.

Simon pulled into the parking lot and nosed the Mustang into the first available space. The school was an ultramodern low rambling building, its roof dotted with skylights. The land around it was flat and green, stretching up to the fringes of a large wooded area to the north, the Interflux property to the east and south, and on the west to a small shopping center, marking the limits of yet another town, DeWitt.

Locking the car, he strode determinedly toward the main entrance, whistling nervously through his teeth. The admissions interviews were being held in the office area. Simon was twenty minutes early for his appointment, so he took a seat in the waiting room in a crowd of hopeful young students. By now, Emile Querada had had over a week to examine his art portfolio. This, then, was the moment of truth. If Querada hated his paintings and threw him out on the street, his father would interpret this as a dead end in art leading to a bright future in Interflux. Simon set his jaw. It must not be. He was good; he knew he was. But would that win him a spot in Querada's small, handpicked painting seminar?

A secretary stood up in front of the group, consulting a list in her hand. "Is Irving Simon here?" she drawled.

Simon stood up. "That's Simon Irving."

"Whatever. Mr. Querada will see you now."

As Simon approached the department head's office, the door opened to reveal a young girl sobbing into a large handkerchief. She brushed by him and ran out of the building. Squaring his shoulders, Simon entered.

Emile Querada, six feet eight inches tall, with a long wispy beard and burning wild eyes, was a fearsome sight. Wide-eyed, Simon eased himself into the chair the artist indicated.

"You are Irving Simon."

"Simon Irving, sir. There seems to be some misunderstanding — "

"It does not matter. Querada has looked at your work. I'm very impressed."

Simon couldn't hold back a foolish grin. He said, "Thank you, sir," and then Querada blew his stack.

"Don't thank me!" the artist bawled, standing up and waving his arms in the air. "You think this is good news? No! This is a curse! I honestly wish I could tell you you stink, and let you get on with your life!" He sat down, breathing hard. "But you chose to be one of my students, which means you have no life."

"Well, this is what I was hoping for, and — "

"Too much work, too much sweat, too much pain,"

said the artist abstractedly. "Is it all worth it?"

"Well, uh — " Simon began.

"Stop!" snapped Querada, thrusting out a large hand as though directing traffic. "That question must never be answered. And you, Mr. Simon, will work more than any of your friends or acquaintances. You will curse Querada on a regular basis. Congratulations, and I'm truly sorry."

Dazed, Simon took the proffered hand. "I'm — I'm accepted, then?"

"Let me tell you a story. When I was in Bologna, I knew a very brilliant and talented artist who had only one problem. He asked stupid questions. When a person was overcome with joy at his work, he would say, 'It's all right, then?' One day he asked one too many stupid questions, and someone shot him. Yes, you are accepted." He scowled. "Even though we stress art as much as we possibly can, the state insists that you also receive a high school education. It must never interfere with your painting. On the first day of school you will register for all that irrelevant stuff. Here is something also to bear in mind. Seven times in the last eight years, a Querada student has won the New York State Vishnik Prize. Last year a creep from Albany won. This year it will be a Querada student again — " his voice rose sharply in pitch, " — *or I will know the reason why!*" He punctuated this last statement by pounding on his desk so hard that a paperweight of Atlantic City took flight and shattered on the floor, spraying water and artificial snow on Simon's shoes. The artist smiled. "Welcome to my class."

Simon tried to stammer out his thanks, but was interrupted when Querada bellowed, "Next!" Another boy came in, and Simon supposed that his interview was over. He all but fled, restraining his ecstasy. Now he could go home and tell his parents he'd been accepted at Nassau Arts. So much for Abercrombie Prep, which led to Harvard Business School, which led to Interflux.

Giddy with exultation, he stopped beside the Mustang and couldn't resist thumbing his nose at the tallest Interflux smokestack, presently belching filth over Greenbush (just within the legal limit, of course).

An amused voice came from a few feet down the line of parked vehicles. "I see you're a big Interflux fan."

Simon wheeled, flushing to the roots of his fair hair. Standing beside a battered, ancient orange Volkswagen Beetle was a slender boy with dark curly hair and an engaging smile that radiated the highest degree of friendliness.

Simon grinned sheepishly, mumbled something about it being a long story, and got into the car. He switched on the ignition, but the only result was a low-power hum. He tried again. Same response. Disgusted, he got out of the car, lifted the hood, and peered inside.

A few vehicles down, the ancient Beetle roared into action in a small blue cloud of burnt oil. The car backed out, leaving a trail of flaked rust in its wake, and came to a creaky stop behind the Mustang. The dark-haired boy leaned out the window. "Sounds like your plugs are wet to me."

"Oh," said Simon, managing to convey his helplessness. "Uh — I don't want to sound stupid, but — what do I do?"

The dark-haired boy pulled a rag from his lidless glove compartment, got out of his car, and approached the Mustang. "The name's Phil Baldwin," he said, drying off the plugs and points. "Nice car. There. That ought to do it," he added, slamming the hood shut.

"Simon Irving. Thanks." The two shook hands, and Simon came away with a handful of grease.

"Oops. Sorry." Phil grinned. "The wreck's not clean, but it gets me where I'm going. I saw you inside in painting. Is it a yes or a no?"

"I'm in. How about you?"

"I got a conditional acceptance in sculpture," said Phil. "They say my stuff isn't any good as it is, but that I show a lot of potential."

"That's pretty good," Simon approved.

"Well — not exactly. You see, I show potential for a lot of things, but I don't usually deliver."

"Pardon?"

"It all started when I was five. I showed the promise to be a concert pianist; but by nine, I was all thumbs. I was going to be a child model, but then my nose grew faster than the rest of my face. They had me pegged for chessmaster, too, because I was wiping up the competition at ten years old. I still play like the best ten-year-old in the business. It's the story of my life. I've got hopes, but I don't intend to be crushed if I bomb out at sculpting, because I've been down that road before."

"That's a good attitude," Simon said politely, not knowing what else to say. "Tell me, do most of the kids enter Nassau Arts at the beginning of high school? I'm in eleventh grade. My family just moved here."

"You should be all right. They come in at all levels. I'm in eleventh, too. I did two years at Greenbush High. It's a write-off. My next-door neighbor's been here since freshman year. He's in painting, too — Sam Stavrinidis. His real name is Sotirios in Greek. He's co-owner of the wreck." He smiled. "As you can see, we were both a little short of cash. I'd just failed to live up to my potential as a short-order cook, and Sotirios had blown the bundle on a lot of art supplies. He's a really cool guy. I'll introduce you. Anyway, I'd better get going. My family eats early because my brother works the night shift at the plant."

"You mean Interflux?" Simon asked weakly.

"The very same. My dad used to work there, too. That's why when I saw you saluting the plant, I couldn't resist sticking my nose in. Have you got some kind of beef, or are you just an ecologist?"

"A little bit of both," said Simon evasively.

"Well, anyway, I'll see you Monday morning at registration. Sotirios says it's a mess." He jumped into his car and rattled off, waving out the window until he was out of sight.

The Mustang started on the first try, much to

Simon's relief, and he turned out of the parking lot and headed for home. The fact of his acceptance at Nassau Arts flooded over him again, providing a feeling of security as he drove past the Interflux plant and took the highway toward Fosterville. He hoped his father wouldn't be too upset at the news. His dad was really a great guy, except for his total devotion and unwavering loyalty to Interflux.

Simon sighed. Luckily, Phil Baldwin jumped around from subject to subject so often that the real reason for Simon's disrespectful gesture toward the smokestack had never come out. He certainly didn't want to go through school wearing the tag "Son of Interflux." He was determined to fit in at Nassau Arts.

* * *

"Hi, Mom; hi, Dad. I'm home. Guess what? I was accepted at Nassau Arts!"

"That's wonderful, dear!" called Mrs. Irving from the kitchen. "Wash up and join us in the dining room. Dinner's almost ready."

Mr. Irving was already at the table. He was very much Simon's father, a fair-haired man of medium height and build who radiated the confidence of his executive position. As was his custom in the evening, he had abandoned his hand-tailored business suit for more casual sports clothes.

"Congratulations, son."

Simon could see his father wasn't too thrilled with the news, but was trying to put a good face on things. He appreciated the effort.

12

"Mr. Querada seemed to like my work."

"Get ready for a surprise," called Mrs. Irving from the doorway. "Vegetarian lasagna." She entered the dining room and placed a steaming casserole dish in the center of the table.

"We're not vegetarians," Simon felt moved to point out.

"I read an article in our new local paper, *The Sun,*" she explained, seating herself opposite her husband and doling out massive portions of what looked like pasta, ketchup, and cottage cheese. "Executives your father's age are prone to heart disease. We don't eat enough healthy foods."

"Quite right, too," agreed Mr. Irving, setting straight to his dinner. He flashed Simon a crooked grin, and unobtrusively held up three fingers, which Simon knew was the signal for "Meet you at Burger King in three hours." This was a common occurrence with the family, as Mrs. Irving was quite prone to sudden dietary experiments and general health kicks. These usually lasted only a few days, but there were notable exceptions. Simon could remember twenty-five straight days of bran, during which time he and his father had dropped a small fortune into the coffers of Howard Johnson's. The manufacturers of Kaopectate had fared pretty well, too.

"Isn't it delicious?" beamed Mrs. Irving.

Her husband nodded enthusiastically, while at the same time changing his signal to only two fingers. Simon nodded his understanding. Even two hours would be a painful wait.

"So," said Mrs. Irving conversationally, "tell us about the famous Mr. Querada."

Simon thought a moment. How would you describe Querada? "He's a little tough to figure out, but I think I'm going to enjoy working with him. He's really somebody, you know. He's exhibited in all the best galleries and museums."

"I'm very impressed," said Mrs. Irving. "And how about you, Cyril? How was your day?"

Her husband's brow clouded over. "Don't ask. The Flake is on the loose again."

Simon stifled a grin. The Flake was his father's name for Kyle Montrose, president and chairman of the board of Interflux. If there was a flaw in the Interflux empire, it was Montrose, who had inherited his position, along with thirty percent of the company, ten years earlier at age twenty-two. The spoiled son of a fabulously wealthy businessman, Montrose cared nothing for his company except that it provided him with the money to lead the wild and reckless life of an international playboy, topping gossip columns with his celebrated antics. The embarrassment invariably fell on Interflux, and lay heavy on the shoulders of Mr. Irving, who always claimed that his true function was not running the company, but absorbing all the hard knocks so that everybody else would be free to run the company. He had come to dread Montrose's every move.

"I thought he'd dropped out of sight for a while," said Mrs. Irving.

"He got bored with his retreat in Indonesia, and

14

decided to take in a little London night life. He attended a Royal Gala Command Performance of the London Ballet, where he — acted wholly inappropriately."

"Good heavens, what did he do?"

"Well," said Mr. Irving reluctantly, "he acted in such a way as to draw untoward attention to himself."

Simon spoke up. "Come on, Dad. This isn't a press conference. Tell us."

Mr. Irving flushed. "If you must know, he mooned a duke and two earls! I was on the phone with reporters all day. You know those London tabloids. They eat you for breakfast! Why don't things like this ever happen to IBM?"

Simon stared into his plate to hide his laughter, but all he saw was his leftover lasagna. He consulted his watch. An hour and a half to Burger King.

Two

Although Simon had not yet met Sam Stavrinidis, he respected his opinion already. Registration really was a mess. Standing in various waiting areas and lines for over an hour and a half, Simon signed himself up for a semester that looked more like a life's work. He had a double period with Querada in addition to art history, and design and composition, not to mention summary courses in math, English, and biology. The whole process took him doubly long since all his information had been inexplicably filed under "Irving Simon."

Though Nassau Arts was a selective school, its attendance area included Long Island itself, New York City, and Westchester County, and its students numbered over fifteen hundred. Each was provided with a Nassau Arts orientation packet, which contained a school map, brochures and course lists, commuter information, and other important papers, including a booklet of money-saving coupons from the nearby DeWitt Shopping Plaza.

Riffling through his packet, Simon pulled out a

small printed business card which read:

T.C. SERRETTE,
EDUCATIONAL AGENT, LOCKER #0750,
YOUR MOUTHPIECE AT NASSAU

Simon looked up in perplexity. There, right beside the guidance office, was a large table. Behind it sat an immaculately groomed dark young man, resplendent in a navy blue three-piece business suit with a tastefully subdued necktie. On the wall behind him hung a sign which read: T.C. SERRETTE AGENCY. He was greeting old acquaintances and chatting engagingly with the passing parade. Intrigued, Simon approached the booth.

"Well, I'm really glad to see you're in business again this year, T.C.," a tall red-haired girl was saying. "I think I might have washed out last term without you to bat for me."

T.C. smiled. "Nice to see you again, Kathy. Call on me anytime." His eyes fell on Simon. "Hi. New here?"

"My first day. If you don't mind my asking, what's this all about?"

"Oh, this is my educational agency. At Nassau Arts you run into a lot of situations — you know, with grades, or teachers, or administration. You need good solid representation. That's where I come in. I know all the staff. I've worked with them all before. And I plead your case."

"You can get people higher grades?" Simon asked in disbelief.

"Well, it's usually not as simple as that. There's give and take. But I can always work something out."

Simon goggled. "Why can't the students speak for themselves?"

"Uh-uh. Too risky. At a regular high school that might be all right, but here you're going to want professional assistance." He noted the incredulous look on Simon's face, and smiled tolerantly. "I can see you're finding this a little hard to swallow, but in a couple of weeks you'll see exactly how it works. Let me guess — you're in painting, right?"

Simon nodded. "How did you know?"

"Just a little hobby of mine. Querada can be tough. And the academics have a habit of creeping up on you. If you have any problems, just come to see me."

"Well, I don't think so, but thanks anyway."

T.C. smiled knowingly. "See you later." It sounded like a promise.

Simon's locker, #1102, was located at the very beginning of a long hall in the music wing. He was stowing his coat, mentally repeating his combination, when a booming voice rang through the hallway.

"Hey! Simon! Over here!"

A little way down the hall stood Phil Baldwin, waving and beckoning. He met Simon halfway and led him to the locker adjacent to the washroom. Phil indicated a tall, olive-skinned boy who was stowing books and art supplies in the next locker. "Hey, Sotirios, get your head out of there. I want you to meet somebody. This is the guy I was telling you about."

Sam emerged, his gear satisfactorily placed, and Phil performed the introductions.

"Hey, I just saw the weirdest thing," Simon told them. "There's this guy who's like an educational agent or something. He speaks for you when you get into a jam."

"Oh, yeah. T.C. Serrette," said Sam. "The school couldn't run without him."

"Have you ever used his services?"

"He's the only person who can get a word in edge-wise with Querada."

"Let me get this straight," said Phil. "Whenever you get in big trouble with grades or something, and the staff is getting ready to hose you, you call in this guy and he gets you out of it?"

"Don't make any big plans to set fire to the building, Philip. T.C. couldn't get you off for that. But he's really good when you need a break. My freshman year, I ended up on geography probation for a term. Any test mark below B and I was out. T.C. bargained them down to B minus. But when the next test came along, I only got a C plus. Then T.C. convinced them to search for a few extra marks in my paper on the grounds that I promised to do a make-up report. It saved my neck."

"Do you have to pay him?" asked Simon.

"In a way. You see, he's from Canada. Somehow or another, he talked them into letting him study here — he's in music — sax — but he doesn't have any-where to live, and he's usually pretty low on cash. So when he works for you, you have to let him come over and stay at your house."

"No way!" laughed Phil.

"Oh, it's okay. Parents love him because he's very polite and always well-dressed."

Phil looked worried. "How long do you have to keep him?"

Sam laughed. "Anticipating trouble, are you, Philip?"

"Oh, you know — if sculpting doesn't pan out, I might need someone to negotiate a transfer."

"Well, the longest he ever stayed at my house was five days. That was probation, which was a pretty big job. But usually it's only two or three."

Simon made a mental note to avoid T.C. Serrette at all costs. Any stay at his house lasting more than five minutes would pinpoint him as the son of Interflux. If a visitor somehow managed to miss the GOOD NEIGHBOR front doormat, there were still the Interflux envelopes, stationery, and Interflux TIME IS MONEY telephone notepads. Then there was the fact that only rarely would ten minutes go by in the Irving household without at least one mention of Interflux.

As the conversation progressed from Serrette to Querada to general school experiences, one thing became abundantly clear to Simon. Sam Stavrinidis was a great favorite among the female population of Nassau Arts. They were coming up to him in droves to ask how his summer had been and to gaze adoringly into his handsome face. Even those who didn't know him stared long and hard as they passed by. Sam was very casual with them, and was always careful to introduce Simon and Phil, who were received politely and instantly dismissed from sight and mind. Phil took it very well, but Simon was developing a massive inferiority complex. He was almost tempted to yell out, "My father is the senior executive vice-president of Interflux!" whereupon the girls would forget Sam, swept away with visions of the Italian Riviera and charge accounts at Bloomingdale's. No. Nothing was worth that. Maybe one day he would achieve the devil-may-care attitude of The Flake and could moon British nobility with impunity. But if he did, it would be as the world's greatest painter, not as a business tycoon.

* * *

Simon and Sam both opened their year in Emile Querada's painting workshop. The painter was at his intimidating best, looking like a combination of Rasputin and Larry Bird.

"You can't get entertainment like this anywhere else in the world, even for money," Sam whispered as Querada launched into the first temper tantrum of the year.

Simon was rigid with shock. This wild-eyed giant was pacing back and forth in front of the class, tearing at his beard, still howling about last year's Vishnik Prize.

"Bad brushwork! *Terrible* brushwork! I still see it in my mind! Oh, it's painful!" Then suddenly, the storm was over, and he looked benignly down at the class. "This year I'd like to concentrate on improving our brushwork."

Weirdest of all was the fact that Simon was the only one in class who was even faintly perturbed by Querada. The other students, Sam included, sat in impassive relaxation, their expressions ranging from mild boredom to vague interest and slight amusement as the teacher discussed each student's recent work, occasionally flying off the handle and just as suddenly calming down.

"Where is your sense of color?" he bellowed at Peter Ashley, stamping his size fourteen construction boot on the boy's desk top as easily as a normal person might have stepped up on a footstool. "No apple is this purple! If I saw an apple this color, I wouldn't paint it. I would take it to Ripley's Believe It or Not."

"I'll try to do better," said Peter casually, right into the teacher's face not four inches away.

"That's all I can ask for," said Querada kindly. "Let me tell you a story. When I was in Munich, there was an artist whose only claim was that he always did his best." His brow clouded. "One night he froze to death in the park, because his best wasn't enough to pay his rent. *He painted purple apples just like this one!"*

"Do the cops know about this guy?" Simon whispered nervously.

Sam grinned. "This is nothing. When Nassau Arts first hired Querada, they had to do over this room in special acoustic tile because the other teachers were complaining about the noise."

Steeling himself to absorb the shocks of Querada's frequent blow-ups, Simon also tried to concentrate on learning something about his fellow classmates. At the top of the talent ladder was junior Laura Dixon, who came in for her share of the ranting as runner-up in last year's Vishnik competition. Also very good were Bob Lawrence and his girlfriend, Grace Chernik, who had first met under the barrage of a Querada tirade. Peter Ashley also seemed to be one of the class's stars, purple apples notwithstanding. The workshop had twelve students in all, but Querada reserved the spotlight of that opening class for Sam Stavrinidis.

"Mr. Stavrinidis, I don't know where my mind was last year, but looking through your portfolio, I made a peculiar discovery. Every picture you submitted had at least one camel in it."

"Well, sir," Sam explained, "that's because I do a lot of Middle Eastern desert scenes, so the camels fit into the subject matter."

"What about your 'View of Central Park,' Mr. Stavrinidis, which I, like an idiot, allowed you to submit for the Vishnik competition? There was a hansom cab pulling two young lovers. My heart is warm. But since Central Park is not in the Middle Eastern desert, why is that hansom cab being pulled by a camel?"

"I felt it was appropriate," said Sam evenly. Simon braced himself for an explosion that would bring the house down, but none came. Instead, Querada marched silently up to the blackboard, reared back, and pounded his forehead against the board so hard that the slate cracked. Simon waited for him to fall unconscious, but he merely stood there, facing away from the group, his head enveloped in a cloud of chalk dust.

"Don't laugh," whispered Sam. "Just hold it in until after class."

Simon hadn't intended to laugh. He was thinking more along the lines of running for his life. In fact, the only thing that kept him in his seat was that not one other student seemed to think that anything out of the ordinary had taken place.

Querada turned to face them, smiling benignly. "One last thing. Everybody welcome our new student, Mr. Simon. Sometimes it's difficult to be new, so let's show a little extra understanding and patience." The artist then asked them each to bring a quick nature sketch tomorrow, and dismissed the class.

Simon was still shaking as he and Sam headed back to their lockers after the double period. "I don't understand how you can just sit there with that — that psychopath!"

"Best art teacher in the world," said Sam with conviction.

Simon looked dubious. "Best!? The man should be locked up! He's dangerous!"

"He's soft as a kitten. His bark is a lot worse than his bite."

"He broke a chalkboard with his face! He yelled at poor Peter Ashley so loud it took the curl out of his hair! And poor Laura Dixon! He insulted her and everyone her height!"

"Querada loves Laura," Sam insisted.

Simon stared at him in disbelief. "Well then, heaven save me from being loved by Querada!"

* * *

Schuyler's Creek was a favorite spot of many of the Nassau Arts students. It was a peaceful location about fifteen minutes' hike along a small trail through the wooded area to the north of the school. Sam brought Simon there after classes. Simon's head was spinning from his first day at Nassau Arts. With Querada's tantrum still ringing in his ears, he'd been hit with five other classes, three of them academics, all of them hard. He was certainly looking forward to a little peaceful sketching in the quiet of the woods, but this was not to be, as Phil also trekked out with them.

"I'm as good as dead in the Sculpture Department," Phil was moaning. "Have you seen some of the stuff those guys do? It's fantastic. I couldn't even dream of dreaming of being that good. I'm in big trouble!"

"You've only been there one day," Sam pointed out.

"And maybe you'll improve," offered Simon.

Phil was not consoled. "I never improve at things I show potential for."

Sam seated himself on a rock, propped up his sketchbook on his knee, and surveyed the area. "We've all got our problems," he said abstractedly, making a few experimental marks on the page.

"Very true," agreed Simon. He could not take his eyes off the tip of the tall Interflux smokestack that, even here, showed above the tops of the trees.

"Hey," Phil said irritably. "Come on, guys. At least give me a little sympathy. I haven't been at Nassau Arts eight hours, and already I'm in the soup!"

Sam shrugged. "Get an agent."

"This is a really nice setting and all that," said Simon. He shook his head. "But is it just me, or is there something about this creek that's — you know — wrong?"

"That's just the water," Sam explained. "You see, the creek snakes over by the Interflux plant."

"So?"

"So they dump some kind of funky stuff in it," supplied Phil. "It contains detergent, and the creek gets a little foamy."

"But aren't there environmental laws regulating that kind of stuff?" Simon asked.

"Oh yeah, but you can't beat Interflux. They took water samples and, sure enough, the plant was dumping too much funk in the creek. So Interflux convinced the town to reclassify Schuyler's Creek officially as a stream, because for some reason you're allowed to put more funk in a stream than in a creek. Anyway, it turned out that they were a half part per million below the legal limit for a stream, so they get to keep on dumping, and we get a creek with suds."

"Tell him about our field," said Sam, still sketching.

Phil grimaced. "It's the Interflux executive parking lot now. Naturally, we didn't have too much say in the matter. And someone's always making a big thing about air pollution. But Interflux usually makes the safety requirements by about a billionth of a smoke particle. Each time it works out that Interflux holds all the aces."

"So everybody in town hates Interflux?" asked Simon.

"I wouldn't exactly call it hate," said Sam.

"Man, half the town works there," Phil added. "It's just that the company is so big that it manages to offend practically everybody in some way."

Simon didn't have the heart to tell them that the existing plant was a mere anthill in comparison to the monstrosity Interflux had planned, including a massive complex of office suites, a tripling of the plant facilities, and warehouses that Simon figured would surround the Nassau Arts building with chrome and gunmetal. With a sigh, he found an angle that appealed to him and began to sketch.

Sam was already well into his work, and Phil was leaning over his shoulder, watching intently. "Hey, Sotirios, what's that thing you've got there in the bushes? It looks like a — "

Simon came to attention. "Sam," he said warily, "you're not putting a camel in there."

Sam grinned. "I'm going to camouflage this one so he'll never find it."

"Why are you looking for trouble?" Simon asked. "You don't tease a lunatic! He'll break up the whole class!"

"You just don't know Querada. You'll get the hang of it soon."

* * *

"Dad, do you know anything about Schuyler's Creek?" Simon asked that night at dinner, largely to detract attention from the fact that he was not eating his vegetarian burrito.

"Stream, son. That's Schuyler's Stream."

"Do you know that the plant is polluting it?"

"Oh no," said his father. "It's government-approved waste disposal, very carefully monitored. It wouldn't be pollution unless — oh, let's say we were putting the same amount of waste material into a creek."

"But it is a creek! And it foams!"

"How's everyone enjoying dinner?" beamed Mrs. Irving.

"Very tasty," said her husband, casually signaling to Simon with three fingers. "Anyway, you don't have to worry about Schuyler's Creek — I mean, Stream. It won't foam anymore. We're digging it up. We'll be laying the foundations for the new ware-housing any time now. What's the big interest?"

Simon concentrated on dismantling the burrito in such a way that it looked at least partially eaten. "Oh, I've been doing some sketching in the woods around there."

"Well, you'd better make it fast, because those trees are coming out, too. We're flattening the whole area at the same time to make it easier and quicker."

"But, Dad, a lot of the kids at school really depend on that green space. It's nice and quiet, attractive, and generally a great place to work and relax."

Mr. Irving looked mystified. "That land has always belonged to Interflux. We let them use it, but now we need it."

"Guess where I got this recipe?" chimed in Mrs. Irving, oblivious to the conversation.

"*The Sun*," chorused her husband and son.

"Fine paper, *The Sun*," said Mr. Irving approvingly.

* * *

As Mr. Irving had promised, the unconquerable will of Interflux soon hit the woods north of the school. The howling sounds of chainsaws in the distance rang through Nassau Arts. In the painting studio, it provided an apocalyptic background for Emile Querada's tantrum upon spotting the camouflaged camel in Sam's nature sketch. In the sculpture wing, it was a mournful wail which symbolized Phil's inner emotional state as he gazed bleakly at the large block of wood that was supposed to turn into his first project. Throughout the school, classes were temporarily halted, either officially or just in the minds of the students, as all said silent goodbyes to Schuyler's Creek (Stream) and its environs. In conversation, Interflux took a real beating, and although he knew he was not responsible, Simon was stricken with guilt.

Life, though, went on, and Simon was amazed at how, even in the first week of school, Nassau Arts was all business. His teachers assigned work wholesale, as though the semester were almost over. Simon shared a math class with Phil, and the two immediately arranged to split the homework 50-50 in an effort at time-saving.

"No point in both of us doing it all," Phil reasoned, "when we can each do half and copy the other guy's stuff before class. We don't have time for this. We're artists."

But Phil's classification as an artist was becoming shakier every day as project number one progressed from a block of wood to a lump of wood. And while it did have human form, it was not quite recognizable as the bust of a person, and certainly not Garibaldi, as Phil had declared it to be.

Simon was having his problems, too. His first English paper came back with a grade of D plus , a bare pass. The teacher, Mr. Durham, who insisted that all his students call him Buzz (which was inexplicable, since his given name was Xerxes), commented, "I didn't feel that you experienced psychic growth in writing this essay." While Simon was in complete agreement with this assessment, it was somewhat alarming, since he didn't anticipate psychic growth in future assignments, either. And while one D plus was nothing to panic about, a whole string of them wouldn't go over too well on the home front.

Simon's only break that week was that his biology teacher, Miss Glandfield, was so upset over the destruction of the woods north of the school that she canceled class and took to her bed, calling plague, catastrophe, and ten-ton flame-balls down on Interflux. Miss Glandfield considered each and every lowly tadpole her little friend, which Simon felt was a trifle inconsistent with her reputation for dissecting her little friends once they grew up to be frogs. But he accepted the spare period as a chance to catch up on other work.

On Friday afternoon, Simon and Phil were walking down the hallway after last class, discussing Phil's sculpture problems. They came upon Sam, seated in front of his locker, oblivious to the admiring looks from passing female students. He was leafing through a thick paperback entitled *The Complete Querada*, the teacher's autobiography.

As Phil opened his locker, a sealed envelope fell out and fluttered to his feet. "Oh boy, that's it. I'm out of here," he moaned, ripping the letter open. "They couldn't even wait till I finished Garibaldi before giving me the boot." He examined the form letter inside. "'Nathan Kruppman requires your participation in his Nassau Arts video film, *Omni*, at first light Saturday morning, Flushing Meadows Corona Park, Southwest entrance, Queens. Enclosed please find your lines. Thank you. Nathan Kruppman, Director.'" Phil looked up, bewildered. "Who's Nathan Kruppman?"

All activity suddenly halted, and everyone within earshot stared at Phil as though he had a cabbage for a head. Dead silence fell.

"You'll have to excuse my friend," Sam explained to the shocked onlookers. "He's new here, and he just got his first part in *Omni*."

There was a chorus of congratulations and nods of understanding, and the hall went back to normal.

Phil dropped his voice to a whisper. "Who's Nathan Kruppman?"

"He's a senior in film and TV," Sam explained. "The top student in the department — probably the whole school. He's been working on this project since day one at Nassau. It's something amazing. He must have upwards of a hundred hours of raw footage shot so far, all on digital video. He writes it, directs it, designs the sets, supplies the costumes, and the actors and crew are one hundred percent Nassau Arts students. Practically everyone's been in it at some point. It's an honor."

"Have you ever had a part?" Simon asked.

"Of course. A few times. I've worked on the crew, too, and I've helped out with set-building and painting. What part did he give you, Philip?"

Phil checked the enclosed script. *"Agamemnon?! What is he filming — the Trojan War?"*

"Probably. He jumps around a lot. I was in the 1952 World Series sequence. I also had a bit part in the Russian Revolution, but my biggest role was Noah, which we filmed during a rainy spell last fall."

Phil was unimpressed. "Just how does this Nathan guy know me?"

"Oh, he probably saw your photo in your confidential file. The staff gives him access to everything. Nobody says no to Nathan."

"Yeah, well, I think he's about to get his first no. I've got enough troubles. I've got Garibaldi to worry about; I don't have time for Agamemnon. Besides, it's never been my ambition to see the sun rise over Queens."

"Look," said Sam seriously, "you can get straight F's in everything, and carve lumps ten times worse than Garibaldi, and with a little help from T.C. here and there, you can still survive at Nassau Arts. But if you refuse to help with Nathan's movie, you can get A pluses by the truckload and carve the 'Pieta,' and you'd still be finished at this school. That's the way it is."

"Sounds pretty weird, if you ask me," said Phil sulkily.

Sam shrugged. "There's always Greenbush High."

"I'll go!" said Phil in disgust. "I hope you don't need the wreck tomorrow, because I certainly don't intend to take the train at five o'clock in the morning."

"Do you think I'll ever get a part in this movie?" asked Simon. He was beginning to feel strangely left out in this conversation, and was certain that he could play as good an Agamemnon as the next guy.

"Oh, sure," said Sam. "I think the whole school was in the War of 1812 last spring."

"Well," said Simon, "I'd better get going. Give me a ring tomorrow, Phil. You can tell me all about your big movie debut."

* * *

That night, Simon had a dream. He was seated in an Interflux warehouse laboriously counting great mountains of zipper teeth, one at a time. There was no escape from this horrible task, since the zipper teeth were piled so high that he was completely shut in on all sides.

Then, suddenly, with the tally up in the fifteen millions, he lost his count and had to start again at one. He woke up in a cold sweat, images of Interflux still whirling in his head. He could see the bulldozers flattening the almost-denuded area north of the school. He pictured the new, expanded installation growing out from the existing plant to surround and suffocate Nassau Arts.

He sat up and turned on his reading lamp, which made the zipper on his windbreaker, thrown over his desk chair, gleam at him mockingly. Awake or asleep, there was really no getting away from zipper teeth. Having spent over ten of his sixteen and a third years as the son of Interflux, Simon was not one to dump on big business. But it did seem a shame to rip up terrific wooded area and a nice creek (stream) which was so much appreciated by fifteen hundred students just to build warehouses for zipper teeth. Not that he begrudged Interflux its zipper teeth or anything like that. It was just that there were so many out-of-the-way places that nobody cared about which were just crying out for zipper teeth. The woods, or at least what was left of them, should live.

Even more important, Simon Irving should be protected from being absorbed by this giant industrial sponge. Sure, he was in Nassau Arts now, but a week on the inside was enough to assure him that the school was no match for the magnetic pull of Interflux and the iron will of Cyril Irving. He could already tell that his father was taking Nassau Arts lightly, could almost hear him announce, "See? I told you he'd outgrow this painting nonsense. It was only a phase." It would take something big to move him, something like the Vishnik Prize.

That was it, then. He would have to win the Vishnik Prize.

Three

On Saturday night, Simon and Phil went to the late movie at the DeWitt Shopping Plaza Cinema. Before the film started, the two stopped in at Burger King, where Simon, now a regular as a result of his mother's recent cooking binge, exchanged friendly greetings with the manager.

In contrast to the day before, Phil had nothing but praise for Nathan Kruppman and his movie. ". . . and I park the wreck, and I'm not in a very good mood, you know, because it's five-thirty in the morning, and I'm not too big on Queens at any time of the day. So I walk into the park, and I almost drop down dead. There it is — Troy, in all its glory! The walls, the horse, everything! And the cast! Hundreds of us, and all people I've seen around school!" He shook his head. "It was amazing! They had armor there for me, and weapons. And the shoot! Oh, wow! We got it in only one take, which is a good thing, because on my order we set fire to the whole city. I'll tell you one thing. Nathan Kruppman is a great man. He's a genius, that's all there is to it. Today was the most moving experience of my life."

"Pass the ketchup," said Simon sourly. He had been secretly hoping that the filming would be an inconvenience and a bore, and that Nathan would turn out to be a jerk. Now, to hear Phil tell it, everyone who had missed it might as well die.

Phil seemed to read his thoughts. "Don't worry. You're sure to be in the next shoot. He's doing Woodstock, so he'll need a lot of people."

The high of Phil's weekend didn't last very long. On Monday the news came that his potential as a sculptor had come to naught, and that Garibaldi was a no-go. Phil was one hundred percent prepared for this, and spent his lunch hour with T.C. Serrette. The two worked out a plan where T.C. would try to keep Phil in Nassau Arts on the grounds that he was switching his area of concentration from sculpture to poetry, where, Phil assured the agent, he was bound to show potential. T.C. wasted no time in setting up an appointment with the admissions director, and in less than half an hour's negotiations, Phil Baldwin was still a Nassau Arts student, pending an interview with the head of the Poetry Department. The cost: up front three days accommodation for T.C. at the Baldwin house, and three more days upon Phil's acceptance into poetry. Phil, weak with relief, was more than happy to oblige.

This switchover did not affect his standing in his and Simon's math class, where the second week's homework turned out to be even heavier than the first. But, as poetry students were known for their resourcefulness, Phil had a solution to this problem as well. He and Simon drafted Wendy Orr, whom Phil knew from Nathan's shoot, into their homework pool so that now the load could be split in thirds rather than halves. Wendy, who was president of the Nassau Arts Student Council, specialized in dance, and while Phil claimed that she'd joined the pool through the sheer logic of the situation, Simon was convinced that her partnership with them came largely from the fact that she knew he and Phil hung out with Sam Stavrinidis.

"What is it with you that you always think the worst of people?" Phil accused as the two headed for their lockers right after Wendy's enlistment.

"I don't always think the worst of people," said Simon defensively. "I just get suspicious when we're trying to discuss divvying up the homework problems and she's firing off questions about Sam like an S.S. interrogation team."

Simon's biology class restarted that week, Miss Glandfield having recovered from her emotional upset. She had apparently decided to hold off the ten-ton flame-balls upon seeing that Interflux seemed content to level only seventy-five percent of the woods. The southernmost quadrant, the part nearest the school, was left standing, which she interpreted as a goodwill gesture on the part of Interflux in response to her own personal sanctions (for she had phoned several times to tell them about it). Being on the inside of things, Simon knew that the surviving trees had only been granted a grace period, as Interflux intended to start construction on the area they'd already cleared before flattening the rest of the grove.

On that day, Miss Glandfield divided the class into lab pairs, which was how Simon became acquainted with Johnny, his partner. Johnny led somewhat of a double life since, in school, he was Jonathan Zulanovitch, top student in the music program and one of the most promising young classical guitarists in the country. But on selected nights and weekends, he became Johnny Zull, lead guitarist of Outer Nimrod, the most exciting and dynamic band in Manhattan's underground rock music scene.

"I can't stand the sight of Long Island!" Johnny announced with much emphasis as he and Simon gathered equipment for their first experiment. "What a hole!"

Stunned that Johnny should feel moved to make such a statement, apropos of nothing, Simon could only manage a weak, "Huh?"

Johnny pointed out the window. "Look at that. It makes me sick. A plastic civilization with paper dolls for people. They're all dead out there. They think they're alive, but they're dead. The only thing that's real on Long Island is the boredom. That's it. Nothing else."

"Uh — uh — is there somewhere — better?"

The sheer absurdity of this question caused Johnny to squeeze his eyedropper, spraying viscous red liquid on Simon's shoes. "The city, man! New York! That's what life is about. But not the city they show in the tourist booklets; the real city! Tenement housing

— cracked sidewalks — garbage — cockroaches — rats! That's real! To freeze all winter and sweat all summer, and write great songs by the light of a bare bulb in an eight-by-eight cold-water walk-up with crumbling plaster and bad plumbing! That's living!"

Simon was sure it wasn't, but said nothing and concentrated on applying the liquid to the leaf on his slide. There was no reaction from the leaf, but his shoes were starting to steam.

"In the city, if you've got something to say, you go right ahead and say it — in five-foot letters on the subway wall. On Long Island you don't say anything. You sit at home worrying because you didn't buy your kid a computer when he was three, so he won't get into the college of his choice, and he'll end up stupid and have to wear plaid shirts forever. In the city, you wake up because they're breaking pavement outside, or because somebody heaved a brick through the front window of the delicatessen you live over. On Long Island, you sleep through the alarm on your fifteen-hundred-dollar Piaget watch, but some poor dog half a block away is driven crazy by the sound and smashes his head against a fence until his brains are scrambled. I hate Long Island!"

Simon, weary of this speech and more than a little nervous about his shoes, said, "If you hate it here so much, why don't you move to the city?"

"Because my mother says that if I move out before I graduate, no one's going to feed my fish."

"Oh."

It was going to be a long semester.

* * *

Both Simon and his father were delighted that night when dinner turned out to be roast beef, signifying the end of the vegetarian era. For the time being at least, they would not have to plan their evenings around the all-important visit to Burger King.

In keeping with the mood, the conversation was light. After dessert, though, Mr. Irving, able to enjoy his coffee on a truly full stomach for the first time in a week, grew chatty.

"Work was like a zoo today. Remember those exotic trees The Flake sent for the office on his trip to that Bengali village? Well, it turns out they had microscopic baby lizards living in the trunks! We know this because the first wave of microscopic baby lizards grew up into not-so-microscopic adolescent lizards, and they're all over the building. My secretary went home screaming — at least, I think she went home. It's entirely possible she's still running."

Mrs. Irving laughed. "It sounds like you'll have to call an exterminator, dear."

"We did, but when we tried to explain our problem, the idiots wouldn't come."

"You know, Dad," grinned Simon, "you shouldn't be surprised if Long Island exterminators aren't always prepared to handle Bengali lizards."

"Yeah, well, then some ninny in production got it into his head to phone The Flake in Burma, who, for some reason, is proud of himself, like he created a new form of life. He immediately called the Bronx Zoo and donated his lizards to their collection, so now we can't use an exterminator. We have to catch them and keep them. Well, my whole executive staff — they thought that was just terrific. You take a guy who spends eight hours a day in offices and boardrooms, and give him a chance to roll up his sleeves and chase lizards, and before you can say 'What about the Atkinson contract?' he's crawling under desks and tables with an empty mayonnaise jar, looking for big game. What a mess!"

"Maybe you should get some tsetse flies for bait," suggested Mrs. Irving thoughtfully.

Mr. Irving shrugged in exasperation. "I suppose I should be grateful. I've only got The Flake's lizards. I could have The Flake, too."

* * *

Three students were in Querada's classroom the next morning before the artist's arrival. Simon and Sam were standing with Peter Ashley, who was showing them his new painting, an abstract. Abstracts were high-risk projects in Querada's class, since the artist had never in living memory approved one, and made no bones about his conviction that most abstracts were done by people who couldn't paint real things.

"Who can tell?" Sam shrugged. "This might be the one he actually likes. *I* like it."

Peter shook his head. "I don't know why I painted it. He'll probably give it one look, stomp on my desk, and say, 'Mr. Ashley, when I was at the South Pole teaching penguins to paint, there was this one little fellow who insisted on painting abstracts. It was because of this that I learned that penguin tastes a lot like chicken if you do the batter right.'"

Simon laughed. "I really like it, Peter. I know it's impossible, but it even seems kind of familiar."

A mischievous smile played around Peter's mouth. "It's a real estate map of Greenbush. My sister works in the Town Hall, and she showed me one. I kind of liked the shapes, so I transferred it to canvas, jazzed it up a little, and here it is."

Instant recognition came to Simon. The abstract matched exactly the real estate map Cyril Irving had up on the wall of his study at home. Mr. Irving's map had the Interflux proposed expansion drawn onto it, but was otherwise the same map, with the same land lot boundaries, except for —

"What's that thing, Peter?" Simon pointed to a small worm-like shape on the canvas, which, if Simon's guess was correct, jutted out from what would be Nassau Arts property and meandered out a fair distance in an uneven crescent. "Surely it isn't a land lot."

Peter frowned. "I think it is." He squinted at the canvas. "Oh, yeah, I know that place. That land is the big joke of my sister's office. Back in the twenties, old man Schuyler won three-quarters of an acre in a poker game, and he took it in this crazy shape just to be a pain. It's the most useless lot in town. It's part trees, part scrub, and part swamp. Nobody's owned it since the old man died, and ever since then, the town's been trying to unload it on someone. They've got it up for sixty-seven hundred dollars back taxes, but nobody's offered sixty-seven cents for it. Who would?"

"How big is that strip?" Sam asked curiously.

Peter shrugged. "Thin. From what I've heard, it's about forty feet at its widest point, but usually it's more like twenty. As for the length — I really couldn't tell you." He grinned at Sam. "You want to buy it?"

"Are you sure Interflux doesn't own it?" Simon asked.

Peter nodded and pointed to his picture. "All the Interflux land is black with orange flames. That strip is pink, which means it's town land. I was pretty careful about that kind of stuff."

All morning, Simon was haunted by the image of that wiggly strip of land. He was positive it didn't appear on the diagram in his father's study. And he had certainly spent enough time staring at that map while Mr. Irving had gone on and on in excruciating detail about the proposed complex. According to Mr. Irving's map, Interflux owned all that land. But Peter's version said they didn't. Wouldn't it be a hoot if — ? No, it couldn't be.

Still, Simon couldn't get the two maps out of his mind. He kept trying to place one over the other, but whenever he did, he ended up with the same impossible result: every one of the proposed access roads to the Interflux construction site at some point crossed over old man Schuyler's big joke. Was Interflux capable of such a blunder? Cyril Irving always said, "In business you leave nothing to chance." Then again, Interflux had bought its Greenbush land thirty years ago, and for all anyone knew, the buyer could have been careless and overlooked this strip.

Simon smiled. Tonight he would tell his father about this, and if it turned out that Interflux had made a mistake, he would bug him about it for the rest of his life.

* * *

The Nassau Arts cafeteria, unlike its counterparts in most high schools, was a splendid place. The ceiling was largely glass, so the room was flooded with natural light, and the walls were decorated with vivid murals painted by students past and present.

Sam Stavrinidis always ate at the table closest to his own contribution, a giant camel, and it was there that Simon and Phil found him at lunch. Soon the three were joined by Wendy Orr, her best friend Barbara, and the quarter-ton couple. Barbara was an attractive redhead, reputed to be a top-notch dance student, and generally known as the quietest girl in the school. During the whole lunch hour, besides "Hello," her entire conversation amounted to "Pretty good," which she said twice, once to "How are you?" and once to "How's the salad?" She spent the rest of the time staring at Sam.

The quarter-ton couple, however, had eyes only for each other. Dino and Dina were truly a match made in heaven. They were both operatic vocal students, he a tenor, she a soprano, both greatly talented. The tag "quarter-ton couple" came from the fact that his weight hovered just below three hundred, and hers just above two hundred, so that, theoretically, if you got them on the same scale together, the reading would be right up there around five hundred pounds. They liked each other just fine that way, and so did the voice coach, who felt that great body mass yielded depth and resonance.

Wendy was complaining about her job as Student Council president. "This school is the pits for student government. I can't get anybody to work. There's no social director, T.C. makes the Student Council obsolete, and my vice-president is a complete write-off. What we need is a combination treasurer/program director who can make good use of the Student Council's money."

While officially it seemed as though she was throwing this position open to anyone, it was clear to Simon that she had the job earmarked for Sam Stavrinidis. Sam, however, showed no signs of volunteering, and sat passively eating his soup.

"What kind of stuff did you have in mind?" asked Dina between bites of a twenty-four-inch hero sandwich that she was sharing with Dino.

"You know — dances, parties, social stuff. The things normal schools do. Just because we're Nassau Arts doesn't mean we have to be boring. We've got a fortune in the treasury, and nothing to spend it on."

"How much is a fortune?" asked Phil.

"More than sixty-seven hundred dollars."

Simon choked on his Pepsi. "What? How much?"

From her purse Wendy produced a gold bankbook and consulted it. "Sixty-seven hundred thirty-four dollars and eighteen cents."

"You're kidding!"

"What are you so surprised about? Everyone here

is so concerned with his own specialty that there's no involvement, and the money builds up."

Simon could barely keep himself from screaming. "I want to get involved! I want to be treasurer!"

Wendy considered this. "Have you ever had any experience at student government?"

Well, thought Simon, it was time to lie. "Oh, sure. I was vice-president of my last school, and I worked on the organizing committee for the school clubs, and I was chairman for prom night, and I organized rallies for the football team, and — "

"Oh, wow!" Wendy exclaimed, looking at Simon with a newfound respect. "You're really an expert."

Simon nodded brazenly. Sorry for the exaggerations, Wendy, but this was important. It was a sign! It had to be! Not three hours after he had found out about the Schuyler land strip from Peter Ashley, here was Wendy with a Student Council bank account containing exactly enough money to pay the back taxes and snap up the land that Interflux forgot. Obviously, this was a setup from no lower office than heaven. Interflux had been riding too high lately, and now it was time for someone to give it to them right in the zipper teeth. Why tell Cyril Irving about the Schuyler land when Simon was only a few slightly dishonest dealings away from the money to buy it himself? Yes! He had to get his hands on that $6,700. "Okay, where's the money?"

Wendy looked at him quizzically. "Why? What's your hurry?" A slow smile came over her face. "I get it. You have so much experience with student activities that you already have some fantastic plan."

Simon nodded, smiling. "You've got it."

"Well, let's hear it! I'm dying to know!"

"It's a secret, but I can assure you it's going to be — memorable. So what we have to do right now is go to the bank and sign the account over to my name, because I want to get started with the preparations right away. Eat up and let's go."

Phil spoke up. "What's so urgent that it has to be done this minute? I mean — " Simon signaled at him madly, and he fell silent.

"I know," said Wendy. She looked excitedly into Simon's eyes. "It's a party with a beach theme, and it has to be soon so that it's still warm enough to wear bathing suits. Right?"

"Something even better than that," Simon promised. He picked up his own tray and hers as well, even though she was only half finished with her dessert. "Come on. If we hurry, we can hit the bank and still make it back for next class."

"Hey, Simon," called Phil, "from one friend to another who's about to come into some money — before you leave the country, remember who your buddies are. The wreck could use a little body work, you know."

* * *

The account was in the bank at the nearby DeWitt Shopping Plaza, and Simon wasted no time hustling Wendy into the Mustang and roaring off, leaving a good deal of tire tread in the Nassau Arts parking lot. For whatever inexplicable reason, Wendy's opinion of

Simon was inflating with each passing minute, and the sight of his black and red sports car helped this immeasurably. It was almost as though she believed that he had somehow acquired the car as a result of his now-legendary career as a student leader.

The bank transfer was done swiftly, and in a matter of minutes, Simon had acquired Wendy's counter-signature on a blank check, delivered her to her locker, made a motion to visit his own, doubled back, ducked into a washroom for a few minutes so she wouldn't see him leaving again, and then scooted back to the car.

On the way to the Greenbush Town Hall, Simon had a brief attack of conscience; how could he do this to his father? The answer came from Cyril Irving's own mouth: "In business you leave nothing to chance." Interflux had left this to chance, and was fair game.

The Greenbush Town Hall was really an old wood-frame house originally owned by the Schuyler family and donated to the city in 1904. It was neat and respectable, but had a vague air of neglect about it. The paint job was obviously old, and weeds were beginning to choke out what little grass showed between the unpruned rose bushes. Inside there was even less evidence of order. The office employees, numbering three, ran around a lot, looking very busy, but not seeming to accomplish anything. The telephone rang constantly, but was never answered.

Eventually, a very young clerk noticed Simon standing by the front desk, and soon she and her two fellow employees were involved in a lively debate over who was in charge of the Land Office and, having settled on someone, which filing cabinet was the Land Office. While this was going on, Simon had a chance to examine the bankbook, and noticed with some shock that Wendy had put his name down as Irving Simon. He wondered why the bank teller hadn't said anything when he'd given his sample signature. He sincerely hoped that it was assumed that he'd signed his last name first, because it would be a tragedy beyond words to pull off the coup of the century only to find that his check had bounced.

By this time, the three had still not located the Land Office files, but had come up with the official town real estate maps and charts, not to mention the results of the 1909 town vote on indoor plumbing (they were against it, 95-87). Even from a distance, Simon could see the long, thin, erratic strip marked out on the map to the northwest of the Interflux property.

"Lot 1346B," he said in a voice that impressed him with its steadiness. "I hear it's available for sixty-seven hundred dollars in back taxes. I'm interested in purchasing it."

"You're kidding!" The three clerks began to stare at Simon and giggle.

"Is something wrong?"

Now the three laughed out loud. The senior clerk consulted a large ledger marked, strangely, MAH JONGG MONEY, APRIL '81 TO OCTOBER '82. "The back taxes are sixty-seven hundred eight dollars thirty-five cents."

"I'll take it," said Simon, and the two junior clerks ran off to a back room and slammed the door. Howls could be heard.

So it was that Simon found himself filling out the documents for the purchase of Greenbush Land Lot 1346B. Under the heading COMPANY NAME he printed, on a wild impulse, *Antiflux*, listed himself as *I. Simon, Program Director*, and gave the address of the school. Then he made out the check, handed it over, accepted the title deed, and fled.

As soon as he stepped out the door, a horrible thought occurred to him. What if he'd been wrong about the map up in his father's study, and he'd just converted the entire Student Council budget into the most useless piece of real estate on Long Island? So strong was the feeling of dread that suddenly took him that he drove straight home. Luckily, his mother was out, which saved him from yet another lie, explaining why he was home in the middle of the day, and why he was pounding up the stairs to his father's study in such frantic haste.

He burst into the room, took in the map, and almost collapsed with relief. He'd been right. Better still, Interflux had been wrong. He drove back to school flooded with the greatest sense of accomplishment he'd ever exprienced.

* * *

Phil caught Simon just inside the door leading from the parking lot. "Hey," he called, jogging up. Then, in a lower voice, "Well, come on. How did it go?"

Simon looked startled.

"Oh, save it. I'm not stupid, you know. It was the most obvious thing I've ever seen in my life. You really had Wendy going with all that student activities stuff, which, no offense, I thought you were shoveling on a little thick. But she actually bought it! Any idiot could see you were making a move on her."

Simon's surprise was genuine. "What are you talking about? I wasn't even thinking about Wendy."

Phil was taken aback. "Huh? Don't tell me you really want to be Wendy's school treasurer then?"

"Yeah, I — "

"I can't believe it!" Phil shook his head. "You mean you *want* to be cruise director on the good ship Nassau Arts? You're actually going to organize a dance?"

"Of course not."

"Then why did you kidnap her away from lunch and haul her off to the bank? What did you need that money for?"

Simon grabbed Phil by the arm, pulled him into the nearby washroom, and checked the stalls to make sure no one else was within earshot. "Land," he said finally.

"What?"

"Land. I took the Student Council's money and bought land."

Phil's face drained of all color. "You mean land?" he whispered. "Like — property?"

"Yeah, land." Simon grinned proudly.

"How much of the budget did you spend?"

"All of it."

"Oh my God! But you were supposed to make parties! Nobody said anything about buying land!"

"Phil, I knew exactly what — "

"Okay, okay — don't panic. It's not too late. We can weasel out of the deal. We'll go back to the guy who sold it to you, give him a little song and dance about temporary insanity, and get him to take it back. We can bring T.C. with us — he'll make it sound better. We'll end up with him staying at our houses for a year, but at least we won't have any more land!"

"But Phil, this is very special land."

Phil held up both hands. "I'm not questioning that. I'm sure it's just terrific land. But good land, bad land — you don't buy land with the Student Council's money!"

"Phil, shut up and listen. Here's the deal." Simon related the story of Interflux's oversight and the bizarre-shaped parcel of land that was so vitally located. He carefully avoided any reference to his father. "That's the land I bought! There isn't a kid or a teacher in this school who hasn't got a gripe against Interflux. But if I'm right about this land, and I'm sure I am, Interflux can't build any of their new stuff without permission to drive trucks over our property. Which means when they start expanding, well be in a position to hassle their brains out!"

The shocked expression on Phil's face dissolved into a toothy grin, and his eyes took on the look of someone who has opened a bin marked SHEEP MANURE and found it full of gold bars. "They really really need this land?"

Simon nodded. "They're in trouble if they can't cross it."

Phil clapped his hands together with glee. "Hah! And they can't cross it if we won't let them!"

"Well, it's not us exactly," Simon explained carefully. "Not the Student Council, that is. I bought it under a company name — Antiflux."

Phil laughed with delight. "It's the perfect name, but what for?"

"We're hassling them, remember? When they hear the name, they'll get the message."

"Wow!" said Phil. "When I first saw you in that parking lot thumbing your nose at Interflux, somewhere in my mind I knew there was something cool going on. I mean, it's tough to look dignified thumbing your nose, but you had the form. And now, not two weeks later, you've got Interflux in a choke hold! Man, the more I think about this, the more I like it! When we tell Sotirios, he's going to freak out!"

* * *

Phil was disappointed in Sam's reaction. "You guys are nuts," Sam said firmly. "Missing Querada's class for nothing is nuts. Blowing the Student Council's money because of Peter Ashley's abstract painting is nuts. Trying to mess with Interflux is nuts. Antiflux is nuts."

"But don't you see the beauty of it?" crowed Phil.

"I see that when you tell Wendy you bought land with her party money, your life won't be worth two cents."

"But when I explain — " Simon began.

"Schuyler Avenue is paved with the bones of people who tried to explain things like this to Wendy.

She's a little high-strung, you know. The girl has the temper of Mount St. Helens and can smoke at the mouth for twice as long. She'll probably kill you first, and then have your remains thrown in jail, because I don't suppose you thought about this, but what you did was illegal."

"No it wasn't," Simon defended himself. "I'm the program director. This is — a program."

"Call it what you like, but remember — that girl can get nasty."

"Quit scaring the guy like that," laughed Phil. "This'll just take a little explaining, that's all."

* * *

Wendy was in the dancers' warm-up studio when Simon and Phil found her to explain the events of the day. Simon spoke clearly and reasonably, discussing in great detail all aspects of the situation. Unfortunately, he had no way of knowing that she and Barbara had already phoned Bloomingdale's, collect, to punch up their wardrobes in anticipation of many smart social events at school. She was very quiet, so Simon was unprepared when she picked up a textbook and flung it at his face. It was such a good shot that it knocked him backward into a row of chairs. Then Wendy, who looked rather good in a leotard (although this was a strange time for Simon to notice it) gathered everything portable within reach and pelted it at him, hurling abuse along with assorted tap shoes, clipboards, music stands, and cups and glasses. *"Land?!"* Running out of projectiles, she made a dash at Simon directly, and the last thing he saw before she descended on him like a vulture was Phil strolling nonchalantly out the studio door.

"Land?!" Throwing chairs effortlessly out of her way in a show of strength that was amazing for one of her trim size, Wendy grabbed Simon by the collar, hauled him to his feet, wrapped him in a microphone cord so tightly that he couldn't move his arms, and pushed him down again. Then she snatched up the nearest fire extinguisher and emptied its entire contents over his inert form. Shouting *"Land?!"* one last time, she snatched up an old ballet slipper, stuffed it into his mouth, and walked off in a huff, leaving him lying there, trussed up like a turkey, in a pile of foam.

"She let you off easy," Sam said later. It was he and Phil who came to rescue Simon after the battle was over.

"Thanks for the support!" Simon gasped at Phil, shaking himself like a dog and spraying foam far and wide.

Phil grinned. "We were outnumbered — one of her and only two of us. I had to go for reinforcements."

"We'd better get you cleaned up," Sam observed.

Simon nodded breathlessly, some of the enchantment gone from his day. He noticed that his nose was bleeding all over his shirt. It gave the fire extinguisher foam a pinkish tint.

"Hey, look on the bright side," Phil wisecracked. "The hardest part is over. From here on in, it'll be smooth sailing for Antiflux."

Simon nodded again. It was true. If he could survive the kind of punishment that Wendy Orr could dish out, what had he to fear from the mighty Interflux?

Four

Simon's first action at school the next day was to storm the student records office and demand that his name be corrected on all school documents. The logic was that, eventually, Interflux was going to find out about Lot 1346B. On that day, they would come roaring down on Nassau Arts, demanding to see I. Simon. And he would be S. Irving.

Otherwise, life went almost back to normal for Simon, and Nassau Arts functioned very much like a school which had *not* had its entire Student Council budget converted to real estate. Wendy, of course, was one of the differences. Though she had once seemed confused as to whether his name was Simon or Irving, now the matter was quite clear in her mind. She referred to him at all times as, "You sleazebag," or when he was not present, "That sleazebag."

"You can do your own stupid math homework, you sleazebag!" she snarled, resigning forthwith from his and Phil's math homework pool.

Simon should have been grateful that she was no longer throwing things at him, but for some reason, he had been finding her increasingly attractive ever since her assault on his person. He could still see her standing there, magnificent in her rage, discharging the fire extinguisher at him, until the whole picture faded into a haze of foam. Now, alas, she would have nothing to do with him, yet another piece of evidence that these things only worked out in the movies.

To make matters worse, on Wednesday morning he found taped to his locker a note which read:

Dear Sleazebag,

If all that money isn't back in the bank account in a week, I'm going to report you to the staff and have you expelled, arrested, and shot.

— W.

Another bit of unpleasantness that came on Wednesday was his return to Querada's class.

"There is something different about this group that I didn't notice yesterday," the teacher began, scanning the room from his remarkable height. The wild eyes stopped on Simon, who barely had a chance to realize that this message was directed at him before Querada was across the room and upon him like a chicken hawk. *"There is only one excuse for missing a Querada class. Death — your own!"*

Then he was back to normal again, pacing in front of the students. "When I was in Kenya, I was teaching a group of artists studying wildlife painting. One man, an Australian, missed one session and fell so far behind that he would never again catch up. He missed more and more sessions, and began taking long walks in the jungle. Poof! He was eaten by a tiger. *If you're in class, you can't be eaten by a tiger!"*

Simon cowered and wished for the tiger. The artist stepped back and turned away. When he spoke again, his voice was soft and tragic. "Only twelve persons in the world have the opportunity to study with Querada. And one insensitive clod has seen fit to give up two hours." He turned to Simon, his eyes impassioned. "Two precious hours — gone, irretrievable, wasted. *You waster of precious hours, on your feet! You are not worthy to occupy this seat!"* As Simon scrambled up, the artist grabbed his chair, lifted it over his head, and hurled it out an open window. Then he returned to the front of the class and began the lesson as though nothing at all had happened.

"Psst," whispered Sam. "Do exactly what I say and everything'll blow over. Pretend that nothing's wrong and you're sitting in a chair like the rest of us."

Not even daring to look away from the front, Simon nodded.

The class dragged on, and when it was finally over, Simon walked out the door and collapsed to sit cross-legged in the hall.

"What are you doing down there?" asked Sam.

"How would you like to stand up straight for two hours?" Simon asked irritably. "It's no picnic, you know."

Sam grinned. "Better than being eaten by a tiger."

"I suppose you think that's funny," said Simon,

massaging a leg cramp. "I came here to learn to be a painter, and all I'm getting out of it is flat feet! That guy's the biggest nutcase it's ever been my misfortune to meet!"

"He's a joy," said Sam wistfully. "I'll never forget the first time I missed a class."

"What happened?"

"He threw my chair out the window."

Wearily, Simon got to his feet. "Well, you may think he's terrific, but I hate him."

"Aw, don't say that. You're just sensitive because he was cracking on you today. You'll look back on these classes as the best time of your life."

"If I live through this," Simon growled, "which I doubt, I don't intend to look back on it at all."

"I'll tell you what I'll do," said Sam. I'll lend you my copy of *The Complete Querada*. You'll understand him a lot better when you've read it."

Simon grimaced, but said nothing.

* * *

Also on Wednesday, Phil was officially accepted into the Poetry Department. The department head believed that the former sculptor's work, while itself not very good, did show signs of a spark that could be developed into real talent.

"In other words, I show potential," Phil said with a crooked smile. "I figured I would."

Coincidentally, T.C. Serrette moved into the Baldwin house on that very day to begin a three-day residence. Since Sam needed the wreck, Phil recruited Simon and the Mustang to move T.C. from the house of Sheila

Hunt, a theater arts student who had needed the agent's services enough to incur a four-day stay-over.

Sheila lived in Brooklyn, so the drive was considerable, through stop-and-go rush-hour traffic. When the Mustang finally pulled up in front of Sheila's house, Simon and Phil both gaped in horror. There on the lawn stood T.C. amid a sea of boxes, bags, suitcases, trunks, totebags, and knapsacks large and small, each item carefully identified with a large red-and-white Canadian flag.

"Just a few of the necessities of life," T.C. said engagingly after Simon had expressed his doubts that all the paraphernalia would fit into the Mustang. "You see, I really enjoy the comforts of home, so I bring as much of it with me as I can."

"But there's no room for all this stuff!" protested Simon for about the seventh time.

"Oh, sure there is," said the agent airily. "One thing I've learned in the agent business is that you can pack any amount of stuff in the smallest of cars if you use a little common sense."

He then started issuing directions, and in twenty minutes, Simon and Phil had all of his possessions off the lawn and into the car. True, some of the boxes had to be tied onto the roof, and the trunk had to be left open because of protruding items, but T.C., who was an expert mover, had all the rope and red flags necessary.

The drive to Greenbush was a little hectic because Simon's rear visibility was zero, and T.C. had to ride on Phil's lap, wedged in between suitcases. The Mustang sat low under the weight of the load, and the traffic was even worse than before. But eventually, T.C. was comfortably moved into the Baldwin house and set up in the basement guest room. The final requirement to establish Phil as a bona fide Nassau Arts poetry student had been met.

Phil Baldwin was on a roll. He immediately began work on several poems and, to maximize his free time, recruited Bill McIntosh, a writer and Nassau Arts' only children's book specialist, into the math homework pool. At seven feet one inch, Bill was the school's tallest student, not to mention America's most promising high school basketball center. His avid interest in writing for the young was a constant source of aggravation for all the colleges that sought to entice him with scholarship offers. Bill thought basketball was relaxing, but was not as concerned with an eventual NBA career as he was with finding a good illustrator for his many stories. He also thought that math homework was the pits, which made him a perfect addition to the pool.

For Phil, things were moving along nicely on the home front as well. His mother thought T.C. was "the most wonderful boy you'll ever meet." The agent, now beginning his fourth year of life as an eternal guest, simply knew all the angles when it came to pleasing his clients' parents. He was the perfect visitor, always liking the food, admiring the decor, and presenting his hostess with a small bunch of flowers. (He had a discount arrangement at the DeWitt Plaza

Flower Shop.) He chatted knowledgeably with Mr. Baldwin about his stamp collection, and Phil's older brother and younger sister admired his saxophone playing. Phil was on cloud nine.

The thing that made Phil happiest was that he was in on the big secret. He now spoke comfortably of "our land," and constantly talked of his excitement over "our next move."

"When the time comes, we'll know what to do," Simon would say vaguely. In fact, he had never really thought beyond buying the land. And all future plans for Antiflux didn't seem half as important as coming up with Wendy's $6,700 by next Wednesday, or facing the consequences.

* * *

That weekend, Nathan Kruppman filmed Woodstock in a field in Passaic, New Jersey. The cast of an estimated eight hundred Nassau Arts students included Sam, Phil, Wendy, Barbara, Johnny Zull, the quarterton couple, Bill McIntosh, and even Laura Dixon. In fact, of all his growing acquaintance at school, Simon was the only one he knew who wasn't in this sequence.

To take his mind off his irritation over this and the new $6,700 Wendy crisis, he spent the weekend leafing through *The Complete Querada* by Emile Querada. On the cover was a picture of the artist, scowling, under which was written, ". . . just like spending an evening with the twentieth century's nastiest and most unpredictable artist."

"God forbid," Simon said aloud. He had to laugh in

spite of himself, though, when he read the foreword, which opened:

> I urge you not to buy this book. It is a gross corruption of my original words. All editors are idiots . . .

Simon skipped ahead to the color plates. Whatever he had to say about Querada as a person, as a painter the man was brilliant. And as he skimmed through some of the chapters, reading a section here and there, he realized that Querada's abrasive personality was a lot more charming on paper than it was faced with the six-feet-eight-inch reality.

ROLLING STONE INTERVIEW, 2005

> RS: Why do you teach at a high school when any university in the world would be dying to have you at three times the money?
> Q: Any artist who has reached the age of eighteen and has never had the benefit of seeing me break something has no future. It is too late for him. The high school years are crucial.

Simon smiled, flipping forward.

> Artistic creativity is related to physical energy, and therefore violence is a legitimate part of the creative process. When I wreck my apartment, I'm trying to change the energy level within myself so as to achieve a new

perspective. The best way to lower energy is to transmit it to inanimate objects through violence. I'm not, as some people say, trying for publicity. If I wanted publicity, I'd wreck someone else's apartment.

Simon shook his head in admiration. The guy was priceless.

The idea for "Theater of Shadows" came when I was working on another painting, which was not going at all well. After I threw myself through the glass patio door, "Theater of Shadows" became clear to me during my ride in the ambulance.

Fascinated, Simon read on.

I painted "Logic of Chaos" in a small cabin in northern Canada loaned to me by a former friend. I did the whole painting sitting outside in the crisp, cold air while the cabin burned to the ground. The picture sold for forty thousand dollars; the cabin cost me forty-two thousand dollars.

The more Simon read, the more impressed he became. He delved with delight through the artist's eccentric stories, some of which he had heard from Querada himself. He laughed at all the jokes and drank in the art commentary. Marveling at the color plates one last time, he tossed the book onto his desk and sat up on his bed. He forgave Emile Querada all the lunacy in the world. He was an absolute genius. It was an honor to have one's chair thrown out the window by such a man.

Suffused with energy, he began work on a painting designed to knock Querada's socks off. It was a dark tavern scene highlighting three men playing darts, and Simon was sure it was his best piece of work ever. The thought of presenting it to Emile Querada excited him, and he was even considering using it as his entry for the Vishnik Prize. His mother lauded it to the skies, and even his father, who thought painting a useless occupation (which was a little hypocritical for a man who manufactured zipper teeth, audio level needles, clipboard hinges, etc.), admitted it was pretty good.

On Sunday, Simon was leafing through *The Sun* when he came upon an article titled: "The Bean Diet: Protein with Low Meat." Most alarming of all, there were recipes for bean stew, bean soup, bean salad, meatless chili, and a host of others that looked equally dangerous. With a great sense of purpose, he ripped out the whole page and burned it in the fireplace. But he was too late. Dinner that night was the beanburger, a sort of bean Sloppy Joe, heavy on slop, low on taste.

"Beans are very good for you," Mrs. Irving informed them.

"Most definitely," her husband agreed. Pretending to yawn, Mr. Irving flashed Simon the crossed-arms signal, the most drastic of all their secret messages, the one that meant a new line of strategy was necessary.

Later the two, both convulsed with heartburn and gas, met in the garden shed in the backyard to plan their defense.

"One of us has to be allergic to beans," Mr. Irving finally decided.

"Good thinking, Dad." Simon always enjoyed these little strategy sessions with his father, and sneaking back into the house under cover of darkness he felt a slight rush of guilt for the aggravation he knew his father was probably going to suffer over the Antiflux land.

Monday was a high day for Johnny Zull, and he zipped around the biology lab with boundless energy, chattering exuberantly about his great weekend. Outer Nimrod had played a gig on Saturday night at a broken-down little club in an area of Manhattan dilapidated enough to impress even Johnny.

"It totally blew my mind," he told Simon, who was trying to concentrate on the various fungus cultures that sat on the counter in front of them. "I mean, some places if they like you, they clap. Or, if they've got a little more class, they whistle and yell. But these guys were the classiest audience I've ever seen. When they appreciate your music, they fight. And let me tell you, there is nothing more gratifying to a performer than seeing two or three hundred people beating the living daylights out of each other in his honor. Man, we just exploded! We blew those fans *away!* Oh, they mashed that club! It was beautiful! When the police came, there was nothing left but splinters, sawdust, and broken glass. And even then the crowd was kicking and punching, and wrestling all over the floor. And loyal! Man, they were still yelling 'You're the greatest' at us from the back of the paddy wagons. I was deeply moved."

"Sounds like it was a riot," said Simon.

Johnny looked at him in disgust. "That was the greatest outpouring of genuine appreciation and true admiration I've ever experienced, and you call it a riot? That's such a typically Long Island attitude. If you weren't my lab partner, I'd get really mad. But I'll tell you what I'm going to do. The next time we get a gig at a really classy place in New York, I'll take you along. Then you'll see what I'm talking about."

"Uh — thanks," said Simon noncommittally.

"Don't mention it," Johnny said magnanimously. "What you need to do is get off Long Island and find out what real life is like."

* * *

"Guys, I've got a problem," said Simon to Phil and Sam at lunch that day. He filled them in on the story of Wendy's $6,700 threat, which was to come due on Wednesday. "So the way I see it, I have two days to live, unless I sell my car to raise the money, and I sure don't intend to do that."

"Hmmm," said Phil thoughtfully. "Well, there's a way out of everything; that's my philosophy. Let's look at what we've got here. We've got no alternatives and a tight time limit. On the surface, pretty bleak, but to a veteran of sticky situations — "

"Even bleaker," said Simon.

"Could I just point out," Sam put in, "that jams like this only happen as the result of stupid, impulsive, harebrained ideas!"

Phil looked vaguely insulted. "My whole life has been a series of stupid, impulsive, harebrained ideas. Do you realize how boring life would be without them? Now, let's use logic."

"It'll be a welcome change," muttered Sam.

"Look," Phil continued, "if you can keep Wendy quiet, everything's fine, right?"

"Okay," said Simon. "But experience tells me she's not so easy to control. And she's mad, too."

"What about a party?" asked Phil. "Do you think we could buy her off with a nice party?"

"We've got twenty-six bucks," Simon pointed out. "What are we going to have — a Hard Times dance?"

"Besides," added Sam, "she feels robbed of sixty-seven hundred dollars' worth of social activities. There's no way she's going to lay off without getting what she considers full compensation." His face turned thoughtful. "Unless — "

"Yeah?" prompted Simon and Phil in unison.

"Well, there's no way you can get Wendy back on your side. She's too mad. What you *can* do is keep her from turning you in."

"How?" asked Simon impatiently.

"She's president, and she's really big on what people think of her. You have to make it unfashionable for her to blow the whistle. She won't do it if she thinks it'll hurt her image."

Simon exploded. "That's *it?* That's the big idea? Oh, no problem then! All I have to do is go over to *The Sun* and *The New York Times* and get them to print the latest popular fad — not turning in Simon Irving! I could get Bloomingdale's to put out 'I-Didn't-Turn-In-Simon-Irving' designer sportswear! It's so simple! Why didn't I think of it?"

"Calm down, stupid. Sotirios is right. I feel an idea coming on already. Now listen, you're still the program director, right?"

"I guess so, but — "

"Well, I think it's high time for a program — right now."

Five

When Wendy Orr came back to her locker after her last class on Monday, she found a folded notice taped to the door. There were similar notices on the doors of every other locker in the school. Intrigued, she opened it. It read:

CONCERNED STUDENTS OF NASSAU ARTS:
- ARE YOU UPSET BY THE DESTRUCTION OF THE NORTH WOODS AND SCHUYLER'S CREEK AREA BY INTERFLUX?
- ARE YOU WORRIED ABOUT THE POSSIBLE SIDE-EFFECTS OF INTERFLUX'S PROPOSED NEW EXPANSION?

THE NASSAU ARTS STUDENT COUNCIL PROGRAM BOARD
PRESENTS
ANTIFLUX
GENERAL STUDENTS' MEETING,
WEDNESDAY, SEPTEMBER 19TH
IN THE NASSAU ARTS CAFETERIA AT 3:30 P.M.
ALL WELCOME

Wendy frowned. She knew from the name Antiflux that it had to be Simon's doing. Because the meeting was on Wednesday after school, she assumed it was a cheap ploy to keep her from informing the proper authorities about his fraud. But the notice made it all seem so reasonable. People would come out for this. What was he going to say to them? If he told them the truth, something that sleazebag was not noted for, they'd kill him, which, of course, he deserved. If he tried to lie, which she fully expected, then she would be there, right at the meeting, to set the record straight. And then she'd go to the authorities and report him.

She smiled, sure of herself once more. Yes, that was exactly what she'd do. She'd hold off on reporting Simon until after his "big meeting." The nerve of that sleazebag, calling a meeting without consulting her!

* * *

Simon had never been much for extracurricular activities. In fact, Wednesday was his first, and he found himself in charge. He was the head of the Nassau Arts Program Board, which consisted of himself, Phil, and a rather reluctant Sam. Sam would have preferred to be counted as one of the attendees of the meeting rather than one of the organizers. But Phil hit him with a strong "taking a stand" lecture, and a few home truths about friendship. Sam finally agreed to take his place on the rostrum, but not without restating his opinions regarding stupid, impulsive, harebrained ideas.

"How can you say that?" Phil challenged. "Remember, this meeting came from your idea, so if anybody's stupid, impulsive, and harebrained, it's you."

"I dispensed calm and sensible advice," Sam said smugly, "and you blew it all out of proportion."

The head count was about eighty, which was excellent considering Nassau Arts students didn't ordinarily turn out for such events. Simon decided it was another sign as to just how unpopular Interflux was among the students. He could see Wendy Orr, tight-lipped with rage, standing at the back of the cafeteria. An expert in body language, Wendy was conveying with the utmost clarity the message "One wrong move and you're dead." Her front of severity was compromised somewhat by her friend Barbara, who stood beside her, staring up at the rollaway platform where Sam was holding a whispered argument with Phil. In fact, Simon could see that Sam's presence on the podium was certainly boosting the image of Antiflux among the girls in the room, even though the meeting had not yet begun.

Simon approached his two friends. "What are we supposed to say, anyway?"

"No problem," said Phil, standing up and walking to the edge of the podium. "Attention, everybody. Thanks for coming out. We're the Nassau Arts Student Council Program Board, and we'd like to welcome you to our Antiflux program. I'm Phil Baldwin, and you probably all know Sam Stavrinidis, and this is our program director, Simon Irving." He paused, groping for something to say and, finding nothing, announced, "We've got a lot to tell you, so — uh — here's Simon."

There were a few seconds of polite applause, during which time Phil returned to his seat beside Sam. As he passed Simon, he tapped him on the arm and whispered, "You're on your own."

"That was a big help!" Simon muttered sarcastically. As he looked nervously over the assembled sea of faces, he had a vision of his ninth grade report card: Public Speaking — F. "Uh — I suppose you're wondering why I called you all here. Ha ha."

His reply was a few discontented murmurs and a lot of restless shuffling. He glanced to the back of the room where Wendy stood, arms folded, looking daggers at him, and realized that if he got an F in this particular public speech, it was curtains for Simon Irving, Irving Simon, and all combinations thereof. He felt a strange cold clamminess, a feeling that he was standing totally alone, and only his ingenuity stood between complete disaster and living to see another day.

"Look," he began, "I'm no talker, so maybe I won't say this right, but it's something you ought to know. We're all here because we're concerned about the way Interflux looks at this whole town, Nassau Arts included, as existing just to serve their plant. It's happening to Greenbush the same way it's happened to a list of towns as long as your arm, except what they're planning here is five times what they've ever done anywhere else. And we can't take it lying down because, two years down the line, Interflux'll build us another hockey rink, or another swimming pool, or put an addition on the library, and we'll be expected to say, 'Oh, thank you, Master, for paving the woods and putting up warehouses, and running more cars through town than the New Jersey Turnpike sees in a month! Thank you for building up smokestacks so high that the pollution is ten hours old before we have to breathe it!' We've got to do something, because the city officials are going to continue to sit on their cans, building up the muscles in their index fingers on their pocket calculators while they add up how much tax money Interflux gave them this month! No one else is going to buck Interflux! It's up to us!"

"Didn't he tell us he flunked public speaking?" Phil whispered to Sam as Simon continued to harangue the crowd with the expertise of a seasoned orator.

Sam shook his head. "There's something about that guy and Interflux. I mean, normally he's this mild-mannered person who minds his own business. But as soon as Interflux comes up, he's off like a shot, half cocked, buying land with someone else's money, and making speeches that would raise the dead to revolution."

Phil shrugged. "Maybe he just got a good look at Wendy and he realizes he's fighting for his life."

By this time, Simon was pacing up and down in his zeal, waving his arms before the captivated audience. "We're an art school, and we've got the right to a peaceful environment to work in. Within reason, of course. We can't expect Interflux to stop everything because of us. But we can fight them over this ridiculous expansion that will have anyone who walks two feet past our parking lot bumping into a warehouse full of zipper teeth!"

Sam sat bolt upright. "Fight the expansion?" he hissed at Phil. "When did this happen? I thought this whole thing was just to keep Wendy off his back!"

A photography student near the front spoke up. "You talk a good game, but what makes you think Interflux is going to listen to us?"

"Yeah!" called someone else. "This isn't exactly the first time people have been after Interflux. They're used to this stuff. What are we going to do — picket? Big deal! Send them a petition?"

"Toilet paper for the executive washroom!" shouted someone from the back.

Several voices added "Yeah!" and some of the students headed for the exit.

"Hold it! Hold it!" called Simon, raising his arms for order. "That's what I was about to tell you. We've already done something." He paused until he was certain of their full attention, then pulled out the town land map that had come with the title deed. "Here's Interflux, here's Nassau Arts. If Interflux wants to build, they're going to have to run trucks over this long black strip of land. Last week we bought it."

Dead silence fell. All eighty of the students stared at Simon in mute wonder as they digested this information. A girl halfway out the large door slowly eased herself back into the room, goggle-eyed. For a few seconds, not a sound was heard in the cafeteria. Then someone tittered; someone else laughed. A contagious wave of mirth swept over the crowd until everyone was laughing to the point of tears. A group in a back corner began to applaud, and that caught on as well, until Simon, Phil, and Sam found themselves on the receiving end of a rousing standing ovation.

Feeling a great rush of elation, Simon surveyed the crowd until his eyes lit on Wendy. He had never seen her angrier, not even when she was in the process of stuffing a ballet slipper into his mouth. And every ounce of approval for Simon and Antiflux that she sensed in the room irked her that much more. For some reason, he had an insane urge to rush over and ask her out, although it was becoming increasingly apparent that he had missed his last chance to do that in the four-hour interval between lunch last Tuesday and that painful scene in the warm-up studio. In a sobering thought, he realized that she still might turn him in, in spite of the success of the meeting and the fact that she was the only person in the room, Barbara included, who was not smiling and cheering. (Barbara, apparently, found the brilliance of Antiflux to be just another one of the many endearing qualities of Sam.)

Simon held up his hands for order, and gradually got some semblance of quiet. "I should also mention that we all owe a great deal of thanks to Student Council president Wendy Orr for making the funds available."

All eyes turned to the back of the room, and at that precise moment, Wendy replaced her scowl with a disarming smile as she acknowledged her many well-wishers.

"Masterful," approved Phil. "He pulled it off perfectly."

"And now," shouted Simon, "it's time for us to take our next step!"

"Next step?" Sam repeated. "What next step?"

"We're going to go out there and fence off our land so that when the Interflux bulldozers and trucks come, they won't be able to get through to the construction site!"

Another cheer went up. By this time, the group had grown to about a hundred, with the addition of students who had come to investigate the source of all the noise.

Sam slumped in his chair. "This is it," he told Phil as everyone raved about Simon's latest suggestion. "We are actually witnessing the birth of a stupid, impulsive, harebrained idea."

Phil was on his feet right at Simon's side. "We need stakes to use as fence posts!" he called out. "As many as you can get! They don't have to be beautiful; they just have to be stakes! Raid the school! Raid the DeWitt Plaza! Your house! Your neighbor's house! And rope — bring twine, string, clothesline, cord — all you can get!"

There was a mad scuffle as the students all scattered in search of fencing materials.

* * *

By seven-thirty that night, the fence was up. It wasn't pretty, but the land now fulfilled all the legal requirements of a fenced-in area.

"This is a fence like Schuyler's Creek is a stream,"

Sam pointed out once the line of fencing had started to grow.

"Exactly," said Phil, pounding a length of discarded bannister into the ground with a heavy hammer. The enterprise had started immediately after the meeting broke up. While the students were combing Greenbush and surrounding areas, Simon, Phil, and Sam trekked out to the land, armed with a surveyor's report, to mark off the exact perimeters of Lot 1346B. They actually found old stakes and official town markers, most of them buried or rotted away, but all of them a welcome confirmation of their own measurements. If Interflux had taken the time to look at the area at some point in the last thirty years, Simon noted with satisfaction, they would have seen the markers, realized the situation, and avoided what he hoped to turn into a real problem.

The three finished the land survey in forty-five minutes, Simon with determination, Phil with clean-cut enjoyment, and Sam with continuous warnings about the futility of the exercise. Fighting the expansion, he pointed out, was only slightly easier than halting the arms race, outlawing chocolate, or slicing off the Himalayas and relocating them in downtown Baltimore.

He had to keep his opinions to himself once the students began at arrive laden with the building materials, ready and eager to participate in "the only decent program this school has ever come up with." Even Sam knew better than to demoralize the troops at the beginning of the war.

The fence required more than two hundred stakes, roped together with everything from fishing line to grocery string. Even then there was a multitude of material left over.

"You'd better save it, just in case," advised Dave Roper, who was emerging as the liaison between the workers and the Antiflux top brass.

"Why?" asked Simon.

"Well, you never know. We could buy more land."

"But there is no more land."

"Still, it could come in handy. If another lot comes open suddenly, we won't be caught off-guard."

It was finally agreed that the extra materials would be heaped at the very rear of the property.

When the fence was finished and the last post, an old broken hockey stick, had been connected to the first, a rotted two-by-four, by means of a few old bicycle chains, the crew of one hundred stood back to survey the finished product.

"It looks too naked," Dave said, reporting the consensus of the masses. "The Interflux bulldozers might not pay any attention to it at all and just run right through it. It's too — you know — insubstantial."

It was then time for Phil Baldwin to add his bit of creativity to the project. With Phil in the lead shouting encouragement, the group stampeded back to the Nassau Arts building, raided the paper supply storeroom, and set to work lettering signs to be placed at ten-foot intervals around the perimeter.

These read:

NO TRESPASSING
PROPERTY OF ANTIFLUX
A BAD NEIGHBOR

Well pleased with themselves, Antiflux went home.

* * *

The next day, Simon found himself the object of much attention as word of Antiflux spread through Nassau Arts. Countless times, students who had been present on Wednesday stopped him in the hall to introduce him to their friends. "Hey, this is the guy I was just telling you about," they would say, "the one who's giving it to Interflux." Then Simon would be congratulated all around, praised to the skies, and offered all the help he might need.

Sam and Phil were receiving some of the same treatment, as was, ironically, Wendy Orr. As Student Council president, it was assumed that she was an important factor in Antiflux, which, in a way, she was, since yesterday's meeting had really started out as a ploy to keep her from shooting Simon down in disgrace. According to reports, she was acting the part pretty well, smiling in all the right places, and making sure to refer any questions to Simon. A few times, Simon experimented with actually approaching Wendy, but every time he got within about twenty feet, the sparks from her eyes would singe his confidence, and he would retreat. He may have been director of the Nassau Arts Program Board, and the father of Antiflux, but to Wendy he was still the sleazebag who cleaned out her party fund.

That week, Emile Querada's elite painting seminar hit its stride, and the first few finished pieces of work were ready for class presentation and analysis. Simon was having a little trouble dealing with his newfound respect for Querada. He had been charmed by the book, but the fact remained that Emile Querada was an escapee from a rubber room with a definite tendency toward sadism.

"Miss Dixon's 'Mother and Child' brings to mind a story you should all hear. When I was in Paris, I was walking down the street, and I came upon a painting very much like this one in an art shop window. Like Miss Dixon's work, it was very well done. The brushwork was good, and the colors were very real. So I asked myself, 'Querada, why do you detest this picture so violently that you would like to destroy it?' And I answered myself, 'Five minutes in the company of these persons *would be like a hundred thousand years in purgtory!* Look at those faces! There's nothing there! These aren't people!"

"That's a picture of my sister and her new baby," said Laura, her calm unruffled.

Querada leaped up so high that his head dislodged a piece of acoustic ceiling tile. "Reality is no excuse for a picture!"

Sam leaned over to Simon. "When he hits the ceiling, he really hits the ceiling."

Now Querada was in the middle of the class, eyes

closed, long arms crossed, hands gripping his shoulders. "When I look at that painting, I have a vision. I see the creep from Albany winning the Vishnik Prize. I see the creep's teacher, also a creep — how happy he looks. Ah! I see Querada —he doesn't look happy at all. I see the judges *yawning* at your sister and her new baby." Then he broke into a tirade about the Vishnik Prize, assured all twelve students that they had no chance of winning it, predicted a Vishnik dynasty for Albany, and very nearly burst into tears. Then he peered into each face individually, pleading, "Somebody please paint something that will make this awful vision go away!"

Wordlessly, he handed back Laura's picture, and Laura accepted it, also wordlessly.

* * *

Phil rushed into the cafeteria in a great state of agitation. Spying Simon and Sam, he dashed over, grabbed Sam's drink, and drained it in one gulp. Cutting off Sam's cry of protest, he took a deep breath and launched into his tale of woe.

"I can't believe it! I just can't believe it! Yesterday everything was so great, and today — this! I've been asked to leave the Poetry Department! In fact, they insist! Man, T.C. just moved out of my house the day before yesterday, and I'm back in the hot seat again!"

"What happened?" Simon asked.

Phil shook his head. "I really thought it would take them longer than this to find out I have no talent for poetry. But just because of one little line — "

Sam sighed and sat back, resigning himself to

being late for next period. "All right, Philip. Let's hear the poem."

"Well, I really should explain the circumstances first. I'm working on this set of four poems representing the seasons, and it's turning out all right. I mean, they're a little boring and all that, but they sound artistic and everything. It's the most poetic poetry I've ever written. Along comes Miss Hotchkiss, and I'm a little behind here because I joined the class late. I still haven't got the last line for 'Winter,' and she's really on my case. So I put the first thing I thought of that rhymed, just to shut her up. It's really her fault, not mine."

"The poem," Sam repeated.

From his pocket, Phil produced a mangled piece of paper.

"Winter"
by Phil Baldwin

The seasons are but four in count
And pass in like parade,
With Autumn's kiss and Winter's nip
Once Spring and Summer fade.

The Winter lays upon the Earth
A frosting smooth as glass
On which young children skate and slide
And you could break your —

"Phil!" exclaimed Simon in horror. "You didn't hand that in!"

"I can see now that it might have been a bad decision," Phil said sheepishly. "But she nagged me. She had it coming. You've never heard Miss Hotchkiss. She's got a voice like forty dolphins holding a sing-along. Anyway, she took one look at my poem and hoofed me out on the spot. Man, it destroys my faith."

Phil was so upset over his untimely ejection from poetry that he consoled himself by adding another member to the math homework pool, bringing the enrolment up to four. Laura Dixon agreed to join after Phil convinced her that she would be able to devote more time to going after the Vishnik Prize if she had seventy-five percent less math to worry about.

Simon figured that Laura joined the pool in a moment of weakness brought on by Querada's bombardment of "Mother and Child." "I was really feeling for you back there, Laura. That wasn't criticism; that was attempted murder."

Laura looked surprised. "Why? He analyzed my work, and now I know exactly what's wrong with it and what I should do to improve it. He was terrific."

"Terrific?! He jumped up so high his head hit the ceiling!"

"What's wrong with that?" challenged Bill Mc-Intosh, who, at five inches above Querada, spent a lot of his time trying not to hit the ceiling.

"You're still pretty new," said Laura, "so you might find Querada a little strange. But to me he's the most wonderful man in the world."

At lunch, the quarter-ton couple made news at Nassau Arts. The two, who had both been present at the Antiflux meeting, took a walk in the woods together and decided to check on the status of the makeshift fence. There they found three large trucks parked along the path which led to the Interflux construction sites, halted at the fence directly facing one of the PROPERTY OF ANTIFLUX signs. The drivers, they said, were awaiting instructions.

The news was extremely well received under the camel in the Nassau Arts cafeteria. "Man, it restores my faith," said Phil, whose faith was on a constant treadmill of destruction and restoration.

Sam was impressed in spite of himself. "I really thought they'd just roll over that bunch of sticks and string."

"They'll check it out first," said Simon, "and when they do, boy are they in for a surprise."

On Simon's advice, none of the students went out to the site to witness Interflux's dilemma. Not so Miss Glandfield, however, who had somehow gotten word of the stopped trucks. She canceled all her remaining classes, Simon's included, and took a lawn chair out to Lot 1346B to spend the whole afternoon enjoying the spectacle of the corporate giant in trouble. She wasn't certain exactly who was responsible for this fence that was causing Interflux such discomfiture. Obviously, it had been inspired by her own strong stand. She hoped that she would soon meet the person or persons involved so she could invite them over for tea and crumpets.

The spare period gave Simon a chance to study for the test in art history that was coming tomorrow. In all the excitement of the year thus far, he had neglected this course to a shameful degree, and had not even paid attention very well during the lectures, because Mr. Monagle had a voice so dull and monotonous that Simon usually spent most of the class asleep. He noticed with some alarm that he had not yet taken the textbook out of the shrink-wrap, and the pace of the course was already ninety pages ahead of him. Large pages. With small print.

Mr. Durham managed to add another complication to Simon's life in last period. Simon entered English class expecting Buzz to close off the day the way he usually did — by babbling about deep hidden meanings until it was time to go home. Simon didn't understand Mr. Durham's lectures, but this didn't bother him, since he was certain that nobody else did either, including, quite possibly, Mr. Durham himself. But today Buzz started with a sharp attack on the class, complaining of the low level of psychic growth so far. To stimulate "this collection of stagnant energies," he assigned *Concepts of Cyclical Symbolism*, and demanded a five-page analysis by Monday.

Dino of the quarter-ton couple nudged Simon. "Is he crazy or something?"

Simon didn't answer. The question was obviously rhetorical.

* * *

There was no mistaking Mr. Irving's mood when he came home from work. Obviously, when the stopped truck drivers had reported their situation, Interflux had contacted the town, and the whole story had come out. Yes, there was a land strip that Interflux didn't own. And no, they couldn't buy it now, because somebody else had bought it just last week.

"Seven roads into that construction site, and every single one of them goes right through — " his face contorted, " — Antiflux!"

"Can't you build another road that goes around this strip?" his wife suggested helpfully.

"It's like a swamp up there, Mary. It would be easier to get a submarine through north of that lot. I can't believe my ninnies didn't think to check on a land purchase that was made thirty years ago! Now if we want to stick with the schedule, we're going to have to deal with — Antiflux!"

Simon's tone was casual. "It sounds to me like you people left something to chance."

Mr. Irving was not amused. "Another county heard from! Don't get smart, kid. The guy who's running this whole scam uses the address of *your* school! Have you ever heard of I. Simon? We can't find anybody there by that name."

Simon studied the carpet. "It's a big school, Dad."

Mr. Irving snorted. "And that Town Hall! Those people are airheads! When brains were being given out, they must have been on coffee break, just like they are every time I try to phone! Do you realize that this one woman kept me on the phone half an hour before telling me she was the cleaning lady? Then when I finally got someone in charge, she wouldn't shut up about a town vote on indoor plumbing from seventy-five years ago! And the laughing that goes on in that place! Let me tell you, those people know as much about running a land office as my behind knows about putting up stovepipes!"

Simon cackled.

"That's enough out of you. This isn't funny."

"Sorry, Dad. I didn't mean to make fun of your problems."

"These aren't problems," Mr. Irving corrected him. "They're nuisances. Like ants at a picnic. It's a hassle, but eventually, you get around to stepping on all of them."

The head ant was insulted.

Six

It poured all weekend, raining out the Sack of Rome, which Nathan had intended to shoot, weather permitting. At the last minute, the crew put a large tarpaulin over the Eternal City and, according to a contingency plan, Nathan filmed the St. Valentine's Day Massacre and some other interior shots in a warehouse in the Bronx. Once again, Simon didn't make the cast, but it was just as well, as the large part of his weekend was devoted to *Concepts of Cyclical Symbolism* and his report. He didn't understand the book, or even its title, so his five pages were a little confused, but this was a plus, he was assured by Sam, who had had Mr. Durham before.

* * *

Interflux stood to lose money every day, paying stopped work crews to sit and look at BAD NEIGHBOR signs. With Cyril Irving in a rabid mood, his people scrambled to gather information on the mysterious Antiflux, without results. I. Simon had literally disappeared off the face of the earth.

There was a twenty-four-hour watch on the land,

but the stakeouts reported that the only people who even went near there were a fat couple who held hands and sang, and sometimes a crazy lady with a lawn chair. The fence, flimsy as it was, held firm; the signs had been all but destroyed by the weekend weather, but the message remained clear. The land belonged to Antiflux, and Antiflux was a bad neighbor.

So Mr. Irving sent for the mayor, one Fred Van Doren, a distant relative of the Schuyler family. Interflux's message was "We put the green in Greenbush," and Van Doren agreed so completely that he all but saluted upon entering the office of the senior executive vice-president. He didn't protest at all when he was told that it was the town's responsibility to get Interflux out of this mess.

Mr. Van Doren was then told what his opinions were: he found it unacceptable that Antiflux had not properly identified themselves thus far, by using the address of a school and the name of a person who couldn't be found. This made them a risk. Therefore, the town would give Antiflux one week to identify themselves properly, or else the purchase would be invalidated. Mr. Van Doren also found out that he was going to announce this in newspaper ads.

Van Doren, who was not noted for his deep thinking, proclaimed that this was exactly what he had been planning to do anyway, and took himself off to carry it out.

* * *

When the town announcement hit the papers, Phil was still in the middle of his latest crisis, and Simon was just scratching the surface on a possible crisis of his own. Mr. Monagle had handed back the art history exam, and there it was. Eleven out of sixty. He had given the teacher one of the few good laughs in an essentially humorless course when he'd looked at his paper and asked, "Is there going to be a bell curve?" Luckily, Mr. Monagle assured him there was "no problem at all," so there was no need for Simon to seek out T.C., who was busy anyway, combing the school for a new department in which he could place Phil.

"First poetry and now *this!*" said Phil, throwing his copy of *The Sun* on the floor and stomping on the town's notice. "This is not doing much for my faith, you know!"

Simon could not take his eyes off the town's advertisement: NOTICE TO PERSON OR PERSONS RESPONSIBLE FOR PURCHASHING GREENBUSH LAND LOT 1346B UNDER PSEUDONYM ANTIFLUX. The message was from the mayor, but Simon knew that the style was all Cyril Irving. Clever guy, Cyril Irving. Leaves nothing to chance.

Simon was disgusted. After catching the Interflux blunder, pouncing on the land, and camouflaging himself so beautifully in the process, already the whole plan had hit a snag. Now he had to show himself to keep the land, in which case his father would see that his own son was the chief ant at the Interflux picnic and kill him. To make matters worse, he couldn't talk to anyone about it, because he'd have to admit to his father's identity. Any normal person who found out that the father of Antiflux was really the son of Interflux couldn't be blamed for saying, "Stay away from this guy. He's crazy." He needed time to think.

"What do you mean *think?*" howled Phil. "What's to think? They're going to take away our land! Let's go down there right now, tell them, 'Here we are. We're Antiflux.' Big deal. We can own land. It's a free country."

Even Sam was beginning to lose his cool a little. "Simon, you've got no choice. No land, no Antiflux, which you may remember is the only thing keeping Wendy from selling you out. And even then there's a little matter of sixty-seven hundred dollars that you can't get back unless you show yourself."

"And the land will be gone, too," added Phil, who was just getting used to the idea of being a man of property. "So what we do is this: we write the town a letter saying we're Antiflux, they can send all their tax bills and notices here, we apologize for any confusion, blah, blah, blah, but we own the land, and you want to make something out of it?"

"That kind of attitude got you booted out of poetry," Sam pointed out.

"It wasn't that at all. It was Miss Hotchkiss. She hated me. So how about it, Simon?"

"I need time to think," Simon insisted.

* * *

The evening was lousy. It was a good thing Simon was left out of Nathan's filming of the rescheduled Sack of Rome, because he was far too preoccupied to perform. A little after nine, he was lying on his bed counting his options to a grand total of zero, and ignoring his open art history textbook, which was, if possible, even more boring than Mr. Monagle's lectures.

A sound penetrated the fog of his thoughts, the sound of a Panzer tank navigating this quiet Fosterville street. He jumped up and ran to the window. Sam Stavrinidis was parking the wreck in the large circular driveway, waiting patiently through forty-five seconds of run-on, during which time a massive blue cloud settled over the carefully kept chrysanthemums like nerve gas. Simon heard the doorbell and his mother answering it. Then she was down the hall, tapping on his bedroom door.

"Simon, there's someone here to see you." Her voice dropped to a whisper. "And he's gorgeous!"

"Yeah, yeah, Mom. I know."

"I found your address in the phone book," Sam explained. "I hope I'm not disturbing you."

"Not at all," said Mrs. Irving. "We're happy to have you. We move around so much that it's nice to see Simon is making friends."

"Yeah, right," said Simon. "Come on in, Sam." The two settled themselves in Simon's room, and Mrs. Irving went back to reading *The Sun*.

"I just came from the Sack of Rome," said Sam. "Offense ten; defense, no score."

Simon smiled vaguely.

"Listen, Simon, I'll get right to the point. I was listening to the news in the wreck on my way home.

They were talking about the Interflux expansion, and it came up that the name of the top man at Interflux is Mr. Irving. Tell me, has this got anything to do with why you're so dead set against identifying ourselves on the land?"

Simon stood up. "Okay, he's my father! You are looking at the son of Interflux! Pure and simple! You may now go ahead and hate my guts!"

Sam shook his head. "I don't get it. Why Antiflux? What have you got against your dad?"

Simon looked surprised. "Nothing. He's a great father. We have a good time together. We play basketball, we laugh a lot, we sneak food together when my mother goes on a health kick — he's a really nice guy."

"It seems to me that Antiflux was a pretty rotten thing to do to a nice guy."

Simon shook his head. "You don't understand. My father is terrific; Interflux I'm not too thrilled about. All my life I've lived breathing Interflux air, eating Interflux food, wearing Interflux clothes, and hearing about the great future I have guess where. The last town I lived in, my friends all turned against me when they found out I was the son of Interflux. That's okay. If they're that shallow, I don't want to know them either. But the bottom line is I'm interested in painting and art. I don't want to have anything to do with Interflux."

"So you're in painting school. What are you complaining about?"

"It just gets to you after a while. Look at this house!

All the coasters say Exxon because Interflux makes splashguards for gas pumps. All our our luggage comes from American Airlines' special offer, because of this two-and-a-half-inch metal doohickey that Interflux makes that no airplane washroom can be without. Every cup, saucer, dish, and bowl in our kitchen is from a free giveaway by some company that Interflux makes a tiny piece of junk for." Impulsively, Simon dashed into his closet and emerged with an enormous carton filled with small toys. "See this? All from Snappy-Wappies! I've never eaten a Snappy-Wappy in my life! 'For your little boy, Mr. Irving!' Because your company manufactures some dumb little gear wheel for the machine that makes the box tops easy to tear off so some other poor little kid can end up saddled with kazoos, secret rings, 3-D animal pictures, two-dimensional plastic dinosaurs, football cards, X-ray glasses, onion-flavored chewing gum, and other stuff like that!" He shuddered. "Sam, I've never been in a town where Interflux wasn't throwing its muscle around. And this time I saw a weak spot, and I went for it!"

Sam nodded. "The original stupid, impulsive, harebrained idea."

"And that's the story," said Simon. "Take it or leave it."

Sam looked thoughtful. "Well, one stupid idea deserves another. What say we write the town a letter and identify ourselves and leave you out of it?"

"But I bought the land."

"As I. Simon," Sam added.

"How do we explain it?"

"Why do we have to? We send them a copy of the deed to show we're on the level, tell them the land is owned by the Student Council, and ignore I. Simon."

"Who signs this letter?" Simon asked, beginning to come alive.

"How about Wendy? She's Student Council president."

"Wendy?!" Simon exploded, his newly formed options vanishing before his eyes like soap bubbles. "Wendy wouldn't give us the skin off a grape!"

"We'll threaten her with unpopularity. If she loses us this land, her name is mud at Nassau Arts. A lot of the kids are really psyched about this, and they want to know what we're doing about those town notices."

"And you'd be willing to do this for me?" Simon asked, toying with the possibility that Antiflux was alive and well and ready to fight another day.

Sam grinned, and Simon noticed that his teeth were perfect, too. "Well, if you think we shouldn't, we can always pack you a lunch and leave you in the crossfire."

"No, no!" said Simon quickly. "Let's do it! Thanks a lot, Sam!"

"Any time. Now, I think we should keep your Interflux connection a secret around the school. But we're going to have to tell Philip, and I figure we might as well get that out of the way right now."

* * *

They found Phil setting up the Baldwins' spare room, preparing for T.C.'s arrival on Wednesday. Phil was now a bona fide photography student, after one of the most difficult negotiations in T.C.'s career. Expert wheeling and dealing and the raw potential Phil demonstrated at the interview got the job done. Such a large service would ordinarily incur a stay of ten to twelve days, but T.C. let the Baldwins off with only eight, explaining that Phil was great for his reputation.

Sam sat Phil down, gave him a milkshake as a pacifier, and told him that there was a new development that might take some getting used to.

"Simon's dad is the senior executive vice-president of Interflux."

Phil choked. "Wow! Really?"

"Just pay attention, Philip. Here's the story." With much prompting from Simon, Sam managed to make the situation reasonably clear to Phil.

"So we're going to write the letter and keep the land?" Phil said.

"Right," said Sam. "We just leave I. Simon out of it, and Wendy signs as president of the Student Council."

"Well, I still have my doubts about that," said Simon. "I think it's an accomplishment that she isn't beating me up anymore. I can't envision her doing us favors."

"No, that part doesn't bother me too much," said Phil. "Worse comes to worst, we'll tie her to the back of the wreck and run her up and down the Long Island Expressway a few times."

"You and what army?" Simon challenged.

"One more thing," said Sam. "We don't tell anybody about Simon's family."

"Good idea," Phil agreed. "You know, this whole thing just gets cooler with each new development. I mean, first Antiflux and the land, and suddenly his dad's Interflux, and he really likes his dad, but we still fight the company — it's got emotional conflict, excitement. And strategy! We make a move, they make a countermove. This is just great! Simon, you are one truly awesome human being!"

"Thanks," said Simon with a strange grin.

"Mark my words, there are glorious days ahead," Phil prophesied. "Life gets so dull sometimes that you forget things can be this good. A little stability is a small price to pay for this kind of excitement."

"Hold on a minute there," said Sam. "Let's get this straight right now. We are *not* trying to make life exciting for *you*. A lot of stupid things have been done, for whatever reason, and now we have to do some even stupider ones to stay afloat. So try and restrain your thrills. We're writing this letter not because we want to make trouble, but because we need the peace and quiet to try and figure out how we're going to get out of this. If we got the chance, we'd be crazy not to give Interflux its land, give Wendy back her party money, and go home happy not to have to worry about tomorrow. I don't care if Interflux puts up a slaughterhouse on Nassau Arts' front lawn. At least when I go to sleep at night, I'll know that no one's plotting against me, whether it's the world's largest corporation, the world's angriest dancer, or someone I haven't even thought of yet."

"Well," said Phil, "either way we've got to write the letter."

Dear Mr. Mayor,

The organization Antiflux that lawfully purchased Land Lot 1346B and has lawfully fenced same is a subsidiary of the Student Council Program Board of the Nassau County High School for Visual, Literary, and Performing Arts. Any communication you may wish to make regarding this property can therefore be sent to the school's address in care of the Program Board. You can be assured that we will respond to any lawful request made by the Town of Greenbush, and pay all taxes promptly. Enclosed is a photocopy of the lawful Title Deed to Land Lot 1346B, as proof of our lawful ownership.

Yours very truly,

Antiflux,

per: Wendy Orr

Student Council President

Wendy looked up. "You want me to sign this?" Sam and Phil nodded. Barbara gazed at Sam. Simon shuffled.

Wendy smiled diabolically. "Read my lips: No."

"But, Wendy," Phil began.

"No," Wendy repeated. "Negative, *nyet*, forget it, put out the light, pull the chain, shut the door. No." Predictably, Barbara had nothing to add.

Simon had expected Wendy's reaction, but had never believed her refusal could become her so well.

"Well, okay," said Sam indifferently. "I guess we'd better tell everyone that we've lost the land."

Wendy stopped short. "What do you mean 'everyone'?"

"The whole school. Practically everybody's interested to see how this turns out. The land belongs to all of us, you know. They'll be pretty upset when they find out that one little signature would have made the difference."

"I won't sign it," she said, less certainly.

"Oh, we understand," said Sam sympathetically, his dejection apparent. "After all, if one person should have the power to dynamite something for the whole school, it may as well be the Student Council president. They probably won't blame you — most of them — maybe."

"You're putting it all on *my* shoulders!" Wendy exploded.

"Of course not," said Sam innocently. "Oh, a few people might get that impression, since you're the only one who could have signed, but you wouldn't."

"What about *him*?" Wendy exclaimed, pointing at Simon, and spitting out the syllable "him" as though it tasted like vitriol. "*He* bought this dumb land! Why doesn't *he* sign?"

"You're the president," Sam explained. "When the mayor sees your name, he'll know that you speak for all fifteen hundred students. You've been involved in community activities before. Sure, we'd all be more than happy to sign, but who's Sam Stavrinidis? When they see 'Wendy Orr,' they'll know we're on the level."

"But you're *not* on the level! This is the slimiest thing I've ever seen! And now I've got to endorse it because, if I don't, you're going to tell everyone it was me who ruined everything!"

"I would never dream of doing such a thing," said Sam, his expression open and sincere.

"I believe you!" blurted Barbara spontaneously, catching all three boys off guard. None of them had ever heard her say anything except in answer to a direct question.

Wendy groaned. "All right! Why do I have to take the rap alone? If I sign, why shouldn't the sleazebag sign, too?"

Sam had no immediate reply, so Phil announced, "For an undisclosed reason, that's why!"

"You're quite right," said Sam quickly. "Your signature should be countersigned by no fewer than two members of the Program Board. I don't want you thinking that we're not fair."

"You don't know the meaning of the word," said Wendy acidly.

So it was that the letter delivered by special messenger to the Town Hall was signed by Wendy Orr and countersigned by Philip Baldwin and Sam Stavrinidis. Antiflux was now out in the open.

Seven

It took the town only two days to respond to the Anti-flux communication. Their letter came through Wendy, who delivered it directly to Simon, saying, "Hey, sleazebag, take this and choke on it. It's for you." Simon was beginning to have very serious doubts about his chances with Wendy.

Dear Ms. Orr,

We appreciate your reply of the day before yesterday, yet there are a number of questions that we feel need answering, particularly those regarding I. Simon. Mr. Simon purchased the land, yet his name appears nowhere in your letter. To us this seems a rather strange omission. We await your explanation.

Yours truly,

F. Van Doren, Mayor

"The nerve of that guy!" Phil exploded. We ought to tell him where he heads into. 'Dear Mr. Mayor. You want to know who I. Simon is? We'll tell you who I. Simon is! None of your business, that's who I. Simon is!'"

That wasn't too far from what the Program Board actually did send to the mayor, which was a politely worded letter reminding the Town of Greenbush of Antiflux's lawful claim to 1346B, and pointing out the fact that it therefore didn't make a particle of difference who I. Simon was. He was Antiflux's old purchasing agent, and had been replaced.

"It's not dishonest," Simon said earnestly. "Irving Simon *was* replaced — by Simon Irving, right when I had my records changed."

* * *

Interflux was baffled. In its history, the company had dealt with every kind of lunatic, environmentalist, and profiteer, and yet here was something completely different — a Student Council that demanded nothing, would speak to no one, and declared only its intention of being a bad neighbor.

On top of this, the bean diet raged mercilessly on, and showed all the potential of being the most destructive marathon in Irving family history. With unpleasantness both at home and at work, Mr. Irving spent an increasing amount of time at the Fosterville Country Club, and Simon often went with him. Mr. Irving felt father and son time took his mind off his problems, for the poor man had no way of knowing that his son *was* his problems.

"Boy, Dad!" gasped Simon after his father had wiped up the court with him at squash. "You were a madman out there! Unbeatable!"

"I'm working off some frustrations, son. I'm paying work crews to sit on their — " He grimaced. "No. I refuse to talk about it. That's the whole point of coming here. I'm going to relax if it kills me."

The two began to walk toward the changing room.

"What time do we have to be back for dinner?" Simon asked.

"Thanks a lot, kid! That's the other thing I'm trying not to think about." He sighed. "Remember steak? I do." He slapped his knee with determination. "I'm going to have one tonight! We're going to find the best restaurant in town and order us up a couple of slabs of meat you can hardly see over! I'll go call your mother." He was so enthused by this idea that he rushed right out to use the phone. When he returned, he was totally cast down. "The bean casserole is already in the oven."

Simon drove home while his father sat in the passenger's seat, complaining. "It gets worse and worse. Antiflux yesterday, bean casserole today. Who knows what's next? It's not worth my while getting up in the morning. Do you know where The Flake spent the night last night? In the Kathmandu city jail! One of his idiot friends dared him to ski down Mount Everest in the nude! They had a drink riding on it!" He shuddered. "The *New York Post* called *me* for comment."

"Take it easy, Dad."

* * *

The following Monday, Mayor Van Doren made another trip to Interflux to find out his opinions on the progress of the Antiflux situation. There he learned that he had decided to discuss Antiflux with the Nassau Arts administration and see if he could make some headway.

The top administration people at Nassau Arts had their offices in an area of the basement known by one and all as The Dungeon. It was to this suite that the mayor was conducted that afternoon, only to be requested to leave twenty minutes later after he referred to the Student Council Program Board as "a pain in the butt." He did come away with one piece of information, however: the administration refused to interfere with the spending of the Student Council budget, even if that budget was spent buying land.

The Dungeon, though, decided to follow up on this, and sent for Wendy Orr. She claimed no responsibility for Antiflux, and put them onto Simon Irving.

Thus, on Tuesday morning, Simon found a note on his locker requesting him to report to The Dungeon at his earliest convenience.

"Look," Sam pleaded, "you don't go to The Dungeon without your agent."

Simon shook his head. "I don't know. I don't think I buy this agent stuff. I can speak for myself."

"You don't understand! This isn't just anything! This is The Dungeon! They say the last student issue that went all the way to The Dungeon was when Nathan first began *Omni* and needed the go-ahead from the top. That's history in this place! And even then, Nathan Kruppman took T.C. Serrette with him for the meeting! Now, T.C. and Philip are practically brothers this week. Philip can get him to drop everything and see you right now."

They found Phil, but Simon was still not convinced that T.C. was the route for him.

"Wait a minute," Phil pointed out. "This Dungeon thing concerns the whole Program Board. We have to take a vote. I vote yes, Sotirios votes with me, all opposed, blah, blah, blah, motion carried. Come on, let's see T.C. before first class."

"All right," Simon conceded, "but I want you to know that I'm only doing this to get you off my back."

* * *

"T.C.'s the greatest!" Simon raved after the meetings were over. "Everyone should have an agent! This is the twenty-first century, after all!"

"Come on," said Sam. "Tell us what happened."

"T.C. was amazing. He knew everything, and he answered all the questions perfectly. And he only charged me two days. And he spoke so well. And — "

"Yeah, yeah," Phil insisted. "What about the Dungeon guys? What did they say?"

Simon shrugged. "Them? They just wanted to make sure we're not crooks or anything. They're not going to interfere at all so long as we don't break any laws and don't get bad publicity for the school."

"Are you sure?" asked Sam seriously.

"What kind of question is that?" snapped Phil. "Of course he's sure! These Dungeon guys must be really cool. Mr. Brownlee would have had us bazooka'd.

He ran Greenbush High like a concentration camp."

"Honestly, Sam," said Simon, "there's nothing to worry about. These people sincerely believe in the students' right to handle their own affairs."

"So we were lucky," said Sam. "This time."

Phil was of a different opinion. "It's destiny, really. I mean, Antiflux comes up against the most impossible obstacles, but she always pulls through. I'm starting to have a lot of faith here."

Sam made a face.

* * *

Work was now coming up for examination regularly in painting class, and Simon found that he was learning a lot. He was impressed with the talents of his fellow students, but no less pleased with his "Tavern Scene," which was now finished.

Querada continued to be a one-man show. "'Saturday at the Beach.' Mr. Stavrinidis, you and I both know there are no camels at a public beach. Yet you, Mr. Stavrinidis, you very annoying person, have put three camels into this picture!" He turned his eyes pleadingly up to heaven. "Why, O great organizing principle of the universe, must I suffer with this idiot who chooses to throw away his talent and make garbage?" He shook his head, snorting like a horse. "I look in the change booth in the background — a camel; there, printed on this child's beach ball — a camel; and this baby in the surf is playing with a little plastic camel!"

"You missed the one reflected in the sunglasses of the lady in the red bikini," Sam said mildly.

Simon held his breath, expecting an explosion. But the artist simply walked quietly back to his seat and, without uttering a sound, overturned his heavy oak desk so quickly that the whole process was complete in a fraction of a second. Simon missed it all in the space of a single sneeze, but there was the wreckage, undeniable proof. The desk was on its side, and dozens of papers were still airborn, settling over the battlefield.

"Mr. Stavrinidis, when I was teaching at the University of Copenhagen, a colleague of mine had a very talented student who thought it was amusing to paint an escaped convict in every crowd scene. Each piece of work, there he was — a little man in a striped suit, hiding. My colleague finally went berserk and ran his student over with a mobile home. Querada does not own a mobile home." He walked across the room and bent down so that his eyes were an inch and a half from Sam's. *But I can rent one! No — more — camels!* He turned to the rest of the class, back to normal once again. "That's all the work handed in to me. Does anybody else have something to present?"

Simon raised his hand. "I've got a painting finished." There was an uncomfortable pause, so he added, "Do you want me to bring it up to the front?"

The artist glared at him pityingly. "Mr. Simon, have I ever told you the story of the young artist who asked stupid questions?"

Simon flushed. "Yes, sir, you have."

Querada stomped on the floor. *"Then set up your picture!"*

Simon was trembling as he placed his canvas on the display stand but, as he stepped back and viewed his "Tavern Scene," all his old confidence returned, and he cast the teacher a look of cautious triumph.

Querada stared at the painting for a long time, cocking his head, stepping back, moving forward, and snapping *"Silence!"* at the slightest shuffling noise or squeak of a chair. For ten full minutes the class waited while he examined "Tavern Scene."

Then he began to point out every single flaw on the entire canvas with such nit-picking precision that Simon could only stare in mute shock as his image of perfection was dashed to pieces. He could almost see the Vishnik Prize, his passport to freedom from Interflux, sprouting white fluffy wings and flying away from him until it was only a tiny speck above the smokestacks on the horizon.

The torture didn't end quickly. After Querada finished his lengthy list of faults, he called the class up to gather around the painting and get a look at these flaws close up. By the time the period ended, Simon was so down that a future in his father's office counting zipper teeth was beginning to look bright.

Then something strange happened. Before leaving the room, several of his classmates came over to Simon and congratulated him on the success of "Tavern Scene." Simon was completely mystified.

"Man, I've never seen Querada like a painting so

much," said Peter Ashley, shaking his head.

"He cut me up for forty-five minutes!" Simon blurted out.

"Forty-five minutes of attention from Querada!" said Laura dreamily. "I've never seen that before."

"I don't get it," Simon said to Sam later. "I took five times as much abuse as anybody else. Why are people congratulating me?"

"Are you kidding? Sometimes I think you'll never adjust. That's the greatest honor Querada can give you. He *loved* that painting."

"Yeah, sure," said Simon sarcastically. "He only made up that part about every single bit of it being wrong so that I wouldn't get a swelled head! I can just go home and take it easy, and they'll mail me the Vishnik Prize!"

"I'll bet Querada feels that if you rework that painting, you've got a good shot at the Vishnik Prize. You've got it made. You could coast on this picture all semester."

"Forget it," said Simon determinedly. "I'm not submitting a picture with forty-five minutes of flaws. I'm going to do something so much better that that nine-foot crackpot won't be able to think of a single thing to say! Not one!"

* * *

Although nothing much had happened, for some reason Antiflux went big time in the school halls that week. Simon found that practically everybody knew him, and he now received full credit from all as the architect of Antiflux's master plan. It was not as much credit, he noticed a little sourly, as Sam Stavrinidis seemed to get for his substantially smaller part in the affair. Nor did it appear to be enough to merit him a role in Nathan's movie (not that he wanted one). And it certainly wasn't enough to earn him anything more promising than a passing snarl from Wendy Orr.

"She shot you with a fire extinguisher!" Phil protested when Simon told him and Sam about his feelings for Wendy.

"Yeah, but she looked so good doing it."

"Love is blind," said Sam wearily, "not to mention stupid."

"Man, I'd never get involved with a girl who shot *me* with a fire extinguisher," Phil stated positively. "I've got a list in my mind of things that I just will not take from women, and that's on it."

"Speaking of women," said Sam casually, concentrating on the far wall rather than his two friends, "and I'm not sure about this, so it might sound stupid, but I'm beginning to get the vague impression that that girl Barbara might kind of like me."

Simon looked at Phil in exasperation. "Well, it sure doesn't take a brick building to fall on him!"

"Of course she likes you, you idiot!" Phil exploded. "Everyone in the building knows it; why don't you?"

Sam shuffled uncomfortably. "Well, I was sort of noticing, but she's so good-looking and so popular, I figured what would she want with me?"

Phil snorted in disgust. "I hate you, you know that? Now, listen very carefully, because I'm only going to say this once. Barbara, along with every other female this side of Montauk Point, thinks you're the greatest thing since the invention of the wheel. Look how they all chase you."

"Aw, come on. They just like me as — you know — a friend."

Phil was screaming now. "You're so stupid! Look, just ask her out, will you? To make me happy, okay?"

"I think I'll just let it slide and see what happens," Sam decided. "If things look good in a little while, then maybe I'll ask her out."

"You know," Phil said later as he and Simon checked T.C. Serrette's accommodation schedule in front of locker #0750, "sometimes that Sotirios ticks me off so much, if we weren't friends from childhood, I'd take the wreck and run him over, if he remembered to put gas in the tank. They wasted that face on him. Man, they could have given it to me!"

Simon examined the sheet. "T.C.'s not coming to my place for a while yet."

Phil snorted "That's because he's spending all his time in my basement. If this keeps up my mother's going to throw me out and adopt him!"

* * *

In math class, the homework pool was working like a charm. Its membership now stood at six, and the only drawback in the whole scheme of things was that Phil, who was not living up to his potential in math, either, was making mistakes that were ultimately duplicated five times. No one had the heart to throw him out, however, since this was, after all, his pool.

"I'm getting the math all right," Phil explained. "It's the numbers that are fouling me up."

"The math and the numbers are the same thing!" said Bill McIntosh as he threatened, in a friendly way, to slam-dunk Phil's face if his accuracy didn't improve.

Phil's new big thing, of course, was photography. He was working very hard at setting up a portfolio good enough to buy him some tenure in the department. He had mastered the darkroom quite well, but his sense of composition was getting a lot of unwelcome attention from the teacher, Mr. Floyd. His best picture to date was a portrait of his mother. However, in that shot, a plant on the table behind her chair was positioned so unluckily that its leaves appeared to be sprouting from her ears.

In addition to these troubles, there was a problem with equipment; more specifically, tripods. Whenever Phil signed out a tripod, it would break before he had a chance to return it. "It's not my fault! Honestly!" he complained. "It's just bad luck. I always get the ones that are hanging by a thread, so when I try to use them, they fall apart."

"Why don't you try checking them before you sign them out?" Sam suggested.

"Well, I do, but there must be — you know — hidden defects. Mr. Floyd is really sore, so he gets on my case a lot. Photography can be a drag sometimes."

The only class Simon seemed to be having no problem at all with was design and composition. This, the teacher informed him, just in case he was considering feeling pride in his A average, was typical of all the Querada students.

That week, Xerxes "Buzz" Durham banned all computers, insisting that he had just discovered they were the worst offenders against psychic growth. Poor Dino, who had all his essays typed by Dina, had neglected to mention to her that penmanship was the new order of the day. Mr. Durham, who held fast behind his convictions, changeable though they were, rejected Dino's latest paper outright.

Biology class was way behind schedule because Miss Glandfield spent so much of her time and energy out at the Antiflux land on patrol to make sure that Interflux didn't try to sneak any trucks through. This vigil was so absorbing that she would often forget to come to class. When Simon walked into the lab on Wednesday and found her there, it was the first he'd seen of her in quite a while. Even more surprising was the reaction he got from Johnny Zull.

"Man, I've been hearing a lot of really heavy-duty things about you lately."

"What things?" asked Simon suspiciously.

"Antiflux, man. All about how you're running it, and how the whole thing was your idea, and how you guys are kicking Interflux upside the head. I'm proud of you, dude! And you know what I said to those people when they told me all the great things you've been doing? I said 'That's *my* lab partner!' And boy, were they impressed! Man, I knew I'd be a good influence on you. Interflux is the worst example of the Long Island establishment. Throwing mud-balls at them goes with everything I've ever stood for! Although I'll never understand how you managed to organize all this and keep it from your lab partner." He shook his head. "Sure, I've been hearing stuff about Simon Irving, but I always thought Irving was your first name. And anyway, I didn't make the connection until now. Man, I can't wait till you meet the guys!"

"The guys?"

"Yeah, the guys. Outer Nimrod. I told them all about you on the phone. They asked if they could meet you, and I said I could swing that, us being lab partners and all. Oops, I guess I spilled the beans and ruined the surprise."

"The surprise," Simon repeated, his heart preparing to sink.

"I'm taking you to our gig Friday night as my personal guest. You'll love this club we're playing! It's one of the classiest places in New York."

"Friday night, Friday night, Friday night," said Simon, trying desperately to come up with a previous engagement.

Johnny looked at him, his face earnest and concerned. "You *can* make it, can't you, Simon?"

Simon sighed. "Of course. Wouldn't miss it for the world. Thanks for inviting me."

"Hey, no problem. Lab partners always pull together."

"Right," said Simon.

* * *

115

On Friday night, while Phil traveled with a Nathan Kruppman video crew to Staten Island to film the first moonwalk, Simon rode in on the Long Island Rail Road with Johnny Zull and his favorite guitar. Their destination: Scuzz, a tiny club located below an all-night drugstore in Manhattan's Lower East Side. Simon was prepared to see a dilapidated old neighborhood, but never in his wildest nightmares had he envisioned anything like Scuzz.

"Doesn't it just blow you away?" asked Johnny, breathing deeply as though he had just walked into a garden of hyacinths.

"Is it safe?" Simon asked.

"Absolutely not," said Johnny with reverence.

"What?"

"Well, that's the whole point. The building was condemned in 1973, but Louie — he's the owner — somehow managed to save it. What a break!"

Simon had a brief giddy vision of a *New York Post* headline: FLUX BOSS'S SON MURDERED IN SLUM BRAWL. He felt like running away, but remembered that the only thing worse than being in this neighborhood was being in this neighborhood alone.

The other members of Outer Nimrod were older than Johnny, ranging from nineteen to twenty-two, but they may as well have been cloned from the same master cell. All were welcoming and friendly, and none of them could seem to get over the group's amazing luck in getting themselves a booking at Scuzz.

Besides Johnny, Outer Nimrod was made up of

Neb, Ig, and Frieda. Frieda was the lead singer, and looked about as much like a Frieda as Scuzz looked like a club. He was a two-hundred-and-seventy-five-pound part-time wrestler with a ring in his nose and enough chest hair to stuff a queen-size mattress. With Neb on drums, Ig on bass, and Johnny Zull on lead guitar, Outer Nimrod was a group formidable enough to face the Friday night crowd at Scuzz, a collection of fans who looked and smelled like cave people.

Simon, who had been somewhat prepared for this by Johnny's tall tales (which he now believed one hundred percent), selected a table which he felt would be good for hiding under just in case things got a little out of hand. But the club filled up quickly, as Scuzz was famous for standing-room only Friday nights, and he was joined by two Neanderthal identical twins with arms like tree trunks, each of whom drank eight beers before even sitting down. In all fairness, Simon had to admit that they were friendly, and tried to involve himself in their conversation about crowbars. He sat listening to them for forty minutes and watching in awe as they ordered beer by what was called "the octo" (eight mugs of draft).

At around twenty after eleven, Louie, the owner, decided the bar receipts had reached his Friday night quota, and he came onstage and said, "Now a bunch of guys are going to come out here and play music."

Frieda led Outer Nimrod onto the stage, grabbed the microphone, and bellowed, "We're Outer Nimrod and I'm Frieda! Anybody want to make something out of it?"

At Simon's table, one Neanderthal nudged the other. "Hey, these guys got potential. Order us up another couple of octos."

Frieda seemed disappointed that no one chose to challenge him. "Okay, let's do stuff."

Outer Nimrod exploded into a cacophony of the heaviest of metal, the brashest of hardcore, and the unmistakable sound of Europe-bound 747s revving their engines. Johnny Zull was spectacular, creating most of the sound, passing his hand over the guitar strings as though by instinct, while Frieda shrieked in a voice that was nothing short of bone-chilling. The Scuzz crowd, obviously a discriminating group of individuals, savored the opening number like wine-tasters, reserving judgment until the full bouquet could be experienced. The two Neanderthals were nodding at each other in appreciation, all the while putting away octos like it was going out of style.

But then the great Jonathan Zulanovitch stepped up to the front of the stage and began his patented guitar solo, calling on all his classical training, intricate knowledge of excruciating noise, showman-ship, and every single last watt the club's amplifiers could deliver.

Simon goggled. Johnny Zull was the greatest guitarist in the world, alternately making his instrument scream, cry, laugh, and moan in rapid succession, all at a decibel level way above tolerance. He was incredible. Spontaneously, Simon leaped to his feet to lead the cheers and applause for his lab partner, not realizing the symbolic value of his gesture. To a Scuzz crowd, looking at the world through a haze of too many octos, the first person to rise was the traditional starter of the fight.

Simon was never sure afterward which Neanderthal lunged at him first, but it wasn't important, as they both hit within a fraction of a second of each other, sandwiching him and knocking the wind out of him so completely that he collapsed to the floor, gasping. This turned out to be a genuine stroke of luck since, at eye level, fists were soon flying in all directions, and on the floor he only had to worry about being stomped on. Within seconds, the brawl encompassed the whole club, and Simon crawled on his hands and knees behind the overturned table. Outer Nimrod played on, encouraged by this show of appreciation. Simon got up the nerve to peer out from behind the table, and found himself staring right into the eyes of one of the Neanderthals, who luckily couldn't get at him, since he was being held in a headlock by a girl with blue hair.

"Hey, man," croaked the twin. "Why aren't you fighting? Don't you like the music?"

Quickly, Simon ducked back down again, cursing the fate that had brought him to be lab partners with Johnny Zull.

* * *

Mr. and Mrs. Irving sat in front of the late movie that night, eating celery sticks with low-cal bean dip, the recipe for which had appeared that morning in *The Sun*. Mr. Irving was concentrating hard on pretending they were potato chips, sometimes holding his breath to weaken the taste.

"I wonder if I. Simon is having fun tonight," he announced suddenly. "I hope not. I hope all of Antiflux isn't having fun tonight. I hope Antiflux never again has fun, and I. Simon has the least fun of all."

"Cyril," protested his wife. "It's the weekend."

"I have no weekend. I have Antiflux." He grimaced. "The part that gets me is that none of this would ever have happened if The Flake hadn't decided that he needed a complex. We figured we'd keep him off our backs for a while, so we sent him to this big international convention. But he just came back, looked at me with those big stupid blue eyes of his, and said, 'Cyril, how come we don't have a complex?' So I explained to him our decentralized production scheme, and he said, 'The guy from Hypertech showed us pictures of all these great big beautiful complexes, just like whole cities. Cyril, we have more money than Hypertech. We should have at least one complex.' So he showed up at a board meeting, and everybody there was so thrilled to see him with his pants on for a change that they were ready to promise him anything." He threw his arms up, almost overturning the bean dip. "Okay, I figured we'd get away with just changing the name of this place from Greenbush Plant to Greenbush Complex, and maybe put an addition on the cafeteria or something. But no. You know what The Flake thinks the key ingredient of a complex is?"

"Please, Cyril — "

"A monorail. Can you believe it? We have to build this monstrosity and reroute business to make it useful so that he can ride the monorail. And finally, after months of planning and preparation so that this complex really will benefit the company, a bunch of snotty, stuck-up, artistic high school kids won't let me build it!"

Mrs. Irving spoke up. "Please don't say that kind of thing in front of Simon. He's very happy at Nassau Arts. He has friends, and he's fitting in beautifully."

"Everything about that school rubs me the wrong way. I don't go for this painting in high school. I think it's great that the boy has a hobby, but there comes a point where a young man should make something of himself — like I did. What has he got against Abercrombie Prep?"

"Nothing, dear. It's just that he's so talented that he deserves his chance to make painting a career."

"Painting isn't a career. There's a future for him in Interflux. That's a career."

"But he doesn't want it," she insisted. "Now, maybe you're right and he will end up with you in the long run. But you have to let him be. If he should decide to stay with painting, then you'll just have to accept it. Why, he's a new person since he's at Nassau — he comes home every day chock-full of stories about friends and classes, and amusing little anecdotes. Even his very first week he was laughing about how, when he registered at the school, the office had his first and last names reversed."

Mr. Irving chuckled in spite of himself. "I guess

that would make him ha, ha — Irving Simon." The smile faded. "Irving Simon? But that's —that's — " He looked up in disbelief. " — *I. Simon.*"

* * *

It was after four when Simon finally arrived home, bone-weary, still aching from the Neanderthal sandwich, and completely drenched with beer. In one night, he had taken off more weight from sheer terror than the bean diet had managed in almost three weeks. The police had cleared Scuzz out around two A.M. but, as was his custom, Johnny decided to take the later train, and he and Simon had taken a leisurely stroll through unsafe neighborhoods. Simon was most sincerely surprised to have arrived home alive.

His parents were waiting in the doorway, which was to be expected at this hour. He'd probably catch a bit of a lecture, but they would be so glad that nothing had happened to him that everything would blow over. Yes, he could see the anxious relief on his mother's face. A typical staying-out-too-late rap. Nothing too heavy. His father's appearance puzzled him a little. His face was bright, bright purple, and there were beads of sweat on his forehead, but he wore a huge artificial grin that looked almost painful to maintain.

"Hi, Mom. Hi, Dad. Sorry I'm so late."

"Thank goodness you're home!" His mother rushed up to embrace him. "Simon — I smell beer!"

"Hi, son," Mr. Irving greeted, his voice somewhat distorted by the obvious effort of maintaining his ridiculous smile.

"Dad, are you all right?" asked Simon in concern.

"You're sweating, and you're all blue."

"Young man," challenged his mother, "you reek of beer!"

"Yeah, I know, Mom. Someone spilled an octo on me."

"You'll be pleased to know, son," said Mr. Irving, the stiffness of his grin still contorting his whole glowing countenance, "that we made a major break-through today. We found out how I. Simon managed to disappear from all records."

"What's an octo?" his mother persisted.

"Eight mugs of beer."

"Aha! You've been drinking!"

"I haven't, Mom. It's just on my clothes."

"How did it get on your clothes?"

"Just a minute, Mom. Hang on a sec." He turned back to his father. "You were saying — ?"

"I was saying that I. Simon never really disappeared. He just changed his name — to Simon I."

Simon's breath caught in his throat. All the unpleasantness of the evening suddenly shriveled to nothing and was replaced by anticipation of the unpleasantness to come. I. Simon had been discovered. The jig was up.

Eight

The bean diet ended on that day, but this blessed event did nothing to cool tempers in the combat zone. For the first time, the bosses of Interflux and Antiflux met face to face, and joined battle.

One might have thought that Simon was hopelessly outclassed in the argument, but he held his own, and whenever the father seemed to be getting the upper hand, the son would always come back with *"Why?"* Simon was finding that he was actually feeling better now that the whole thing was out in the open. Hardened by his night at Scuzz, and educated by having seen T.C. at work, he was not afraid to trade verbal blows with anybody, even Cyril Irving.

The confrontation had three basic stages. First, the "How could you do this to me, your own father?" stage, which was the most emotional, and easily the loudest. In it, Mr. Irving was the dominant figure, issuing challenges designed to make Simon feel guilty. It was working beautifully, except that Simon was far too stubborn to allow his father to see that he felt like a worm. Then came the second stage, the theme of which was "Give me back my land." Once again, Mr. Irving did most of the talking/shouting. He doubled, tripled, and then quintupled the price of the land, but Simon explained that it belonged to the Student Council, and was most emphatically not for sale, certainly not for warehouses full of zipper teeth. The students were not interested in profit; they were making a point. This led nicely into the third stage, which was a philosophical debate between the two Fluxes, Anti and Inter. Here Simon dominated the floor, waxing eloquent over the Antiflux point of view while his father sat in mute wonder. He tried turning the conversation back to stage one, where he had been in control, but once Simon was started on the subject of Interflux, nothing short of a movement of the earth could stop him.

By this time, it was almost seven A.M., and the war was called on account of sleep. Mr. Irving made it clear that it was only a ceasefire, and that Simon was by no means off the hook. Both father and son slept till half past one in the afternoon, and when they awoke, they found Mrs. Irving already up, and a large lunch awaiting them. That was when the bean diet hit its official close. Mrs. Irving decided that, if ever there was a moment to serve a meal unendorsed by *The Sun*, this was it. She had prepared roast chicken, heaps of mashed potatoes, thick rich gravy, freshly baked bread, a chocolate layer cake that was nothing short of tremendous, and most important of all, nary a bean in sight. She hoped that full stomachs would help smooth over the animosity between her husband and son.

It didn't work. As Simon was sitting down, his father announced, "Oh, no, no, no. You don't want to eat this food. Interflux paid for this food."

"Now you stop that, Cyril. The boy is hungry."

"He has the courage of his convictions. He'd be angry at us if we let him compromise his principles that way. Right, son?"

"If you'd prefer, I'll go to Burger King and eat there," said Simon tersely.

"Well, there's just one problem with that," his father replied. "You'd pay for your burger out of your allowance, which of course comes from me, making it dirty, tainted, filthy Interflux money, extorted from the common people as Interflux ruthlessly mows them down in pursuit of corporate goals."

"Cyril, I insist you stop this!"

"Well, if you want," said Simon, with a stubbornness that could have been acquired only through heredity, "I'll take the money from my college account. Some of it, you may remember, was deposited before you started to work for Interflux."

"And how will you get to the bank and to Burger King?" challenged his father. "Certainly, you can't take your car, as you've probably realized by now that the money to pay for it came from you-know-who."

"I'll walk," said Simon stoutly. "I won't take my watch. I'll tell time by the sun. I'll wear only clothes that I got as presents from non-Interflux people. And on my feet I'll wear the bowling shoes that I won at Bowlerama for getting a strike when the lucky pin was out. If you want, I'll even muss up my hair so there'll be no trace of the last haircut that you and Interflux paid for."

"That sounds fine, son. But it just occurred to me that this house was paid for with money that, at some point or another, passed through the hands of Interflux — "

"I'll stay with friends."

"Every night?"

"It's been done."

Just when Mr. Irving was about to go after Simon with a chicken bone, Mrs. Irving jumped up from her chair and announced, in a voice filled with more authority and volume than Simon and his father had ever heard from her:

"I've had enough!"

Father and son stared in shock.

"You're both acting like a couple of two-year-olds, and this is where it ends! I will not have this senseless fighting in my house! Now, I'm not going to say anything about your silly land, because it has no place in our home! What you're bickering about is business!" She turned to her husband. "You keep it at the office!" And to Simon, "You keep it at school! You can meet in a boardroom somewhere and slaughter one another, but in this house you are father and son, and you love each other! Cyril, how *dare* you make your son feel guilty about living in his home? Simon, how *dare* you fight with your father, who's been nothing but good to you since before you were born? I have no authority at all over how you two conduct your lives from nine to five, but when those hours are over, you are members of the Irving family, regardless of what has gone on during the day! That's it! The issue is absolutely closed!" She sat back down and continued to eat her lunch quietly, as though nothing had happened.

Simon and his father were so utterly cowed by this performance that they finished the meal in complete silence. The truce came over the cake.

"Son," said Mr. Irving, "your mother is right. I apologize for bringing up a business matter at home, and I promise that, at home, it won't be mentioned again. We're father and son and it's Saturday afternoon. What say we go down to the club and shoot some hoops?"

"Right, Dad. And I apologize if I was in any way disrespectful, and I promise that, at home, I won't discuss these things, either. And I think some basketball sounds like a great idea."

Mrs. Irving beamed.

But as soon as the two were out the door, Mr. Irving turned to his son. "But you'd better know that, as the head of Interflux, I intend to crush the life out of Antiflux, nail your carcasses to the wall, and put my zipper teeth wherever it suits me."

"And as the head of Antiflux," Simon said, just as readily, "it's my job to make sure you don't."

Then the two shook hands in a peculiar gesture of

agreeing to disagree. And strangely, despite all that had happened, Simon felt as close to his father as he had ever been.

* * *

"So how did he take it?" Sam asked before first class Monday morning.

"Well, let me put it this way," Simon replied. "If my mother hadn't been there, he probably would have ripped my lungs out. But I think it's all for the best that it's finally out. What worries me is that, in business, he's going to hit twice as hard now that he knows it's me. He said he intends to crush the life out of Antiflux."

"Do you think he'd go for a deal where we give him the land and he gives us the original sixty-seven hundred dollars, which we can give to Wendy to smooth everything over?" Sam asked hopefully.

"I wouldn't take it," said Simon. "He offered me five times what we paid, and I still said no."

Sam's face fell a mile and a half.

"Way to go!" cheered Phil. "Make them sweat!"

"I can't believe this!" Sam exploded. "I jump into your mess, get involved, save your neck a couple of times, and this is how you reward me! We could be out of this hole! Instead, you've dug it deeper!"

"It's just like you told Wendy," said Simon righteously. "If we took a poll of every kid in school, I think they'd vote to keep the land and fight. Antiflux is bigger than just the three of us now."

"But it's the three of us who are going to end up on the firing line!"

"It's my father," said Simon. "I'll take all the blame."

"No you won't!" said Phil dramatically. "I'm with you all the way. When my friends are in trouble, I'm in trouble." He added, "I spend enough time in trouble for both myself *and* my friends."

Sam sighed. "The only difference between playing with my dog and hanging out with you guys is that my dog has a lot more common sense. All right, all right. If you guys want to go to war with peashooters against cruise missiles, I may as well stand with you at ground zero. I just want to lodge my formal protest right here and now."

"You already lodged your formal protest back on fence-building day," Phil pointed out.

"That was for before; this is for now. If I'm going to end up charging into the thick of the battle under the banner of stupid, impulsive, harebrained ideas, I reserve the right to complain as much as I want. You guys are both nuts."

"I knew you'd come around to our way of thinking," Phil said smugly. "Hey, have either of you guys seen T.C. around? There's nobody at #0750."

"You can't be thrown out of photography already!" said Simon. "The week hasn't even started yet."

"No, another tripod committed suicide at my house this weekend. Mr. Floyd said one more and I was on equipment probation. I need T.C. with me when I return the pieces."

"I think you're going to have a lot of trouble getting him today," said Sam. "The word is Nathan's in school."

"Nathan Kruppman?" Phil exclaimed with reverence. "Here? Why? Is he shooting?"

"No. He's meeting with some teachers to talk about his progress and things like that. You can't do everything by correspondence, you know. Also, he's got to work out a mid-term exam schedule that won't interfere with *Omni*."

"Wow! Let's go see him!"

Several hundred students turned out in the large school foyer to greet Nathan that day. When the director himself appeared, with T.C. a respectful half-step behind, the crowd broke into polite, admiring applause, and Nathan smiled and waved casually. He was a short young man, pleasantly homely, but there was an air about him that proclaimed an almost infinite competence. He was the kind of guy, Simon figured, who, if he asked you to jump off a bridge, you'd do it without bothering to ask why, because Nathan must have a good reason. Simon frowned. What was the great one's good reason for opting not to cast Simon Irving in his extravaganza?

Nathan agreed to say a few words. "Hi, guys. Nice to be with you all again. See you on the set."

Then T.C. announced, "Nathan's really busy, everybody. We've got a lot of meetings to go to, so please give us some room."

Instantly, the crowd melted away in front of Nassau Arts' most illustrious student, and he and his agent were off to their meetings, but not before T.C. had promised to find a few free minutes to attend the handing-in of Phil's tripod fragments.

"Has anybody actually seen parts of this movie?" Simon asked as he, Phil, and Sam headed back for their lockers.

"Not even the teacher," said Sam.

"But what if it's lousy?"

"Be real, will you?" said Phil. "Nathan could never make a lousy movie."

* * *

Nothing was accomplished in painting that day, as Emile Querada was plagued by self-doubts.

"This happens three or four times a year," Sam whispered as the artist stood in front of the class, bemoaning his meaningless life and making a terrible fuss. "He talks about it in his book."

"I must have skimmed over that part," Simon responded.

"The one thing to remember is don't say anything. Even if he asks you a direct question, even if he screams in your face, keep quiet."

"What is the point in painting pictures for people to look at?" Querada moaned. "People are cretins! Cretins don't know good pictures from bad pictures! Miss Dixon, why are there so many cretins? Answer me!"

Laura just sat there, tight-lipped.

"What if the cretins are right and I'm wrong? What if I paint terrible pictures? What if I, Querada, *stink*? Mr. Ashley, speak!"

Peter said nothing.

The artist walked right up to Simon and looked straight into his face. "Mr. Simon, *do − I − stink?*"

Simon sat like a statue, determined not to crack.

"No one will answer me! Why can I not get an answer from my own students, my twelve chosen? Someone will answer me!" He rushed to the door, threw it open, reached a long arm out into the hall, and grabbed a student at random. When he pulled his hand back, he had Phil Baldwin by the collar.

"Hey, what's the big idea here? Oh, hi, Sotirios — Simon."

"You! Impartial person! I want a simple, honest answer to a question! Does Querada stink?"

Phil looked shocked. "Pardon?"

"Do I *stink?*"

Oblivious to frantic signaling from Simon and Sam, Phil looked Querada right in the eye and said, "Well, not especially, but if you don't mind my saying so, your cologne is a little tacky."

Simon shut his eyes.

Querada walked over to his desk, sat down heavily, and thumped his head down to the blotter in total dejection. "Go away," he mumbled to Phil, the class, and quite possibly the whole world. "Maybe tomorrow will be a better day."

* * *

A new, unforeseen force began to emerge at Nassau Arts. With Simon and Phil still in the cafeteria line, Sam sat down with his tray under the camel and, like a shot, Barbara was seated opposite him. When Simon and Phil emerged from the line, they found a lively conversation in progress. Half the cafeteria was staring at Barbara, who was not only bubbling with chit-chat but laughing, joking, and gesturing with her hands.

Smiling absurdly at Sam, Simon and Phil left him to his fate, and sat down at a nearby table, where Bill McIntosh had a bet going with Dino that he could sink a half-eaten Nassau Arts rubber hamburger into a cafeteria garbage bin forty-five feet away. The stakes: $100,000 cash.

"Where's Sam?" asked Bill, sucking on a Lifesaver.

Phil tossed his head in the direction of the camel. "The Red Baroness has him in her diabolical clutches."

"I see," said Bill knowingly. "He finally got up the courage to talk to her?"

"No," Simon laughed. "He sat down to wait for us, and by the time we got there, he was kidnapped."

Later, when Sam discreetly reserved the use of the wreck for Friday night, Simon and Phil were on full ribbing alert.

"Why? Have to do a couple of errands for your mom?"

"Well — uh — not exactly."

"I know," said Simon. "Charity work. Sam, you're a prince."

"Aw, get off my back," said Sam sheepishly. "You know darn well I'm going out with Barbara."

Phil pretended to look confused. "Barbara — Barbara — oh yes, Barbara. Red hair and the I.Q. of a geranium."

"Cut it out!" napped Sam. "Besides, she's not that stupid."

"Not stupid?" repeated Phil. "Barbara? Give me a

break, Sotirios! I'll admit that she's great looking, and a really nice person, but don't you think you're over-doing it a little with 'not stupid'?"

Sam made a face. "She's just quiet, that's all."

"So are geraniums."

"Leave him alone," said Simon. Sam was beginning to look dangerous.

* * *

Meanwhile, things were rushed in biology class because Miss Glandfield was so often absent. But those mystical, invisible bonds that exist between lab partners continued to strengthen with Simon and Johnny Zull.

"Man, I knew Scuzz would be a real treat for you, but I never dreamed it would turn out so great. When I saw you standing up to start the fight, I got all choked up. It's great for a guy to see his lab partner supporting him like that. The group thought you were terrific. You're invited to all our gigs."

"Uh — thanks."

Johnny beamed. "So what's the word? What's doing with Antiflux?"

"Right now, nothing."

"Nothing?" Johnny repeated. "Are you sure that's wise?"

"Well, it's not exactly nothing," Simon amended. "You see, we have to wait to see what Interflux does next."

"I get it. We're going to force them to come to us, and then hit them with a counterattack."

Simon grinned weakly. "Something like that."

* * *

The next move came on Tuesday, once again via the town. The Greenbush weed inspector had just so happened to pass by Lot 1346B, and there he saw tall ragweed, goldenrod, and dandelions. The owners were informed that they had forty-eight hours to cut down these noxious weeds or be subject to heavy fines.

"We can't afford heavy fines," Sam said positively. "We can't even afford light fines."

"There are weeds all over town," protested Phil. "Why are they picking on ours?"

"Interflux isn't interested in all over town," Simon said grimly. "They just want to hassle us."

"If this is the biggest hassle they can come up with," said Phil, "then they're not going to last too long in the ring with Antiflux. Why, we could cut those weeds in — "

"Three weeks," finished Sam. "And we've got forty-eight hours. Then — heavy fines."

Simon slapped his knee. "The Student Council has only twenty-six bucks left, and Wendy would cut her own throat before giving us one cent of it. Geez, after all we've been through, I refuse to take the fall over something as stupid as a weed rap!"

"Guys, I don't know what you're getting so upset about," said Phil. "Antiflux is big time. We just call in our troops, and those weeds are history."

Sam was skeptical. "Oh, sure. Fifteen hundred kids who hide all weekend just to get out of doing their own yard work are going to drop everything and volunteer to rid a whole land lot of weeds."

"What's your problem, Sam? Are you afraid to get a little dirt under the fingernails and ruin your good looks for the Red Baroness Friday night?"

"I'll work just as hard as anyone else," Sam said defensively, "and I'll bet you the wreck's next tank of gas that, fifteen minutes into this operation, I'm working and you're figuring out ways to slack off."

"Oh, yeah?"

"Yeah!"

Simon thought it over. Who in his right mind would volunteer to break his back cutting weeds? But then he had a vision of the fence-building. And all those students who had greeted him in the hall, introduced him to friends, and congratulated him on Antiflux. And Johnny Zull's words, often repeated: "Hey man, if there's ever anything I can do . . . " Still, weed-cutting was never going to rank up high on anybody's list of favorite pastimes. So it would probably be a good idea to play up the spirit of Antiflux and de-emphasize the actual operation.

"Okay," he said to Phil and Sam, who were still bickering. "I've got an idea."

* * *

ANTIFLUX
PROGRAM BOARD EMERGENCY MEETING
WEDNESDAY, OCTOBER 24TH, IN THE CAFETERIA AT 3:30
NEW ANTIFLUX PROGRAM
LIMITED NUMBER OF VOLUNTEERS ACCEPTED

"When people hear 'limited volunteers,' they'll break their necks to get in," said Phil by way of self-congratulation.

"Right," Sam agreed. "And when they hear 'weed-cutting,' they'll break *our* necks to get out."

"Keep it quiet until the meeting," said Simon. "I intend to hit them with it in such a way that they won't mind."

There was one problem, however, and that was equipment. A quick inventory of the school's gardening resources turned up three big scythes, and fifteen clippers and trimmers of varying sizes that would not need electrical power. That was not nearly enough to equip the "limited" number of volunteers that Simon was hoping for. Between Simon, Phil, and Sam, they could collect only another nine or ten pieces, so it was unanimously decided to ask a few closer friends to bring tools from home. The only problem with this was that, as they canvassed, Simon was finding with increasing alarm that weed-cutting was even less popular than the Program Board had anticipated.

"Man," said Johnny Zull in true pain, "I'll help you out with this because you're my lab partner and all that, but let me tell you, it's going to be just you and me out there because, no offense, weed-cutting is the ultimate bad news."

Bill McIntosh didn't react much better. "There's only one thing I hate more than cutting weeds, and that's short people who try to get me to cut weeds."

"We could really use you out there," Phil wheedled.

"Oh, all right! But only if it's made absolutely clear that this isn't my idea of a good time. If it starts to get around that I like cutting weeds, I'm finished."

Of the people in Querada's painting class, Sam selected Peter Ashley to recruit. Peter had a reputation for being game for anything, but even he balked when he heard the nature of the job at hand. "This is your big new program? Cutting weeds?" He shook his head. "I don't get it."

"I happen to know that there's going to be a very successful turnout tomorrow," said Sam.

"For cutting weeds?"

"We'll see you there. Don't forget to bring all the cutters you can get together."

In fact, the only people who didn't find the idea completely repulsive were Dino and Dina. The quarter-ton couple had no great love for gardening, but they were interested in supporting Antiflux. And nothing could be that bad if they could do it together. Also, Dino had a neighbor who was a professional gardener, so there was a good chance that he would be able to bring along a lot of equipment.

On Wednesday afternoon, the cafeteria was jam-packed with students waiting to hear the next installment of the Antiflux game plan. Phil was overjoyed with the turnout, and was fighting with Sam over headcount estimates. But Simon was nervous. All through dinner last night, his father had grinned maliciously at him, proving beyond a shadow of a doubt that Interflux had pulled the strings that had sent a town weed inspector to Lot 1346B. Simon had looked back haughtily, although not a word was spoken by either of them for fear of violating Mrs. Irving's household business ban. Simon's feelings now were that this just had to work, even if for no other reason than to wipe that grin off Cyril Irving's face. He glanced anxiously at the closed door to the school kitchen, behind which he knew Bill McIntosh stood guard over a hundred and fifty-odd pieces of cutting equipment. Then he gazed out over the crowd, easily six hundred strong. Bleakly, he realized that in a few short minutes, he would have to hit up this mob to engage in what might well be the least-loved activity of teenage life. He would have to get that equipment into those hands and then coax the whole lot out to 1346B. Impossible? Probably, but maybe Phil was right, and someone up there in the destiny department really did have a soft spot for Antiflux.

At the back of the assembly, Wendy stood beside Barbara, who was gazing up at the platform in unconcealed adoration.

Wendy smiled. "Keep looking, Barbara, because your boy isn't going to be so pretty anymore when this afternoon is over."

"What are you talking about?"

"I know the reason for this big meeting. Remember, all the Antiflux letters come to me first. So I happen to know that the sleazebag, your Sam, and that jackass Phil Baldwin have dragged everybody in here thinking they're going to be consulted on something important. And you know what's really going to happen? Those three idiots are going to try and get the whole school out to their dumb land to cut down the weeds. The town says they have to."

Barbara turned pale.

"No telling how mad the kids'll get," Wendy said cheerfully. "They might even storm the platform and slaughter the Program Board. Oh, look. The sleaze-bag is standing up. I don't want to miss a word of this."

Simon began by listing the sins of Interflux, past and present and, as always, it was a subject he could really warm to. In no time at all, he had the crowd eating out of his hand, but he knew he was a long way from home free.

"But now we have a new enemy! A political enemy! The Town of Greenbush is Interflux's ally against us! The town runs the Land Office, and the Land Office is in a position to push us around! They're making it difficult for us to hang on to our lawful land, which is holding the Interflux expansion at bay! Are we going to stand for this?"

"No!" chorused the crowd in one single powerful voice.

"You know," whispered Phil to Sam, "this man might be president one day. It looks like he's going to pull this off."

"He hasn't mentioned weeds yet," said Sam mournfully. "Then you'll see how fast the lynch mob forms."

"Are we going to sit back and watch while Interflux pulls strings to hassle us?" Simon was howling to the enraptured crowd.

"*No!*"

"Are we going to lose our land to the town and Interflux on the basis of a few political technicalities?"

"*No!*"

"Are we going to give up our fight so easily?"

"*No!*"

"*No!*" Simon shouted along with the crowd. "Of course we won't! We're going to fight!"

"*Yeah!*"

"We're going to match Interflux technicality for technicality!"

"*Yeah!*"

"Triviality for triviality!"

"*Yeah!*"

"We're going to work to see that the town can't touch us!"

"*Yeah!*"

"And we're going to go out to our land and cut down all those weeds!"

Another "yeah" died in every throat and, in its place, a strange murmur arose, a kind of hum, tinged with confusion and vague discontent. All through the crowd, students talked to each other in whispers, until someone finally piped,

"Hey, wait! What's all this about *weeds?*"

"The dirtiest of dirty tricks!" Simon pronounced darkly. "Interflux sent a town weed inspector to our lot, and if the weeds aren't cut by tomorrow, we'll be hit with fines so heavy, we'll lose our land!"

A nervous buzz passed back and forth through the

crowd until finally Dave Roper, who had spearheaded the work crew on fence-building day, shouted, "We'll cut the weeds!"

"Nah!" came the voices of several hundred people in the seconds that followed. Others still muttered, "No way!" — "Forget it!" — "Cut 'em yourself!" and "I still don't understand what's going on here!"

"Interflux thinks that Nassau Arts doesn't have the dedication to do what is necessary!" Simon shouted. "They think they can beat us on our own laziness!"

"They've got another think coming!" howled someone.

"Yeah!"

"Cut those weeds!" bellowed Dave Roper.

There was a weak "Yeah," but the spirit was growing. Phil was with Simon on the edge of the platform, coaxing that syllable out of reluctant throats. Even Sam was on his feet, bowled over by the realization that Antiflux was going to keep its land even if it had to, God forbid, cut weeds.

At that opportune moment, Bill McIntosh opened the door to the kitchen and watched in fascination as the students lined up to equip themselves.

On the podium, Phil slapped Simon on the back hard enough to dislocate both shoulders. "Your mouth — I'm going to have it bronzed!"

"That's my lab partner!" shouted Johnny Zull to anyone who would listen.

"Unbelievable!" muttered Wendy, shaking her head. "He did it! That sleazebag!"

* * *

Inside the boundaries of the makeshift Antiflux fence lived a formidable expanse of weeds. To this spot marched the grim reapers of Antiflux, a gloomy but determined lot, accepting this responsibility as they accepted exams, nuclear proliferation, pestilence, and rained-out Mets games.

The procession halted at the fence, and the students gazed in quiet resignation at the noxious flora laid out before them.

"Oh wow," Phil said bleakly. "You could hide a rhinoceros in there."

"Man," echoed Dino, "you could hide *me* in there."

The crew set to work after Dave Roper finally consented to the removal of a section of fence for purposes of a gate. His distress was so genuine, his protestations so loud, and his love for the fence so comical that the entire work crew indulged in a good laugh at Dave's expense, and started this distasteful job in a better frame of mind for it. The lightheartedness soon grew, as students realized that working side by side with friends and colleagues against a common enemy could be an uplifting experience. Making the job even more tolerable was the fact that there were several times as many volunteers as there were pieces of equipment, so the work was done in very short shifts, and those students not working cheered and heckled those who were.

About a half-hour into the job, a full-fledged carnival atmosphere was in effect, and the dreaded weed-cutting expedition was turning into the social event of the season. Although it was obvious that there was far more goofing off than real work going on, Simon was delighted. Not only would the job get done, but the Program Board would emerge with its image higher than ever. He also took great satisfaction in the fact that he and his weeds had achieved exactly what Wendy had expected to get out of countless parties and social activities. Dare he hope that she would see this, too, and forgive him? he asked of a three-foot goldenrod. Even it didn't think so. With a single swing of his big scythe, he killed the offending weed and its whole family.

Even greater mirth was provided when Miss Glandfield arrived on the scene, eager to strike a blow for freedom by lending her lawnmower to the cause. She roared into the fray, but soon her gas-powered mower was hopelessly jammed by long grasses and tough stems. There was a small explosion, which threw Miss Glandfield into the startled arms of Johnny Zull. Unhurt, she withdrew, pulling the remains of her mower behind her. This, she announced to the convulsed crowd, was sabotage by Interflux, which had traced her phone calls and was after her, just as it had arranged for her septic tank to malfunction yesterday.

By this time there was as much play going on as work. It was not known who started the weed war, but by the time the entire land lot had been cut down to a height of three inches — about six-thirty P.M. — there were more than fifty soldiers involved. Cut weeds were flying in all directions and students were skulking around planning high strategy.

When Simon announced it was time to go home, there were genuine cries of protest.

* * *

It was after seven P.M. when Simon arrived home.

"You're filthy!" his mother exclaimed in horror. "You're all covered with dirt and grass, and there are stains all over your clothes! And you've got goldenrod in your hair! What have you been doing?"

Simon looked past his mother to where his father sat peering sharply over the top of the evening paper. "Everybody else in school looks like this, too, Mom. We had something important to do." He added meaningfully, "And we did it."

Mr. Irving's eyes disappeared behind the paper once more, but Simon was sure his father wasn't smiling. So he smiled instead.

Nine

The wreck died on Friday night, leaving Sam stranded with Barbara on South Bellmore, about halfway between the movie they had just seen and home. In a state of total humiliation, he phoned Simon for a lift, his one stipulation, "Don't tell Philip." But it was already too late. Phil was over at the Irvings' for the evening and would not be put off. And when he found out that his wreck was in trouble, he became completely hysterical.

"What did you do to my wreck?" he howled into the telephone, having finally succeeded in grabbing the receiver from Simon's hand.

"Put Simon back on, Philip. I'm not in a good mood."

"I can't believe this!" muttered Phil as he and Simon climbed into the Mustang and headed toward South Bellmore.

Simon just laughed. "Be grateful you're not Sam."

Following Sam's directions, they found the stranded couple standing by the orange Beetle. Barbara was looking tolerant, though clearly unhappy, but Sam's face radiated deep mortification. He was so upset that even Phil's attempts to start an argument failed to get a rise out of him.

After some discussion, it was decided that Phil and Sam would stay with their wreck, and Simon would drive Barbara home. As the Mustang drove off, officially ending the date, Barbara stared out the back window until Sam was out of sight. Then she turned to Simon and poured out her entire heart, telling of her feelings, hopes, and frustrations regarding Sam Stavrinidis and men in general. Poor Simon could only marvel at how the formerly silent Barbara suddenly found so much to say while talking with or about Sam.

"He's so nice! We get along so well together! I can't believe this happened tonight!"

"Gee, Barbara, I don't know what to tell you," said Simon lamely, making a mental note to check his driver's license to see that the name there was Simon Irving, not Dr. Phil.

Then, for some reason, Barbara started to tell about the history of her love life, about her first boyfriend, Steven, her second, Freddie, her third, fourth, and fifth, who were all named Mark, and her most recent, Cahill. (What kind of name was *Cahill?*) She made it pretty obvious that the number seven spot was all Sam's, and slyly began probing for information on how Sam felt about her.

"I don't know what to tell you," Simon said again. When he finally pulled up in front of Barbara's Massapequa home, she kissed him on the cheek, thanked him for being the most wonderful person in the world to talk with, said she felt much better now, and ran into the house.

When Simon got back to the disaster site, the wreck had mysteriously started up again, and neither Phil nor Sam could explain how. The car was exactly as it had been before, still idling like an armored Panzer division, still belching blue smoke. The body, however, bore one more scar — a small dent in the driver's door which matched in size the toe of Sam's shoe.

"It's an intermittent defect," Phil diagnosed.

"Oh, thank you, Mr. Car Expert!" Sam wailed. "I could have told you that!"

"I was only trying to help," said Phil defensively.

"Well, don't!" He turned his face to the sky. "Why tonight, huh? I don't mind a breakdown, but — why tonight? She'll probably never speak to me again!"

Simon was pretty sure she'd used up all her words on him and would never speak to anyone again.

"Look," said Phil, "there's only one cure for what you've experienced tonight."

"What's that?"

"A hamburger. Let's buzz on over to Burger King. I'm buying."

"You're broke this week," Sam reminded him.

"Well, you'll pay and I'll get you back next trip. This is no time to get technical. You need the company of other males, and eventually you'll realize that relationships with women are supposed to drive you crazy. That's the way it's set up. That's what makes it so good when things finally do work out."

"Unless she shoots you with a fire extinguisher," Simon added.

"Right," Phil agreed. "Let's move out."

* * *

Simon was now working on a new painting called "Assembly Line." It depicted a typical assembly line plant, concentrating on the faces of the individual workers. It was his most ambitious effort to date, with interesting people and good perspective, and Simon felt it just might be the one to leave Querada speechless and bring home the Vishnik Prize.

He didn't get too much work done on the picture that weekend, though, because he spent most of his time at the Fosterville Country Club, trying desperately to keep up with his father. Mr. Irving's athletic ability seemed to increase exponentially with each Antiflux triumph. He was a dervish on the squash court, a killer at basketball, and a virtual torpedo in the club's Olympic-size pool. He was also gaining renown in the weight room, and had only yesterday pedaled one of the exercise bikes into a smoldering ruin. Simon was chided by the regulars that his physique was so far inferior to his father's, a man twenty-five years his senior. And yes, it was true that if Antiflux held out for any significant length of time, Cyril Irving would be an excellent candidate for Mr. Universe, if one disregarded the telltale worry lines on his forehead.

Mrs. Irving, however, considered her husband's excellent condition to be a direct result of *The Sun*'s good eating program. Slyly, she began to ease beans back into the family menu. What she didn't know was that, while Interflux and Antiflux agreed on nothing, the two leaders had gotten together on this most vital issue and drawn up what Mr. Irving liked to call The Strategic Bean Limitations Treaty. This stated simply that beans would be tolerated as a side dish only, and when the meat started to disappear again, the men of the family would protest. Regardless of what was going on in the forum of Antiflux versus Interflux, Simon and his father would continue to trade hand signals across the dinner table and hold strategy sessions in the toolshed.

Nathan Kruppman gave everybody the weekend off and reportedly went into seclusion to do some special effects work. He had consulted by phone with several members of the painting class, but Simon had not been one of these. No, his mother had assured him after repeated questioning, no one had phoned while he was out.

At school, though, Simon could walk tall. He was the chief executive and spiritual leader of Antiflux, and it put a certain spring in his gait. Even Phil noticed this confident strut, commenting, "Hey, Simon, are your pants too tight or something?"

The previous week's weed-cutting had rocketed Antiflux to stardom at Nassau Arts, and the Program Board was famous not only for the fight against Interflux but also as the source of a good time. The veterans all agreed that the explosion of Miss Glandfield's lawnmower was the most enjoyable spectator event since the quarter-ton couple had tried to ride a bicycle built for two.

Dave Roper was also helping to keep Antiflux's profile high. Right after the weed-cutting, he had gathered together a small crew to maintain and improve the Antiflux fence. Despite harsh budgetary restrictions (they had no money), Dave and his group worked all weekend, managing to build in a gate, replace about forty substandard fence posts, and paint the raw wood, all using donations from people's garages. While Dave did this as a matter of pride, Simon approved of it for an entirely different reason. He could easily picture his father having the fence officially disallowed by the Greenbush Fence Council; and if there was no Fence Council, he was sure Interflux would have no trouble convincing Mayor Van Doren to create one.

On Monday, Querada's session let out half an hour early, and Simon and Sam dropped by the cafeteria for a snack before their next class.

"I thought I'd seen everything," Simon marveled as the two settled themselves beneath the camel, "but this tops it all!"

"I'm glad to see Querada's over his depression and back to normal again," said Sam.

"Normal? He *ate* a piece of chalk! You call that normal?"

"It was just a little piece," said Sam. "And besides, you'll notice that as soon as he did it, Peter paid attention to what he was talking about. I think he was great this morning."

At this point, Phil entered the cafeteria, his face careworn. He joined them under the camel, grabbed half of Sam's french fries, crammed them all into his mouth, and chewed forlornly.

"What's wrong?" Simon asked.

"Remember when I told you that if you're in trouble, I'm in trouble? Well, it works in reverse, and you guys are both in big trouble in photography. Today I got that feeling that this is the beginning of the end. I'm an authority, because it happens to me more than anybody else."

Sam opted not to fight over his french fries. "Are you that bad?"

"No, but I'm not that good, either. There are serious photographers in this class, and I'm just a guy who isn't living up to his potential. Today Mr. Floyd said to me, 'Baldwin, I can see you're trying really hard, but I honestly don't think we're getting anywhere here, and frankly, it's not worth the bite you put in my tripod budget.' I give him twenty-four hours before he makes it official. Man, T.C.'s going to freak when he finds out I'm on my derrière again."

"It's getting kind of late to join up with a new department," said Sam worriedly.

"Tell me about it," said Phil. "And it's going to cost me plenty to have T.C. dig up a spot for me. My folks'll get suspicious about why he's at the house so often." He squared his jaw. "Well, I'm not going to sit back and wait for Floyd to lower the boom."

"What are you going to do?"

"Quit," said Phil. "As soon as I talk to T.C."

* * *

Sam ate his lunch with Barbara again that day, and Simon and Phil took their places in the peanut gallery to watch from a discreet distance. They were soon distracted by the goings-on at their own table, however. Bill McIntosh had just had his first manuscript, *The Legend of the Glass Caves*, rejected outright by Kidsbeat Press, and he was in a terrible snit.

"I can't believe it! They didn't want my *Glass Caves*! What's the matter with those people?"

"Maybe they have no taste," suggested Dina diplomatically.

"Well, that's obvious! Listen to this." He opened the manuscript at random.

> Every seventy-two years, the great star Ecinreb, brightest in the summer sky, is positioned so that its light shines through The Passage of the Ages, and the caves glow like diamonds. This is the time of Niknar Tap, when the evil Lord Nodrog quakes upon his dark throne, for now the powers of good are at their strongest.

"Now, what twelve-year-old wouldn't give his right arm to read this book?"

"Beats me," said Phil, kicking Simon under the table.

"I liked it," said Dino.

"What's Niknar Tap?" asked Dave Roper, who had arrived in the middle of the reading.

"It's the name in the language of the land of the Glass Caves for the time when the powers of good are strongest," Bill explained seriously.

"Where?"

"In my book, you dope! And those lunatics at Kidsbeat turned it down!"

"Maybe they didn't understand it, either," Dave suggested helpfully, as everyone else at the table tried in vain to signal Dave that this was a very touchy subject for the seven-feet-one-inch basketball star.

"Look," said Bill in great exasperation, "my sisters are thirteen and eleven, and they both *love* this book. Every kid on my street *loves* this book. And if *you* are not subtle enough to understand the plot, may the black fires of Nodrog consume you!"

"There are other publishers," said Simon soothingly.

"Now that is the first intelligent advice I've heard all day. And I intend to submit my *Glass Caves* to every single one of them until someone has the vision to publish it."

At that point, Sam came over to the table. "Hi, everybody." To Phil he whispered, "I think I'm going to need the wreck on Friday, because — "

"Yeah, yeah, I figured it out. Only, try not to kill it this time, will you?"

* * *

On Monday afternoon, Simon was just about to head out to his car when he spied Wendy bearing down on him like a Yankee Clipper under full sail.

"Hey, sleazebag, you got a letter." She came up and handed him an official Town of Greenbush envelope which, he noted in some annoyance, she had opened. "Are you still Antiflux, or have you sleazed out of that one, too?"

"You know I am." He would have liked to come up with something a little more sarcastic and perhaps a touch wittier, but she was in ballet tights, which was interfering with his concentration.

"Lots of luck with this one." She smiled maliciously. "I think this time you're out of your league. It's a beaut."

Simon finished watching her walk away, sighed heavily, and unfolded the letter.

Dear Ms. Orr,

Re: Lot 1346B

Thank you for your prompt response to the weed problem. There is another circumstance which requires your attention. Please be advised that your lot, now excluded from the Interflux industrial expansion, has been rezoned for commercial development. Therefore you have exactly one week to submit a proposed plan for said commercial development.

Cordially yours,

F. Van Doren, Mayor

Simon stared down at the terrazzo floor. Wendy was right; this was a beaut. He ran out to the parking lot, intending to drive over and see Phil and Sam.

But there were the two remaining members of the Program Board, still on the lot, tinkering with the wreck.

"It's the intermittent defect," called Phil, his voice echoing from under the hood, which was where the trunk should have been.

Simon handed the letter to Sam, who read it and made a remarkably Querada-like gesture, tearing at an imaginary beard. "This is all we needed! Your father really knows how to go for the jugular!"

Phil emerged, grease-spattered, and was duly shown the fateful letter. "So what's the big deal? We'll open up a Kool-Aid stand and hawk a few brownies on the side."

Sam looked vaguely hopeful. "That counts as a commercial enterprise, doesn't it? I mean, we don't have to open Macy's here."

Simon shook his head. "We'd get hassled to the skies."

"Why?" asked Phil. "When I was a kid, I used to open up those little stands left, right, and center, and nobody would hassle me. The police even used to stop by on hot days."

"Your Kool-Aid stands were never blocking the way to Interflux International," Simon pointed out. "Kool-Aid and brownies is food-handling, and they'll be forcing us into restaurant licenses we can't afford, and sending us health and quality control inspectors. They'll see to it that anyone who comes within fifty feet of that stand has to get a complete medical examination, including x-rays and blood tests. And you know the kind of money that would run us."

Phil nodded sagely. "Sharp guy," he told Sam.

"Too sharp."

"I live with the other side," Simon reminded them, "and I know the way his mind works. He's figuring on us to sell lemonade or something, so he's all ready to start the attack."

"Well, what *can* we do?" asked Sam in annoyance. "We have no resources."

"We have fifteen hundred devoted students ready to follow Simon and Antiflux anywhere," said Phil stoutly. "I personally am not worried at all. You've got to have faith. We can't burn out after coming this far."

"We've got a week," Simon amended, "and a lot of praying to do."

* * *

The smile was back on Cyril Irving's face at dinner that night, and though the beans were there in slightly larger portion than the night before, this was the furthest thing from his mind as he announced that no, he didn't feel like going to the club tonight.

"Well, son," he announced, grinning broadly. "How's school?"

"Oh, really great, Dad," Simon replied, matching the arc of his father's grin degree for degree.

"Anything new lately?"

"Well, the school has been infested by *pests*."

"Pests?" his mother asked in concern.

"You know, kind of like termites," Simon explained meaningfully. "Sometimes they think they own the world."

"No they don't," said Mr. Irving. "They just want what's rightfully theirs."

"Termites don't have rights," Mrs. Irving pointed out, puzzled. "My goodness, I hope they're going to get an exterminator."

"Oh, sure they will," said Simon. "This is really no problem."

"Some termites are stronger than others," beamed Mr. Irving, "and a lot of the exterminators around these parts are highly overrated."

* * *

A Program Board think-tank went out at noon the next day to Lot 1346B, hoping for inspiration. This group consisted of the Program Board itself and Johnny Zull, honorary board member by virtue of the fact that he was lab partner of the chairman. Sam had asked permission to bring Barbara, but Phil had pointed out, "Sotirios, this is a *think*-tank," and nothing further was heard on the subject.

"Man, this is an uncool deal," pronounced Johnny, looking around the Antiflux acreage. "It belongs in Long Island."

"There's no way we can put a commercial enterprise on this strip," Sam said unhappily. "What can you do with a skinny zigzag in the middle of nowhere, thirty-five feet wide and a million miles long?"

"It's not even straight enough to be a bowling alley," said Phil bleakly.

Simon looked around in frustration. "Geez! This place is really useless! What kind of idiot would pay sixty-seven hundred dollars for this — this worm-hole? I mean, it smells like worms, it's shaped like a worm, the only things that live here are worms — "

"There aren't even very many weeds anymore," Phil added wanly.

A smile suddenly appeared on Simon's face. "Worms. *Worms!*"

"It's my lab partner!" announced Johnny excitedly. "He's getting another brilliant idea! Let's hear it, Simon!"

"Worms!"

"And — ?" Phil prompted expectantly.

"We'll sell worms!"

There was the general air of a letdown.

"I don't want to put a damper on your enthusiasm," said Sam, "but I don't know how much of a market there is for worms this time of year. And besides, everybody's backyard has worms."

"Yeah, but most people don't want to dig their own."

Sam made a face. "I don't suppose it occurs to you that Nassau Arts students will have the same sentiments?"

Simon shook his head impatiently. "We got them to cut weeds; we can get them to dig worms."

Phil nodded vigorously. "That makes sense. I'm beginning to like this idea."

"Don't you see?" Simon insisted. "It doesn't matter whether or not we have any customers. We just have to open a business. I don't care if we never sell a single worm. We can't go bankrupt, because we have virtually no costs. Everything we need we can get kids to bring in. And the best part of all is that there's no way for Interflux to hassle us with fancy inspectors and stuff. A worm is a worm, and the worst they can do is force us to get a license to be a bait shop. And how much can that be?"

"Too much," said Sam, "considering our treasury stands at nil."

"Look," reasoned Phil, "no matter what we decide to do, we're going to need some kind of license or permit, and that means we're going to have to raise some bucks. Don't be such a wet blanket, Sotirios. This is so great! And how much can that license be? Fifty — seventy-five bucks?"

"If that much," said Simon. "Now let's see — well, we could always pass the hat around school, and — "

"Nope." Johnny Zull shook his head. "That's got no dignity. You don't take a big-time outfit like Antiflux and turn it into a charity case."

"He's right," said Phil. "We can't hurt our image. We've got to do something with style." He paused thoughtfully. "Look at it this way: the Program Board was appointed by the program director, who was in turn appointed by the Student Council president, who was duly elected by the students. That makes Antiflux a government agency. And what does a government do when it needs money?"

Ten

TAX DAY

announced the giant poster in the cafeteria on
Wednesday. Beneath it sat Simon and Phil at a large
desk. On the desk was a cardboard carton bearing a
sign which read:

STUDENT COUNCIL PROGRAM BOARD
HALLOWEEN TAX LEVY
FOR THE CONTINUED OPERATION OF
ANTIFLUX PROGRAM
PLEASE REMIT 10¢ PER STUDENT
ONE THIN DIME

"You know, Simon," Phil announced philosophically, "I know I may seem kind of flaky at times, like
a stowaway on the ship of life where everyone else
pays the fare, but once in a while I really tear off a
good one. This idea is perfect. I mean, it's taxation, so

we come off looking official, and it's only one lousy dime, so no one can complain."

A tall, slim girl, a freshman specializing in theater, duly deposited two nickels in the carton.

"Thank you," said Phil briskly. "Name, please?"

"Lisa Fitzpatrick."

Simon sifted through several sheets as though looking for her name. It was an act, of course, since Antiflux had no school list, and the sheets were really pages out of a racing form which Phil had rescued from a garbage bin outside the staff lounge. "Fitzpatrick," Simon announced, placing a tick mark beside Under the Rainbow, a three-year-old filly running in the fifth race at Aqueduct that weekend. "Thank you."

Lisa looked at Simon with great admiration. "I think it's wonderful what you're doing with Antiflux."

"We try," said Simon modestly. When she had gone, he turned to Phil and whispered, "Eat your heart out, Sam Stavrinidis."

At that particular moment, Sam was having lunch with Barbara, and Wendy had joined them, almost beside herself with anger. "I can't believe it! On Halloween, practically every other school in the country does something special! Kids wear costumes to class, or there's a costume party, or a costume contest! They bob for apples, carve pumpkins, have a good time! At Nassau Arts we have a tax levy!" She glared at Sam. "Your sleazy friend and that jackass Phil Baldwin can't make ends meet on the original sixty-seven hundred dollars they stole! They have to extort ten stupid cents from every living soul in this place! I could kill somebody!"

"Wendy doesn't like your tax levy," Sam reported as he replaced Phil at the tax booth.

Simon shrugged. "She doesn't like my face, either," he muttered.

Sam looked into the box, which was piled high with coins. "Wow! Think we've got enough for that license yet?"

"More than enough," said Phil smugly.

In fact, when the final tally was taken, Tax Day had turned up $126.40, meaning that the tax had reached about eighty percent of the school. They had made the most money in the two main lunch periods, although there had also been a great resurgence of interest in paying near the end of the day when T.C. came to the booth on the instructions of Nathan Kruppman to pay the movie mogul's dime. This didn't impress Simon very much, but Phil was practically in tears over the honor.

Simon used a school phone to call the town, and found in some embarrassment that the license was to cost only $60. Phil suggested that the surplus $66.40 be bet on Under the Rainbow across the board, because he had a gut feeling about that horse. Simon and Sam shouted him down, however, and the Anti-flux surplus was finally placed in a shoebox on the top shelf of Simon's locker. (This ultimately turned out to be a mistake, as Under the Rainbow ran first on Saturday, paying 19-1.)

The three stayed late after school, drawing up an official proposal for the Antiflux Worm Shop, including Phil's Statement of Intent, which explained that, in a warm year with a late frost, fishing could be greatly encouraged by the increased availability of November worms. Then the documents were sealed in a manila envelope, which was affixed to a small burlap sack containing $60 in dimes, nickels, and pennies. Simon, Phil, and Sam all rode over to the Town Hall to make the submission. Naturally, the employees on duty had trouble locating the License Office, and by the time they found it, filed under "P" for "Permit," it was four-forty P.M., time to get ready for knocking off fifteen minutes early. They told the Program Board to come back tomorrow, issued a receipt for their money and papers, and sent them on their way.

* * *

Antiflux's proposal and $60 were never seen again. The official story was that, during the night, a goat gained access to the town offices and ate the entire submission, although rumors were circulating that it had been not a goat but Mayor Van Doren's Saint Bernard which had been found with a mouthful of burlap at nine the next morning. Simon didn't see how either a goat or a Saint Bernard could stomach $60 in small change, which gave rise to a third theory. Peter Ashley reported that his sister and her colleagues had gotten together for a massive nickel and dime Mah Jongg tournament. The only thing that could be proven was that the money and papers had been there, as Simon had a signed receipt attesting to this. Thus, while Interflux had been poised and ready to shoot full of holes any proposal Antiflux might submit, the mysterious circumstances gave them nothing to aim at. The license was issued after a debate that was not long enough to get Simon worried, but took just enough time to cause him to miss Querada's painting session.

* * *

Over a thousand students packed into the Nassau Arts gym and cheered ecstatically as Simon informed them that they were now proprietors of a worm establishment. Enthusiasm was so high that, by the time Simon arrived at school the next morning, the sign-up sheet for the first week of the Antiflux Worm Shop was completely filled, including the duty roster of worm diggers. He felt a touch left out that he, the shop's mastermind, had not managed to snag a single hour's duty.

"The least you could have done was sign me up for some time," he said accusingly to Phil.

Phil shrugged. "I was lucky to get some myself. You should have seen it — it was inspirational! This worm store is going to be awesome!"

* * *

That old familiar aching feeling gripped Simon from ankles to knees as he stood behind his desk in painting class, trying to act as though nothing was out of the ordinary, and he was sitting in a chair like everybody else.

Querada was revving up for a critique of Laura

Dixon's reworked "Mother and Child," and he stood facing away from the class, his hand resting on the tray of the chalkboard, as though he were gathering energy for what was to come. Then, almost immediately, he was beside the painting on the front easel, a benevolent expression on his face.

"Ah, Miss Dixon's sister and her new baby. There is a slight improvement. Nice work. No longer do these people have no expressions on their faces." In a split second, his complexion was suffused with red. "They have expressions like the dummies in Macy's Christmas window!" Great tears ran from his wild eyes and rolled down his cheeks into his beard. "Miss Dixon, do you hate me so much that you would call *this* the fruit of my suggestions? How dare you? I refuse to believe that your sister and her new baby really look like this! If they do, then the great organizing principle of the universe is cruel indeed, and cruelest of all to Querada, who must go to the Vishnik Gallery and quite possibly commit suicide rather than face the ridicule of his peers because of your sister and her new baby!"

Sam nudged Simon. "Now that's a contender."

"There is only one problem, Miss Dixon!" Querada suddenly thundered, just when it looked as though an air of calm were about to descend. "At the rate you're going, by the time this picture has reached a state where it is not an embarrassment to Querada, your sister will be on social security, and her new baby will be a stockbroker! *Work faster!*

"The deadline for this year's Vishnik entries is

November thirtieth," Querada went on in a pleasant, informative tone. "Just a little reminder. Three years ago, one of my students, an idiot, forgot to make his submission. Today he works in a car wash in Terre Haute. Submissions must be made to the New York Vishnik Gallery like always. Last year Mr. Lawrence mailed his entry to the Museum of Modern Art, and only minutely escaped death by my hand when the Vishnik people turned out to be understanding — not that it did any good. A creep from Albany — but that is another story. Kindly get your entries in, to the right place, on time."

Next was "Assembly Line," and Simon creaked up on stiff legs to place it on the front easel. When he saw the picture in the bright light of Querada's custom-designed classroom, it looked better to him than it ever had before, and he flashed Sam a grin of cautious triumph as he awaited Querada's rave review.

"What happened to 'Tavern Scene'?" the artist asked, strangely unawed.

"I decided to go on to something different."

It was déjà vu for Simon as Querada began to list every single nit-picky fault that he found in "Assembly Line." Simon felt like bashing his own head against the blackboard as the idea slowly sank in that, in the process of doing a picture that avoided Querada's forty-five minutes of flaws from "Tavern Scene," he had committed a new block of offenses that took the artist — yes, forty-five minutes to explain.

As he returned to his "seat," Laura, Peter, and a few of the other students congratulated him on the terrific reception Querada had accorded "Assembly Line." He smiled in spite of himself. Maybe forty-five minutes of lambasting was a great compliment from Emile Querada, but there had to be a more positive reaction trapped somewhere in that six-feet-eight-inch funny-farm fugitive.

"Good stuff," whispered Sam as Simon settled himself into a comfortable stance. "Are you going to work on that one or 'Tavern Scene' for the Vishnik?"

"Neither," replied Simon with determination. "I've got another idea, and this one'll hit that lunatic so hard, he might even come out sane!"

"Well, you certainly are turning out — "

"Shut up, Mr. Stavrinidis!" bellowed Querada. "I have something important to say to you! I refuse to discuss your new painting because it had something in it that I hate very much, and we all know what that is! We will discuss this in my office at three-thirty!"

Later, while Simon sat massaging his leg cramps, he put to Sam a major question. "What's with you and camels anyway?"

"I don't know. They're great. I love painting them. Why?"

"Well, look at today — a perfectly mild day for Querada. Okay, he threw my chair out the window and had a few tantrums, but on the whole, things were calm. Then you came along with your camel and got him all riled up."

"I like that part. It's important for our student-teacher relationship."

"But you're the one who's always talking about

other people's stupid, impulsive, harebrained ideas. What would you call this?"

Sam smiled. "A blind spot? Look, Querada and I understand each other perfectly."

"Then why did he order you to come to his office?"

Sam shrugged. "We'll find out at three-thirty. Probably just a little extra chewing out. Sure, T.C. and I are going to end up sitting through a few stories about people who don't do what Querada tells them to and die as a direct result. But we've heard most of those already, and wouldn't mind hearing them again. They're great stories."

At that point, Phil came running up to his locker, his face glowing with excitement. "Hey, guys, guess what? You are looking at Nassau Arts' latest addition to the Innovative Arts Department!"

Sam's jaw dropped. "You're kidding! That's the toughest specialty to get into in the whole school! How'd you pull it off?"

Phil bristled. "I'll have you know, Sotirios, that there was nothing to 'pull off,' because I happen to show a great deal of potential for innovative arts. And besides, T.C. got three weeks out of this one. It was a major event."

"What's innovative arts?" asked Simon.

Phil shrugged expansively. "Oh, I don't know. It's hard to tell. I must understand it, though, because Mr. Copadrick was very impressed at my interview. Basically, we innovative artists believe that the series of actions which create the work of art are more important than the work itself."

"That's garbage!" scoffed Sam.

"Exactly why this whole thing's so perfect," Phil argued. "Garibaldi was garbage. 'The Seasons' was all a bunch of garbage. And in photography, I took a stack of junk pictures, and converted their tripods into garbage. But here I've got a whole department that accepts garbage. They even encourage it."

"That doesn't even make sense," said Simon.

"It's not supposed to. This is innovative arts. That's another rule."

"You're going to make a big joke out of one of the most respected departments at Nassau Arts," Sam accused.

"Why, thank you for your vote of confidence," Phil said sarcastically. "Mr. Copadrick thinks I've got what it takes, and he's one of the top innovative artists in the country. This could be really big for me, so quit dumping on it."

In art history, the results of yesterday's pop-quiz were in, and Simon had scored a pathetic one out of five. He went up to speak to the teacher, but was told, "No problem. There's nothing to worry about." Then he learned that classmate Bob Lawrence was repeating art history, having believed Mr. Monagle's reassurances last year.

"The day before the final, I had a thirty-eight percent average. Monagle said, 'Don't worry,' so I didn't worry, and he flunked me." (Simon later discovered that Mr. Monagle was so worried about soil erosion that the matter of a student passing or failing seemed overwhelmingly irrelevant.)

The math homework pool had grown rather unwieldy, now standing at eleven members, a number which comprised more than a third of the class. Simon was sure that more math was being done divvying up the homework in elevenths than in doing the actual work itself, but Phil was irrepressible. He had divided the eleven up into Group A and Group B, five each, with himself the odd man out. Theoretically, this was designed to leave him no homework at all, but Bill McIntosh always made sure that a few questions were thrown Phil's way.

After school, Phil and Sam intended to make a concerted effort to locate and correct the intermittent defect, since tonight was round two in the Sam and Barbara epic. If he had car trouble tonight, Sam declared, he would push the wreck off a cliff and shoot himself.

First, however, was his meeting with Querada, and Simon and Phil waited for him and his agent in front of Phil's locker. Simon was in a sour mood, having just found out that he had not been recruited for the Boston Tea Party, which Nathan was recreating off Fire Island. This was particularly disturbing because rumors were circulating that *Omni* was nearing completion. With only a few shoots remaining, it was beginning to look as though he, Simon Irving, father of Antiflux, son of Interflux, program chairman, lab partner of Johnny Zull, and all-around nice guy, would be the only student to have had absolutely no part in the film.

"Gee, it's too bad you didn't get picked," said Phil,

examining his own summons from Nathan.

"Hah!" Simon sneered. "You think I want to stand on a wooden boat in front of a dumb camera and throw bags of tea into the water? Forget it. That sure isn't my idea of a big weekend."

About five minutes later, Sam and T.C. came down the hall, glassy-eyed and coughing.

"What's the word?" Simon asked.

"The word is I'm getting too old for this business," T.C. declared, ripping off his tie and undoing his shirt halfway to his waist.

"*Un*-believable!" said Sam in an awed whisper.

"I've seen Querada do a lot of pretty strange things, but this was just beyond anything! He started out sweet as pie, sat us down in nice comfortable chairs — and very calmly he struck a match and set the drapes on fire! Then he said he wasn't going to let us go for a fire extinguisher until I promised never to bring another camel into his classroom!"

"Did you negotiate?" Phil asked.

"No," said T.C. "We ran. But he blocked the door-way."

"What happened?" Simon prompted.

"*What happened?*" Sam repeated. "What do you *think* happened? I swore up and down that never again would a picture with a camel in it violate the walls of his sacred classroom!"

"We held a hurried consultation," T.C. amended. "On the grounds that the room was filling up with smoke, I recommended surrender, and my client agreed."

"You're not kidding!" said Sam feelingly. T.C. wasn't finished.

"I looked into Querada's eyes, and I believe, as sure as I'm standing here, that he was prepared to burn down the office, himself, me, Sam, and the whole school if we had tried to be stubborn."

"You can't call the bluff of a guy who's not bluffing!" Sam put in breathlessly. "You read his book, Simon! I can almost picture the extra chapter added onto the end, explaining how Querada went up in smoke with one of his students, trying to make a point!"

"What about me?" asked T.C. angrily. "Agents burn, too, you know!"

Phil looked pale. "And I told this guy his cologne was tacky?"

"Don't worry about it, Phil," said Simon sarcastically. "There was never any real danger. You see, Sam and Querada understand each other perfectly."

Sam shuddered. "We do now!"

Eleven

The Antiflux Worm Shop was opened without much fanfare on Lot 1346B on Monday morning. In lieu of a brass band, Dave Roper played "We Shall Overcome" on the bassoon as Simon cut the ribbon. Then Dino and Dina took their places as the store's first clerks amidst the applause of about fifty students who had turned out for the official opening. Dave, as the first shift's worm-digger, should have been manning his shovel, but since there were no customers, he used this opportunity to explain to disinterested observers how he had constructed the gate in the Antiflux fence.

The actual worm store itself was unspectacular. It was located on the part of Lot 1346B that adjoined the school, and consisted of a desk, a tent, and signs. The desk was Mr. Durham's, freely donated since the English teacher had sworn off furniture. (It interfered with communication, according to Buzz, and therefore impeded psychic growth. He now convened all his classes cross-legged on the floor in a room that was bare to the walls and free of "energy flow obstructors.") The tent, which bore a sign over the entrance reading EMPLOYEES ONLY, belonged to Dave, and was there for bad weather and to give the employees somewhere to relax at times of slow business. Simon could not seem to explain to Dave that slow business, if any, was all they could expect, and that he was missing the point entirely in believing this to be the beginning of a worm empire. Dave seemed so upset that no members of the public were there to take advantage of his opening specials that Simon announced that he and his father did a lot of night fishing, and that he needed a five-pack of worms right away. Dino, however, would not hear of this, and refused to sell him anything less than a twelve-pack, which, at two dollars was a much better buy than the five-pack at one dollar. The fifty spectators were so inspired by the sight of the Anti-flux boss patronizing the worm shop that they all bought worms, too, and soon Dave was out in the field digging up more stock, with several of his friends watching him from a spot designated by a sign as WORM EXCAVATION SCENIC OVERVIEW.

Simon had originally intended to spill his Dixie cupful of worms out in a field somewhere, but Phil forbade this absolutely.

"It'll ruin your image if you're seen dumping those worms out! Everybody heard your story about the night fishing. Theyll lose confidence in your leadership."

"What am I supposed to do?" Simon retorted. "Keep them?"

"Yes! None of these other people need worms any

more than you do, and they're not throwing them away. It's kind of like the unwritten law. Your problem is you know nothing about psychology. Throw away those worms, and Antiflux is a charity case. But if you keep them, we've got a winning proposition here. Just put them in your locker or something. Then, if you're so keen on 'born free,' you can throw them in your garden when you get home. Even a worm needs a change of scenery now and then."

By this time, it was eleven-thirty, and Simon and Phil decided that class was no longer an alternative and that they would take a long lunch period. The worm store had already made $80, which was more than Simon had figured to pull in over the store's entire lifespan.

"We should tell Sam about this," said Simon. "He'll get a real kick out of it."

"I wouldn't be too sure of that," Phil replied skeptically. "You see, Sam's a boyfriend now."

"Huh?"

"A boyfriend. It happened this weekend, around the same time as Barbara became a girlfriend. That's the way it works. They come in pairs."

"Yeah, but what's that got to do with him wanting to hear about the eighty bucks?"

"Oh, boyfriends never concern themselves with matters as trivial as worm stores. All their brain cells are taken up with thinking about the people they're boyfriends of. It's the same with girlfriends, only their brain cells are all taken up with making sure the boyfriends' brain cells are all taken up with the girlfriends."

Simon laughed. "Aw, come on, Phil. Don't tell me you're jealous."

"It's not jealousy; it's aggravation. Dig this: one date goes well, and Barbara, the timid little kid who can only worship from afar, gets cocky. You know what she did? She insulted the wreck! And what did Sam say? He said, 'Yeah, I know. Phil and I have been thinking about getting a new one for a long time.' Give me a break!"

"Well, you've got to figure that he's trying to make a good impression," said Simon, who could have easily pictured himself bending the truth into a pretzel over Wendy had he not established himself in her heart as Public Enemy Number One. "He wants the relationship to work out."

"Big deal! This is *the wreck* we're talking about — the most beautiful, wonderful '68 Volkswagen ever to rust, rattle, and heave! He should have told her, 'Listen, carrot-top, this is a great car, and if you want to be driven around in a limo, well then *that's too bad!*' Let me tell you, this is a textbook case of boyfriend syndrome."

Simon was sure that Phil was overreacting. But during lunch, even he noticed a tendency in Sam to use the expression "Barbara says" with alarming frequency. "Barbara's a big fan of the Rolling Stones," Sam was saying.

"I think I'm going to go home and break all my CDs," Phil muttered under his breath. Aloud, he said pleasantly, "Where *is* the little woman?"

"Oh, she's in a rehearsal that's running a little late. She should be by any minute."

The big news buzzing around the cafeteria was, of course, the opening of the worm store, although not much was said about it under the camel, since Barbara felt worms weren't fitting table conversation. But fitting or not, weeds were out and worms were in, and Nassau Arts was in a festive mood. Shortly after noon, Dino and Dina came back from their shift and reported that business was picking up again as students on lunch hour ventured out to see the store first-hand. Dave Roper, who was still out there even though he'd been replaced, refused to leave, predicting a big run on the worms over the two main lunch periods, and therefore a need for additional staff.

Everyone was buying worms, though for what reason Simon couldn't imagine. Maybe they, like Dave, had lost sight of the real purpose of the exercise, and wanted to see the store become a success. Or perhaps they had somehow decided that each worm purchased was a nail in Interflux's coffin. One way or another, the worms were going like hotcakes, and the students were apparently obeying Phil's unwritten law for, by the later periods of the day, the halls of Nassau Arts were crawling with escaped worms. Whoever had designed the lockers hadn't anticipated worm storage, for there were large air holes close to the floor. These were perfect tickets to freedom for the aggressive November worm, and

soon the janitorial staff was up in arms over the unfa-
vorable turn the job had taken. An urgent commu-
niqué was dispatched to the head of the Custodians'
Union, Local 237, but ironically, he was away on a
fishing trip, and no doubt had his own worms to
worry about.

After school, Sam commandeered the wreck to give
Barbara a ride home, so Simon and Phil went out to
check on the progress of the Antiflux Worm Shop. It
was mobbed. Students who hadn't had a chance to
get out to the store between classes now lined up to
participate in the phenomenon.

Bill McIntosh was one of these, commenting, "If
I'm going to sit all day in a school filled with creepy
crawlies, I'm at least going to have the pleasure of
contributing to the problem."

Simon was almost afraid to open up his locker
again, but his twelve turned out to be the only worms
docile enough to stay put. This was largely because
eleven of them had died.

"Owner incompetence," commented Phil darkly.
He confiscated the sole survivor, named him Keith,
and took him under his wing. The rest received a
"burial at sea" in the nearby washroom.

After dinner, Simon and Phil returned to the worm
store to supervise the seven o'clock closing. Dave
Roper was still there, gray with fatigue, having
skipped an entire day of classes. Simon reacted half
with amusement and half with horror when Dave
informed him that the day's take totaled $946. In
all that business, only one customer had been a non-

student. One-hundred-and-two-year-old Jedediah O'Dell, the self-proclaimed oldest man on Long Island, fished every day year-round, and was delighted to find reasonably priced November bait.

The $946, most of it in ones, was crammed into a bulging shoebox and presented to Simon.

"I'm going to be a real hit at the bank tomorrow," he told Phil as they climbed into the Mustang. "I suppose I should bring that other sixty bucks worth of change from Tax Day with me, too. That way they'll think I held up a candy store."

"If you'd have bet that money like I told you, we'd be swimming in dough. We could have fixed up the wreck — put in bucket seats, and maybe even a sound system so that her royal red-headed majesty could listen to the Rolling Stones while complaining about the car. Man, this is a strange world. You think you know a guy, and zap! He turns into a boyfriend. Bing. The end."

"Give him some time," said Simon soothingly.

* * *

That night Simon was invited over to the Baldwins' to witness the birth of Phil's first project for innovative arts, and was shocked to find that the materials consisted of a large art board, a high-speed electric fan, yellow, red, and blue dye, and a peeled banana on a bent coat hanger.

"What are you going to do with this stuff?"

"I'm going to dip the banana in each of the colors ten times," Phil said evenly. "Then, before it has a chance to drip, I'm going to feed it through the fan, which will spray it onto the board. Then I'll wait for it to harden, and throw a few coats of shellac over it so it doesn't rot and stink out the world." He paused thoughtfully. "It should look pretty good — or not. It's the creation that's important."

Simon goggled. "Look, Phil, I don't know much about innovative arts, but don't you think you'd better do something a little more — you know —normal?"

"No. Normal is what you guys do in Querada's class. Mr. Copadrick says that anybody can slop paint on a canvas and have it look like something, but it takes a real innovative artist to shoot it from across the room out of an air rifle and have it look like nothing."

"But at least that's paint! This is — " he paused, " — a banana!"

"Well," Phil said as he flicked the switch to start the fan, "we can't very well knock it until we've tried it, right?"

Phil came very close to being thrown out of the house that evening. Mrs. Baldwin said her basement would never be the same again, and Simon was inclined to agree.

"I guess when they designed these electric fans," Phil commented, "they weren't really thinking about getting bananas to splatter back on an art board. It's got a pretty wide spray. Maybe I should have used the Cuisinart."

"Look at my basement!" howled Mrs. Baldwin for the thirtieth time. "Philip, how *could* you? There's banana on my walls! The floor! The ceiling! T.C.'s room!"

"He isn't coming back till January," said Phil irritably. "There's plenty of time to clean it up."

"We'll have mice! Mice and rats!"

"And monkeys," Phil added helpfully.

Simon wiped some of the multicolored banana slime from his pants. "Did any of it get on the art board?"

"Oh, plenty," said Phil. "You know, I've got a real respect for the banana after this. It's a miracle of packaging." He motioned around the room where colored slop was oozing down the walls and furniture. "All that came from one little yellow tube-thing. It's a remarkable fruit."

"Philip Lester Baldwin, will you quit talking nonsense and help me clean this mess up!"

Afterward, with the room cleaned up but still smelling strongly of banana, and Mrs. Baldwin claiming that her son had definitely not heard the last of this, Phil put the finishing coat of shellac on the work of art.

"It's terrible," said Simon honestly.

"Yeah, I know. Kind of gross, too. But innovative, and that's what counts."

* * *

As the week progressed, business dropped practically to zero at the Antiflux Worm Shop as patronage was reduced to the handful of students who had missed the big opening, and loyal customer Jedediah O'Dell. O'Dell, who went through twenty-four worms a day, expressed concern over the store's future with the decline in business. The staff absorbed this new situation with no loss of dedication, and since Simon had no assigned hours, he was beginning to get the feeling that he had virtually no connection at all with this worm store. Dave Roper was definitely in charge.

Distraught over the drop in revenues, Dave ordered an enormous batch of signs. These he directed to be set up all over town, even along the Long Island Expressway route. Interflux, however, was right on top of the situation, and had the town confiscating these signs as illegal advertising. The first Simon heard of all this was when the notice of the fine arrived. It was the happiest he'd seen Wendy since she'd been convinced there were going to be parties and socials galore at Nassau Arts.

"A hundred and fifty bucks down the pipe!" Phil exclaimed. "Do you know what the loss of a hundred and fifty bucks is like to a guy who goes broke Tuesdays and alternate Thursdays? It's like — like — really bad!"

Dave was unconcerned, and began nagging Simon to take out TV and newspaper ads.

The worm problem in the school halls was well on its way to solving itself, as the life expectancy of a worm (even the wily November variety) in a crowded building was tragically short. This pleased the janitors, and Local 237 calmed down. Phil's worm, Keith, was one of the lucky ones, living to squirm again in the Baldwins' geranium bed.

On Tuesday night, T.C. Serrette moved lock, stock, and barrel into the Irving household to take up a forty-eight-hour residence. Simon made a point of warning his new houseguest about Cyril Irving's position in Interflux. He had been secretly scared stiff that the agent would come across an Interflux official paper, or Mr. Irving's Interflux briefcase, or notice Mr. Irving's Interflux ring, and freak out. But T.C. took the news in stride, his professional calm back to normal after the incident with Querada.

"Oh, I know that, Simon. As soon as I saw your father's name in the paper, I figured out who you were."

Simon was taken aback. "You mean, you knew all this time, and you didn't say anything? Didn't you figure it was kind of — weird?"

T.C. shrugged. "It was none of my business."

Although the Irvings were a little taken aback with the amount of baggage their house guest had brought, they took to T.C. immediately. Mrs. Irving found him charming, and Mr. Irving was won over after Simon explained to him that T.C. was not an Antiflux member. (It never came up that he was Antiflux's agent, and that this was, in fact, the sole reason for his stay.) Best of all, Mrs. Irving cooked special dinners, including steak.

"Why does he have to leave so soon?" Mr. Irving ended up saying when the two days were over. "I was getting used to the nourishment. And besides, that's a fine boy — sharp, serious, knowledgeable about business. He's wasting his time at Nassau Arts. He looks to me like an excellent candidate for Abercrombie Prep."

* * *

On Thursday, Simon was surprised when Barbara came rushing up to him. "Simon, I've just *got* to talk to you."

"What about?" Simon asked warily. He had no desire to play Dr. Phil again.

"Let's go somewhere we can talk." Furtively, she led him to a deserted stairwell.

"Look, Barbara, if this is about Sam, I don't think —"

"Shh! It's not about Sam; it's about Wendy."

Well, this was it, Simon decided. Wendy had a gun, and this was his fair warning to get out of the country. Aloud, he said noncommittally, "Yeah?"

"She's crazy about you."

"Wendy *Orr?*"

"Of course!"

"No, no, no," Simon explained. "You see, Wendy hates my guts."

"That's all an act. Oh, sure, she was mad at you at first, but that's all changed. You see she secretly admires you for all the stuff you've been doing, but because she's afraid she blew her chances when she beat you up, she pretends she's still mad. But she never stops talking about you. Take it from me, she definitely likes you."

"I see."

"Now, all you have to do is be aggressive. If you're straightforward and forceful, she'll forget her act completely."

Simon examined his fingernails critically. "What makes you think I'm interested?"

Barbara looked motherly. "Because Sam told me that you're really nuts about her."

Simon found Phil on duty, sitting at Mr. Durham's old desk at the worm store. "Everything you said about Sam Stavrinidis goes double! What a *boyfriend!*" In a rage, he summarized his meeting with Barbara.

Phil seemed pleased. "Congratulations. Wendy likes you. That's what you want, isn't it?"

"It's obviously a joke! They want me to ask her out so she can make me look like a complete idiot!"

Phil shook his head. "Don't you see? It can't be a joke. This is Barbara. She hasn't got the" — he tapped his temple meaningfully — "to make a joke."

"That stupid next-door neighbor of yours!" Simon seethed. "He has a mouth on him like the Grand Canyon! He told *my* personal business — communicated in confidence — to Barbara! Why didn't he just take out an ad in *The Sun?*"

Phil shook his head. "It's just another symptom of boyfriend syndrome. And if I were you, I wouldn't say too much about this, considering you could be fighting off the effects of the same thing pretty soon, what with Wendy liking you and all."

"There's nothing more to that than carefully calculated cruelty."

"I don't know," said Phil speculatively, "but it's just bizarre enough for me to believe it. You and Wendy. Hmmm."

* * *

Sometime that afternoon, the duty roster went up for the next week of the Antiflux Worm Shop. By the time

Simon saw it, it was completely filled with the names of the volunteers. Simon could see the name Dave Roper liberally sprinkled all across the board, Monday through Friday. But there were a few surprises, too. Bill McIntosh and Dino appeared repeatedly on the sheet. They were in the midst of the $250,000 Antiflux Worm Shop Invitational Crazy-Eights Tournament, which Dino presently led, forty-eight games to forty-six. The second week promised even more strategy, action, and tantrums.

Not that much Crazy-Eights was played at the end of that first week, however, for business suddenly began to pick up. Junior and middle school students, who had heard about the store through their older brothers and sisters, began to flock to the Antiflux land to see what the big deal was about. With them they brought a swarm of parents, some of whom were even more interested than their children to see Antiflux in operation. So once again the Antiflux Worm Shop was moving stock at capacity to droves of customers, none of whom had any use for worms. By closing Friday, Antiflux had over $1,500.

Simon spent the weekend working on a new painting, but his mind kept wandering to what Barbara had told him about Wendy, to Sam and his boyfriend syndrome, and to the fact that he had not been picked to venture out to Greenwich, Connecticut, with a Nathan Kruppman film crew. Phil, Dino, and Dina were among those chosen to act in the establishment of Earth's first space station on Pluto. Rumor had it that the quarter-ton couple was going to perform a spectacular weightlessness scene.

Simon decided privately that if Nathan Kruppman actually did come up with a role for him, which wasn't very likely, he would tell him to stuff it. On its worst day, Antiflux was every bit as important as Nathan's stupid movie, and Simon Irving was not a man to be taken lightly.

At home, the pressure was off Simon because The Flake had made headlines again. After a rather long night (which, according to reports, had lasted over a week), Kyle Montrose had been found skinny-dipping in the reflecting pools of the Taj Mahal. On top of this, *The Sun* published an article entitled "Exciting Green Vegetables," and big salads were now a cause for alarm. These two developments had Mr. Irving too wrapped up in his own problems to cause any discomfort for Simon.

On Monday, a new dimension hit the worm shop. Word of mouth had spread around Long Island to such an extent that *The Sun* sent a reporter and photographer over to take pictures of the operation and get the Antiflux story. The interview was handled by Phil, but Dave Roper could not be restrained from getting in his two cents here and there, and several other students who happened to be on the scene were questioned briefly. Simon avoided the whole exercise for fear that his name might connect him with his father, although it was let slip that somewhere in the background was a student silently masterminding the Antiflux game plan. The article, complete with pictures, appeared in the next morning's edition under the headline: STUDENTS WORM THEIR WAY OUT FROM UNDER INTERFLUX BOOT.

Cyril Irving expected the worst. He knew from experience that Interflux versus The Little Guy was a favorite football for the national press to throw around. He was not surprised when the New York papers picked up the story the very next day, and he knew the wire services would not be far behind.

The dilemma was discussed and rediscussed at length over the Interflux boardroom table until finally Mr. Hardy spoke. Although he was only a junior lawyer, all the men in the room gave him their absolute undivided attention, for he had drawn the shortest straw out in the hall before the meeting. It was therefore his responsibility to put to Cyril Irving the question that was on everyone's mind.

"Look, Cyril, aren't we ignoring a much simpler solution? Everyone here knows the head of Antiflux is your son, Simon. I mean, it really seems like we're going through an awful lot of trouble when you could just — you know — tell him to stop."

"I can't do that," said Mr. Irving shortly. "My son is working with school money, and he can't sell me the land without the approval of fifteen hundred kids who won't give it."

There was a babble of protest, then everyone looked at poor Mr. Hardy, indicating that it was time for him to further the argument.

"But, Cyril, Simon's a real big shot at that school. The kids all think he's a genius, and would follow him anywhere. I'm sure he could convince them. But first, you have to convince *him*."

Mr. Irving looked out over the table icily. "Do you mean to tell me that, with all our resources, our experience, our wealth and power, and our *overpaid executives*, the only way out of this is for me to bully my son? Are you saying that, if Simon weren't my son, we'd have to pack up our plant and move elsewhere? That's a little silly, isn't it?" He stood up. "December seventh is the key day. We must initiate full construction by then. You people have my word that that date will never be in jeopardy. If the papers want to print David and Goliath stories, let them. They know we haven't used real muscle yet." He paused. "But I ask — no, I insist — that you remember this: Simon Irving is a coincidence in this affair, and nothing more. Now, if you'll excuse me, Mayor Van Doren is in my office."

Twelve

"So according to this letter," Simon summarized, "the town — in other words, Interflux — is accusing our worm store of being of no value to the community."

Two thirds of the Program Board were meeting in a music practice room. The other third, still in the throes of boyfriend syndrome, had not been seen for some time.

"We've got satisfied customers," said Phil. "How can they prove we're not valuable to the community?"

"They can do that," said Simon. "They're the government. Van Doren says here that we have to devote a certain amount of space and personnel to community service or they'll close us up. And a week later they can confiscate our land."

Phil was no longer intrigued with the strategy game. "I'm getting sick of all this cat and mouse business. How long do these guys intend to keep cooking up technicalities to catch us on? What do they mean by 'service to the community'?"

"The letter says 'of educational, cultural, or charitable benefit to the general public.'"

Phil slapped his knee. "Well, that's so easy I'm surprised at your dad for even thinking it might work. Man, we've got fifteen hundred artists here. We've got so much education and culture it's coming out our ears. Sometimes I want to throw up when I think of how much education and culture there is in this place. As for charity — " he reached into his pockets, "well, I'm a little short this week. We can always give away free worms or something."

Simon looked thoughtful. "You mean a cultural exhibition kind of thing?"

"Yeah. We'll put all the paintings and sculptures and photographs out on display. The writers can give readings; in music or theater or dance, whenever there's a rehearsal, we'll just hold it outside and call it a performance. Yeah." He looked vaguely surprised. "You know, this is even better than I thought. We've got the problem solved already, and we haven't even been working on it ten minutes yet."

Simon shook his head. "It's the fifteenth of November. It just so happens that the weather's been like summer lately, but that's a freak. It's definitely going to get colder. For all we know it could snow the day after tomorrow. It's crazy to plan an outdoor exhibition."

"We've got fifteen hundred bucks. I'm sure we can work something out."

"You can't build Lincoln Center for fifteen hundred dollars, Phil. And if we try and do it on the cheap, we'll get a blizzard for sure."

"Ah, but don't you see?" said Phil whimsically.

"That's where faith comes in. Sure, the logic of the situation may be against us a little, but if you went by logic, Antiflux shouldn't be here at all, considering what we're up against. But faith — that's the ticket. What made the office switch around your name so that it took your dad weeks to figure out what was going on? What made the Town Hall people such a bunch of bumbling nincompoops who wound up giving us the jump on Interflux? What kept the weather warm so we could cut weeds and dig worms? I tell you, Simon, we've been getting some extra help from somewhere, and there's no reason why whoever's giving it isn't going to support us for one more thing."

"Forget it," Simon replied. "This whole idea has more holes in it than a gravy strainer. And you can't fix that by saying 'faith.'"

To this Phil made no reply, but there was a great deal of discontented muttering going on. Simon ignored it. Although he had no plan on the spot, even doing nothing would be more advisable than letting Phil try to spin straw into gold, aided only by the belief that the cards would continue to come up aces. Cities and towns spent millions of dollars on cultural exhibitions and still ran over budget, yet Phil expected to pull it off with $1,500 worm money, high school artists, and faith, commercial value: zero. He had to think. But who had time for thinking?

It was coming down to the wire for the Vishnik Prize, and with the deadline two weeks away, Emile Querada was in a frenzy, flying around the room with the destructive potential of a trapped moose.

"A catastrophe! A disaster! A cataclysmic apocalypse! Where is your work? Mr. Ashley! Mr. Lawrence! Mr. Stavrinidis, where is your brilliant piece without camels? Miss Dixon, where are your sister and her new baby? Mr. Simon, first you had a tavern scene, then you had an assembly line! Now you have nothing!" He lifted up his long beard. "Here! Here is my unprotected throat! Each of you — take a slash! More merciful to do that than to subject me to this torment!" Then he became deathly quiet, and when he spoke again, the class could barely hear him. "I can see it as clearly as if it had happened five minutes ago. When the creep from Albany won the Vishnik Prize, a part of me turned to stone. And now this is to happen again. Soon Querada will be all stone, and they will roll me out to Central Park, where pigeons will defile me, and someone will spray-paint 'RAOUL' on my stomach. And they will put up a sign: 'This used to be Querada before his students threw away the Vishnik Prize and destroyed him.'"

As the teacher launched into a monologue, asking the great organizing principle of the universe what he had done to deserve this, Simon found his mind wandering to his own Vishnik entry, all but finished at home. He called it "Subway Breakdown," since it depicted the interior of a stranded subway car, its occupants coping with the inconvenience and discomfort by working on crossword puzzles, reading the paper, knitting, crying, sweating, and sleeping. Everything that was wrong with the "Tavern Scene" and "Assembly Line" was right with this painting, and Simon was almost overconfident that there would be nothing better in the competition. Lately, he'd been thinking a great deal about the Vishnik Prize. It was so beautifully straightforward — you painted the best picture, and they gave you the prize. If he won the Vishnik Prize, he'd have something that would still be there when the dust cleared after the final battle of the Fluxes. And if "Subway Breakdown" didn't win him that prize, nothing would.

Up at the front of the class, Querada was threatening to take poison, and suddenly Simon realized that this did not bother him in the slightest. He'd become a real Querada student, able to sit through the most violent tantrums without batting an eyelash or even considering dialing 911.

Sam showed no signs of recovery in his bout with boyfriend syndrome, and between Barbara and the problem of coming up with a Vishnik entry without camels, his time was pretty much taken up.

"Sotirios has got it really bad," commented Phil between classes after Sam had pranced off to help Barbara do some setting up in one of the studios. "I've seen boyfriend syndrome before, but our man is really a victim. If you and Wendy get together, do me a favor and try to retain at least a little bit of the old Simon."

"Don't make me laugh," said Simon darkly. "There is no such thing as me and Wendy. I refuse to take the bait for an obvious set-up so my face can be published on the cover of the next issue of *Idiot Magazine*."

"But what if Barbara was telling the truth? You'd be blowing a pretty big opportunity."

Simon glared at him. "Thank you for putting my mind at ease like that. Obviously, I have nothing else to think about, and welcome the chance to agonize over Wendy. You're a real pal."

"But, Simon, I really think — "

"Listen. I have the situation perfectly under control. I intend to treat it like the joke it really is, and if it turns out that I'm wrong, I intend to throw myself off a building. And if you're a good little boy, I'll let you put an art board on the street below, and you can shellac me, hand me in, and hang me up in your new fifteen-hundred-dollar art gallery! Deal?"

Phil shrugged. Simon was surprised he didn't pick up on the art center theme and start nagging. Could it be that that idea was so impractical that even Phil had written it off? He hoped so, since it would be a lot easier to think of something that actually could work if he didn't have to listen to Phil's grandiose plans. He frowned. The one-week time limit made him nervous.

* * *

That afternoon, Nathan Kruppman made another appearance at school, and Simon was very careful to point out that he, for one, didn't care. He avoided the impromptu gathering in the front hall, and did his best to shut Nathan entirely out of his mind. So he was the last person in the building to find out that Nathan, on his arrival, had expressed his desire to meet Simon

Irving. In fact, the first he knew of it was when the great one himself was already upon him, oozing charm.

"I've been hearing a lot of great things about you and Antiflux," said Nathan, after T.C. had performed the introductions. "I wanted to shake the hand of the man who could do all that."

Well, thought Simon, here it was — the perfect opportunity to mouth off at Nathan Kruppman, and Nathan was spoiling it all by being nice. "I hear you've been doing a lot of pretty fantastic things, too." He couldn't resist adding, "Naturally, I wouldn't know anything about it firsthand."

Nathan smiled, instantly understanding the situation, and making Simon feel childish and petty. "You should be hearing from me pretty soon. I've had a part in mind for you for a while now."

"Really?" For some reason, refusing the part, as had been the plan, did not even occur to Simon.

Nathan nodded crisply, engaged Simon in a firm handshake, pledged his support for Antiflux, and bustled off, T.C. in tow.

"You just may have been right about Nathan Kruppman," Simon told Phil when he finally caught up with him at the end of the school day. "I was pretty impressed by him. There's logic behind everything he does. You know why I haven't had a part yet? Because he's been saving me for this special role that's coming up."

"I'm glad to see you're starting to have some respect for Nathan," Phil replied, but he seemed abstracted, and soon went off, mumbling something about a new innovative arts project.

With Phil gone, and Sam engaged in Barbara-related activities, Simon had no one with whom to discuss his upcoming starring role in *Omni*. The only person around seemed to be Dave Roper, but he was just going to the bathroom, after which he was needed at the worm store, and had no time for small talk. Disgusted, Simon headed out to the parking lot. He was just inserting the key in the ignition of the Mustang when the passenger door was wrenched open, and Bill McIntosh insinuated his long lean frame into the bucket seat. He shut the door behind him, assumed the pose of a deeply troubled man, and gazed bleakly out the front window, his eyes twin pools of melancholy.

Simon looked at him quizzically. "Can I do something for you, Bill?"

Bill heaved a sigh. "I've got writer's block."

"Huh?"

"Writer's block. I haven't written a word since *The Legend of the Glass Caves*."

"Uh — I'm sorry to hear that." Simon's mind raced. He and Bill were friends, but they had certainly not progressed to the soul-baring stage. From what Simon had heard, Bill was a very private person, not noted for heavy conversations.

Bill nodded sadly. "Yeah. I guess it's not so bad. I can always play ball. But you know, when I see some of the kids in my neighborhood reading *The Glass Caves* and getting so into it, it kills me that I can't write like that anymore. I tried. I really tried. But everything I write now comes off sounding stupid."

Simon put the key back in his pocket and unbuckled his seat belt to get comfortable. "Well, have you spoken to anyone about this — you know, your parents, your teacher, any of the guys?"

Bill shook his head. "Nobody knows anything about it. Mr. Ferdinand may suspect something, but I doubt he knows how big the problem really is. I came to you because, you know, you're such a 'together' kind of guy."

Simon, whose life seemed to grow more complicated with each passing hour, nodded numbly.

"I mean, you're one of the top artists in the school, and the head of Antiflux, nothing bothers you, and when you've got a problem, you just hit it straight on. People admire you, Simon. So I figured if there's one guy I could really talk to, it's you."

Yes, thought Simon as Bill went on at great length, here was one for the books. One of the country's most promising young athletes, who should have nothing but confidence, telling his troubles to the guy whose worm store was on the verge of being torpedoed by the world's largest corporation. "Well, Bill, I don't know what to tell you," he said in a "together," well-adjusted way.

"Yeah, I know, man. I didn't expect there to be an easy way out. But thanks a lot for listening." He climbed back out of the car. "See you."

Dazed, Simon drove home.

* * *

On Friday, Simon found himself pretty much on his own, with Phil still tied up somewhere and Sam unavailable as usual. He tried an experiment with Wendy when he saw her in the hall before classes. As he passed, he risked a friendly "Hi," and her answering growl made the hair stand up on the back of his neck. Well, so much for the theory that Wendy liked him. Barbara was either crazy or sadistic. Simon Irving was completely safe from boyfriend syndrome, even though he wouldn't have minded a mild case, something on the order of the German measles.

Querada's class was the area of much excitement as the students were caught up in Vishnik fever, and the teacher began to develop sparse patches from clawing at his beard. Simon's thoughts were all "Subway Breakdown," and he could smell the Vishnik Prize, dangling like a carrot on a stick right before his nose. But the competition would be stiff, as that day Lawrence and Chernik presented their latest collaboration, which was bound to be an impressive contender. Also on display was Sam's entry, "Traffic Jam," a camel-less picture of a horrendous highway jam-up on the elevated Brooklyn-Queens Expressway, with the Manhattan skyline in the background. It was good, Simon supposed, but it definitely lacked Sam's vitality. There were two possible reasons for this: first, that his romance with Barbara had him so distracted that it was affecting his work, or second, that Sam Stavrinidis really couldn't do a painting without camels, or at least the knowledge that he would be in some way riling up Querada.

"Nice work, Sam," said Simon.

"Thanks," said Sam, his expression inscrutable.

* * *

That weekend, Simon's special starring appearance in *Omni* didn't make the shooting schedule, although Nathan and his crew did film some chariot racing in Westchester.

Mr. Irving was becoming smug again, secure in the knowledge that it was downright impossible to make a worm store beneficial to a community. This did not stop him from making frequent trips to the club, however, as he now went out of sheer force of habit. Simon still went with him on occasion, but not this weekend, as he had Antiflux to worry about. Making matters more complicated, green vegetables became a full-blown crisis at the Irving table, where meat had passed out of the picture yet again.

"And remember," said Mr. Irving as he and his son wolfed down hamburgers at Burger King at two o'clock in the morning while Mrs. Irving slept, "we've still got beans to worry about. You'll notice *they* haven't disappeared yet either."

"You think maybe green vegetables are just a decoy and she's planning to hit us with beans again?"

"Exactly. And when it happens, we've got to be ready."

"Can't we just tell her?" Simon suggested.

His father shook his head. "Too risky. My plan is to have lots of guests home for dinner, and you invite some of your friends, too. Remember T.C.? We got steak. Steak!"

Simon thought it over. "Sounds good, Dad. Are you sure our — uh — political differences aren't going to get in the way? I mean, my people and yours are probably going to be on different teams."

"We'll declare the table a neutral zone," Mr. Irving said with determination. "This is important."

* * *

When Simon drove into the Nassau Arts parking lot on Monday, he had a plan — not a good plan, but at least it was something. Simply, the worm store would continue operation, and donate one third of its proceeds to a local charity. It wasn't cultural or educational, so Interflux was bound to shoot it down in the long run. Still, it would keep Antiflux alive for a little bit longer, which was all anyone could ask for.

As he got out of the car, he was surprised to see a small tractor chugging onto the edge of the school property from Lot 1346B. His first thought was that Interflux had assembled a militia and was mining the Antiflux land. Then he noticed a towline behind the tractor, and before he had time to think what this might mean, an enormous blue-and-white striped tent rose out of nowhere. It billowed, shuddered, and finally settled firmly along the tip of the thin land strip. Distant cheering wafted over from the woods.

His heart in this mouth, Simon ran headlong across the school's large side lawn to the Antiflux land. There he found about thirty students gathered around the entrance to the tent, congratulating themselves heartily. At the center of it all was Phil Baldwin, obviously in charge.

Simon was tight-lipped. "Tell me the circus is in town and this tent has nothing to do with me. Explain how Ringling Brothers needed a place for their Big Top, and they picked our land, but we aren't involved in this. And make it good, Phil, because I'm not feeling too cool right now."

Phil smiled proudly. "It's our new cultural center. Isn't it great?"

Simon exploded. "You *idiot!* How could you be such an *idiot?* Only an *idiot* could do such an *idiotic* thing!" He would have gone on, but Phil interrupted him by announcing,

"Hey, everybody, Simon's here! Let's show our appreciation! *For he's a jolly good fellow . . .*"

By the time the singing was over, Simon could not get his hands around Phil's neck because he was mobbed by well-wishers, all of them assuring him that this was his best idea ever.

"Sorry to go over your head like this, but it was the only way," whispered Phil, as Johnny Zull declared what an honor it was to be the lab partner of such a man.

"What," hissed Simon through clenched teeth, "did you use for money?"

"I've been meaning to get to that, Simon," Phil said seriously. "We're going to have to hit the bank today, because we owe some big bucks. We've got a five-hundred-dollar deposit due on this tent."

"Aw, Phil!" moaned Simon in true pain. "How could you do this to me? It's costing a fortune, and now we have to find stuff to put in this dumb tent, which is the size of Pittsburgh and twice as ugly. And we've got to get volunteers and figure out ways to organize the whole business! What a pain!"

"But, Simon, that's all been taken care of. I've already got the exhibit and performance schedule completely worked out."

"Oh yeah? How?"

"Okay, picture this. It's Thursday, right? You've just dumped on the idea, but it's looking better to me all the time. So quietly, I talk it up with some of the kids, and they all really go for it. They put me on to the teachers, who like it, too. Then I go to the department heads, and I finally end up down in The Dungeon, and by this time I've got T.C. with me because things are looking pretty heavy-duty. But the Dungeon guys just love your new idea."

"*My* new idea?"

"You may not realize it, Simon, but a lot of people are really proud of you for this. I mean, think about it. We've got the tent, the volunteers, staff support, and any equipment we need from the school. I've alerted the newspapers, and The Dungeon has authorized a door-to-door flyer, so we should have people, too. Man, this is going to be the most awesome cultural center in the world! And the best part is that you, me, and Sotirios are splitting T.C.'s services in even thirds, four nights each."

Simon snorted. "I don't suppose you consulted Sam, either."

"There was no point," said Phil. "But I figure that when he gets over his boyfriend syndrome, he'll be happy that we didn't leave him out of this. You know, if I say so myself, I've handled this whole thing pretty well."

"All right," Simon mumbled in resignation. "Let's have a cultural center."

Thirteen

The sign read:

NASSAU ARTS STUDENT COUNCIL
PROGRAM BOARD PRESENTS
THE ANTIFLUX CULTURAL CENTER
AND WORM SHOP

"That's the stupidest thing I've ever seen in my life," was Simon's considered opinion. But Dave Roper and his following refused to participate without equal billing for the worm store, so the sign was a bit of a compromise. In fact, if it hadn't been for the worm store, which had now been moved behind the big tent, Simon felt he could almost lose sight of the fact that the Cultural Center had started out as a ploy to keep Lot 1346B from Interflux's greedy hands. Over the last couple of days, he had really gotten caught up in the preparations for the big Wednesday night opening, much different from the man who had threatened to take Phil's life early Monday morning. The Cultural Center appealed to him for three reasons: first, it was the perfect activity for Nassau Arts; second, with the whole idea so widely attributed to him, he had become a genuine superstar on the student scene; and third, with the staff so enthusiastically involved, he felt far safer than in the early days when it always looked as though he were about to take the fall over his unauthorized actions.

There were about sixty pieces of work on display on opening night, about half of them paintings, the rest sculptures, prints, innovative arts projects, and photographs. The setup was impressive, as Nassau Arts' display facilities were among the very best, with attractive mounts, professional glass cases, and carefully placed spotlights. A string quartet played background music for the three hundred or so staff, students, and parents who attended the Wednesday night pre-Thanksgiving sneak preview. The Center was to have its regular opening for the public Saturday afternoon.

While Simon was acknowledged as the mastermind behind the Cultural Center, the true father was definitely Phil Baldwin. Although he seemed content to let Simon take the credit, he toured the exhibits in obvious pride and pleasure. For Phil, who despite his potential failed at so much so often, the Cultural Center was a triumph beyond measure.

"These handshakes should really be yours, you know," Simon said to him in the middle of the evening. "If you ask me, I'd say you show a lot of potential at organizing cultural centers."

Phil grinned. "Shh! The tent still might cave in."

Simon was somewhat distracted by the fact that Wendy was also there in her capacity as president of the Student Council, and his conscious effort not to think about her was making him think about her. Because she was playing the hostess, the scowl she usually reserved for him was absent, and she looked so good that he found himself toying with the idea that there was still a chance, however remote, that Barbara had been telling the truth and that Wendy liked him. With grim determination, he decided that it would be better to make a complete idiot of himself in front of these hundreds of people than to live five more minutes agonizing over the possibility that there was no joke and that he was passing up this terrific opportunity.

Okay, thought Simon. This was it. Zero hour. Time to settle the matter for better or worse — probably worse. Mentally, he laid in a course for where Wendy was standing, and commanded his feet to await orders from the bridge. All right — go.

His heart was pounding in his throat. Hold on a second. Why was he so scared of her? She was just another face in the Nassau Arts dance studio, and he was Simon Irving, a big man to whom seven-foot basketball centers came for help and guidance. Confidence surged through his body and the racing of his heart slowed as he faced her. "Hi, Wendy. Having a nice time?"

"Until you got here. What do you want?"

The pounding returned to Simon's throat as his confidence deserted him. His feet were frantically signaling the bridge, begging for orders — retreat, retreat! No. There was no turning back. He looked her right in the eye and blurted, "I want you to go to a movie with me Friday night." As soon as the words left his lips, he knew he'd made the fatal mistake. She would cut him down in front of all these people, and everyone would know that he wasn't Simon Irving, big man; he was Simon Irving, idiot.

"What time?"

"Huh?"

"What time are you going to pick me up?"

"Seven-thirty," he managed in a strangled voice as the string quartet swung into "Love is a Many-Splendored Thing." Simon was fighting a new battle now, that of restraining the goofy grin that was on the verge of blooming on his face. A big man would accept this triumph as a standard matter of course; it was the idiot in him that wanted to run around cheering. So he committed her address to memory, tore himself from her side, and continued to mingle with gold-medal nonchalance. But when Phil (who showed great potential at lip-reading) flashed him a triumphant grin and gave him the thumbs-up signal, the wide smile broke through Simon's artificial calm. He was then forced to flee the tent and do his grinning in the woods.

By the time he had calmed down enough to re-enter the tent, the pre-Thanksgiving sneak preview had grown into an unqualified success, and hopes for the Cultural Center were high. For Simon it was definitely a good night, possibly the best in sixteen and a third years. Here he was, with Wendy in his back pocket, the Vishnik Prize in the palm of his hand, and Interflux once more on the run.

* * *

Simon and his father took no chances with Thanksgiving dinner. After much searching, Mr. Irving managed to locate a single, nineteen-year-old mail clerk from Kansas City to drag home for the major meal. Simon brought T.C. Serrette, whose current hosts were dining with relatives. This was the first time T.C. had ever accepted hospitality for which he had performed no service, but since Simon was a high dignitary on the Nassau Arts scene, the exception seemed okay. The strategy worked, too, since neither beans nor greens made it to the table, so the heads of Interflux and Antiflux spent Thanksgiving side by side, being thankful.

If Mr. Irving had been briefed on the Nassau Arts Cultural Center at all, he certainly didn't show it, or at least Simon didn't notice anything. But Simon himself was so overwhelmed by the prospect of his upcoming date with Wendy that he wasn't noticing much.

The only other matter he could seem to think about with any clarity was the Vishnik Prize, and on the Friday exactly one week before the deadline, he put the final touches on "Subway Breakdown." He was so pleased with his entry that the only thing that kept him from going out to buy a trophy case was the fact that he didn't want to get any dust on the Mustang, which he had spent all morning waxing and polishing.

* * *

"A horror movie," Phil had said. "Take her to a horror movie. Trust me."

Killville was the most appalling experience of Simon's life, although Wendy didn't seem affected in the least. When it was over, Simon excused himself, went to the washroom, and applied a wet towelette to the back of his neck. This restored some of the color to his face. He was now ready to continue the date. Wendy wanted to go out for a bite to eat. Okay, they would go.

"Salads," Phil had advised on that subject. "A burger's got no class, and steaks'll have you in the poorhouse. You want salads with cheese and rolls, but watch those poppyseeds. If they get in your teeth, you're dead."

Mars, located in Fosterville, was a trendy sort of place for a late bite, and it was quite noisy and crowded when Simon and Wendy were escorted to their table. It was so dark that Simon fell down, and only the fact that Wendy had taken his hand kept it from being a total wipe-out.

"I guess you must think I'm a pretty big idiot," he said as he very carefully eased himself into his chair. One leg was shorter than the others, and it rocked.

Wendy smiled. "Simon, you're nervous."

"No," lied Simon. "It was dark. I didn't see the step."

She laughed, indicating that she didn't buy it, but her expression was so totally open and friendly that

212

Simon could hardly believe it was Wendy. This was the girl who hadn't called him anything but "sleaze-bag" since she'd done a number on him in the warm-up studio so many weeks ago.

He was beginning to relax, and suddenly Phil's voice came to haunt him once more. "Keep the conversation going. Any silence longer than five seconds, and she can nail you on a 'nothing in common' rap. It doesn't matter what you talk about, so long as you talk."

"So, Wendy — uh — what do you think about all this warm weather we've been having?"

"I don't think about it at all," said Wendy honestly. "Simon, we're not robots. Let's just talk, okay? I'm not going to shoot you with a fire extinguisher this time."

"That's good," grinned Simon, "because I think I'm allergic to the foam. I had hives for a week."

The tension disintegrated, and the two began laughing and joking about the events that had led up to the glory that was now Antiflux. The light chatter continued in an easy manner as they gave their orders and, later, set to their food. By this time, the conversation was going so well that they were actually talking about the bad old days, speaking with amused tolerance about their past feud. (Simon wisely refrained from pointing out that the only person feuding had been Wendy. He had been willing to submit to the perils of boyfriend syndrome from day one.)

"Simon, when you convinced all the kids to go out

there and cut weeds, I almost died! I figured they'd run up on the platform and choke you."

Simon shrugged. "I was the most surprised guy in the place. A good gust of wind would have flattened me."

Wendy laughed again, and Simon beamed. So this was a date. The only other date he'd ever been on in his life had been a night on the town in Albuquerque with the fifteen-year-old daughter of Interflux's regional vice-president, an experience so boring and so uncomfortable that a lesser man might have sworn off women for life. Nothing like tonight, a perfect evening with the girl of his dreams.

"If it's going well," Phil had said, "don't get cocky. You're bound to say something stupid and blow it." Well, Phil, what do *you* know? When a girl likes you so much that she doesn't get turned off by you taking a spill in the restaurant, nothing can go wrong. Besides, he decided, the rest of tonight was going to be pure finesse.

They lingered at the table long after the food had disappeared, putting down Coke after Coke, discussing anything and everything, from world politics to Nassau Arts. Feeling he could share almost anything with this girl, Simon mentioned how he felt a little hurt over how Sam had disappeared off the face of the earth ever since he'd started going out with Barbara.

Wendy nodded in agreement. "It won't last. They're not a good pair. Barbara is a girl with so much going for her, while Sam has exactly one thing going for him — his looks. Now, *we*, on the other hand — "

A sour note struck Simon in the midst of the gorgeous symphony he'd been hearing for the last two hours, jarring him from his image of tonight as perfection. He must have looked strange, because Wendy asked, "Simon, are you okay? All of a sudden you're in another world."

"No, it's nothing. You were saying— "

"Well, I was talking about how we get along because we're so similar, but that Sam and Barbara won't work out. It's just like Bill McIntosh. A lot of girls are really dying to go out with him. Why do you think that is? Because they like *The Legend of the Glass Caves*? Be real. If he was five-one instead of seven-one, it'd be a lot different."

"Well," Simon said carefully, "a lot of people at school are really good at one thing. Take Johnny Zull, who's probably the best young guitarist in the country."

"That's my point," said Wendy smugly. "If a girl dated him just because she admired his guitar playing, it wouldn't work out. He needs someone who likes him for himself, like — uh — " She began to chuckle. "I wonder if Marilyn Manson has a kid sister."

"But people are more complicated than that," Simon argued. "Look at someone like Phil. He's good at a lot of things."

She laughed. "Or nothing, depending on how you want to look at it. What's the story with him, Simon?

I've heard rumors that he blows from department to department until he gets thrown out. Do you think it's good for the school that people can do that? I sure don't."

Simon sat very still and made no reply, heedless of Phil's guidelines. He had nothing he felt like adding to what she had just said. He reached into his wallet, tossed some bills onto the table, and stood up. "Let's go for a drive," he said grimly.

"Sure. Where to?"

"It's a surprise."

Wendy seemed to get the idea that his humorless manner was some kind of game. "Okay," she said, forcing an artificial scowl onto her face, "we'll both be really serious." She held her expression as they got into the Mustang and drove off. Soon, though, she began to giggle. "Oh, come on, Simon, where are we going?"

"I don't want to spoil the surprise." In five minutes, he pulled up in front of her house. "Surprise."

"Why are we here? I don't get it."

"Think a little harder."

Now the scowl was real. "Do you mean to tell me that you're sore because of what I said about your friends? I was only trying to open your eyes to — "

Simon hit the button that unlocked the passenger door. "I like it fine with my eyes closed."

She seemed mystified. "Look, I'm sorry, okay? I didn't know you were going to be so sensitive about it. I promise not to say anything more about your friends."

"You've said enough."

Face flaming red, she jumped out of the car and slammed the door hard enough to bend the frame. "I wouldn't have anything to do with you if you were the last man in the universe! I was right the first time! You're a sleazebag!"

She wheeled and headed for her front door, so she may or may not have heard Simon's next comment, spoken to no one in particular.

"I'm not, you know," he mused thoughtfully. "If I was a real sleazebag, you'd be walking now."

* * *

It was a little before midnight, and Simon didn't feel like going home. He pulled onto the Sunrise Highway and began to drive at the speed of traffic. He felt very calm, not sure whether his spirits were up or down, and he put on a little mood music. Slow riffs, blues guitar — perfect.

He was sub-dazed, he decided, very cool, very mellow. The Mustang rode like silk and, out the windows, Long Island rolled by, punctuated by carloads of young locals out for their Friday night cruise. Few moments, he decided, were as well put-together as this one.

As he waited for a traffic light to change, the voice of a well-known blues singer intoned, "You ain't nobody if you ain't got somebody," and the perfection of the moment vanished in a puff of smoke.

"What have I *done?*" he howled aloud as the traffic behind began to honk for him to move out. In anguish, he pulled over to the side of the road and beat his forehead rhythmically against the padded steering wheel. All year he had agonized over Wendy Orr, through times when the mere mention of his name had been enough to make her snarl. For months, he had hoped against hope that he would be able to get near her. All his life, he'd never been able to get a girl to look at him twice, but someone as attractive as Wendy had seemed totally out of reach. Yet he'd had not one, but two opportunities with this great-looking dancer. The first time, he'd burned her for $6,700, and now he'd just thrown her out of his car. What was he — crazy? Ah, but he'd done it for his friends, the people who'd taken in a lonely Simon Irving in a new town and a new school. In the case of Phil and Sam, that was friendship above and beyond the call of duty, not caring if he was stupid, or impulsive, or harebrained, or the son of Interflux. These people deserved the stand he'd taken for them tonight.

Yeah, so big deal. So what if Wendy didn't like Phil, Sam, Bill, and Johnny Zull? He couldn't imagine any of them sitting down and sobbing because Wendy didn't think they were up to scratch. It was all nothing but a bunch of words. Yes, for the sake of a few stupid words, he had thrown away the girl of his dreams, thereby earning himself a place in history as a class-A boob. Just another typical night in the life of Simon Irving, genius extraordinaire.

He drove straight home. It was not sensible for such a fool to be loose on the streets.

As the Irvings' automatic garage door rolled up, the Mustang's headlights illuminated a shadowy figure sitting on the woodpile just inside. Simon stopped short and squinted through the gloom. It was almost one o'clock in the morning. What was Johnny Zull doing camped out in his garage? He parked the car in the driveway, got out, and approached cautiously.

"Johnny? Is that you?'

"Yeah, man, it's me." The voice seemed exhausted and empty, and the guitarist spoke much more slowly than was his habit. "What's up?"

"Uh — nothing much. I've had a rotten night. How about you?"

Johnny was silent for a moment. His eyes scouted the deserted block. "What a lousy neighborhood. How can you stand this place?"

"Yeah, well, we've been petitioning the Town Hall for some tenements, but so far no luck. Is that why you're here — to pass judgment on my street?"

"There are times, man, when a guy needs his lab partner."

"Yeah," Simon agreed irritably. "In the lab. Doing experiments. Writing reports."

"Not that stuff. I'm talking about when things go really bad. Not just ordinary bad, but when it's like all the kicks in the face in the world come together for the ultimate negativity trip."

Simon stared at him. "What happened?"

Johnny's face mirrored a deep sense of loss. "I just can't believe it. I think about it now, and I still can't believe it's all over. Outer Nimrod, man. We busted up the group today."

Simon sighed. "Aw, Johnny, I'm sorry."

Johnny shifted on the woodpile, and a large log tumbled onto Simon's toe. "This afternoon, I went into the city to meet the guys, because the band's been planning some new gigs lately. We ended up going out for a glass of tomato juice at this great condemned restaurant near Frieda's place. We got to talking about why we're so much better than everybody else, and I said that our secret was that we'd never sell out. I mean, even if we got rich and famous, we wouldn't buy big houses or fancy cars or gold chains, we wouldn't give big parties, or take baths in expensive champagne, or live high. And we wouldn't play places like Shea Stadium or Madison Square Garden; we'd stick to the classy clubs, like Scuzz. And I must have said the wrong thing, because this big fight started. And then I found out that those three guys, who I thought were special, were just as big sell-outs as anybody else. They want *this*, man!" He made a sweeping gesture to take in their surroundings. "Long Island. Money. Plastic. Ig said he wanted to marry some rich guy's daughter, so Frieda threatened to go on the wrestling circuit full time, and Neb challenged them both, saying he could always go back to Harvard and finish up his Ph.D. And before I knew it, just because of *money*, Outer Nimrod, the most meaningful thing in my life, was in the toilet."

"So you came here," said Simon lamely.

Johnny shrugged. "Where else would I go? I showed up around ten, and your old man told me you weren't home, and I didn't think he'd be into me hanging out for a while, so I decided to wait in here and maybe catch a few z's until you got back. But I couldn't sleep, man. I had to talk to you. And it's not just because you're my lab partner either. It's because you're just such a with-it kind of guy. You know exactly where your head's at. I mean, you're cool as an average dude in the school hall, you're cool leading us all in Antiflux, and even in a place like Scuzz, you're cool enough to be the first guy to stand up. And that's why I thought of you when my whole life converted itself into a piece of junk."

Simon swallowed hard. *Why* were people coming to him with their troubles? He didn't even have the judgment to decide whether this evening had been a noble defense of his friends or an act of cataclysmic stupidity. "Well, Johnny, I don't know what to tell you," he said in a with-it sort of way.

Johnny nodded resignedly. "Yeah, man, I know. But I really appreciate you taking the time to listen. By the way, you know you got poppyseeds in your teeth?"

* * *

Somehow, both Johnny Zull and Bill McIntosh found the strength to keep on going, so Simon felt it behooved him to do the same. Against his better judgment, he got out of bed on Saturday morning (he hadn't been planning to), and went down to his basement studio. There sat "Subway Breakdown," a reminder that he could still paint, even though he was a wash-out at everything else.

He didn't particularly feel like going to the Cultural Center. Wendy would probably be there, and staying away from her was number one on his new list of priorities.

He went, though, head high, and found to his surprise that Wendy was not there. She seemed to be the only one who wasn't. Good coverage in local press and even the New York papers, coupled with a keen interest in high school talent and a healthy dislike of Interflux, had combined to bring a large crowd to Antiflux's doorstep. Straight through from ten to three, the Center's Saturday hours, a steady stream of visitors packed the Antiflux tent and surrounding land where, due to continuing good weather, further exhibits had been set up outside. T.C.'s stage band performed behind the tent near the worm store, alternating with a student playing ragtime piano. At various points during the day, poetry students gave short readings, and groups of actors performed vignettes from classical and modern theater.

It took until three-thirty to clear so many people off the property, by which time it was discovered that Antiflux had pulled in over $300 in donations. This was strange, because there was no donation box, but a senior specializing in decorative pottery had a large replica of an ancient Greek vase on display, and today's satisfied patrons had literally stuffed it with cash.

"This is great!" Phil crowed. "If this keeps up, we'll be able to stay open all year!" He and Simon remained at the Center to clean up the tent and lock up until the exhibits reopened on Monday afternoon. Naturally, the first thing Phil wanted to know was how the big date with Wendy had gone.

"Put it this way," said Simon grimly. "At half past one in the morning, I was in my garage sitting on the woodpile with Zull, and it was a lot less aggravating than the stuff that came before it. Get the picture?"

Phil looked disgusted. "You mean to tell me that after all my advice and coaching, you struck out?"

"I didn't strike out," Simon said defensively. "I got sick of her company, so I took her home."

"Sick of her company? What kind of talk is that? This is a date, not a discussion group! You've been moaning about this girl for months!"

"Well, I'll tell you one thing. I won't moan about her anymore. I don't want to hear another word about Wendy Orr."

Phil shook his head in disillusionment. "I can't believe it. I spend hours bestowing my own personal secret wisdom on you so that your date can go well, and somehow you blow it and make me look like an idiot! What did you do? Poppyseeds in the teeth? I bet it was poppyseeds in the teeth!"

"It wasn't poppyseeds in the teeth!" Simon exclaimed in annoyance. "If you must know, she said rotten things about my friends!"

Phil clutched at his head. "That's *it*? You dumped her for *that*? You clod, they're *supposed* to say rotten things about your friends! It's traditional, like not swinging at the first pitch!"

Simon glared at him. "I feel much better now. Thanks for the understanding."

They finished straightening up the exhibits, and Phil fastened the three large padlocks to the door of the tent. "I still feel cheated," he said as they began to walk to their cars. "I came here expecting to hear stories that would — "

"Drop it, Phil."

Phil sighed. "At least you didn't get boyfriend syndrome. By the way, did I mention the patient called me up last night?"

Simon stopped walking. "Who, Sam? Anything important?"

Phil shrugged. "It was kind of weird. I'm figuring carrot-top wants to go somewhere and he needs the wreck. But no. He just wants to talk. Only neither of us has anything to say. So he starts asking me all these questions about Antiflux and what's been going on lately, which is stuff he already knows. But get this — he doesn't chew me out, or moan and groan, or anything. He just listens. Freaky, huh?"

Simon started walking again. "Freaky," he agreed.

* * *

Although it was the last week in November, the weather stayed unseasonably mild, and there was no need for the emergency heaters that had come with the tent. Denver was under four feet of snow, blizzards wracked the Midwest, and both Boston and Washington had had storms, but Phil's faith formed a protective umbrella over the New York metropolitan area.

The Cultural Center prospered, and attendance was steady as people came from all over to see what Nassau Arts had to offer. Even Phil was surprised that the Sunday papers had mentioned the Center again, and *The Sun* critic had commented, ". . . a professional caliber exhibition, tent and worm store notwithstanding." Success was almost assured.

The only casualty of the Cultural Center was, ironically, the worm store. Stuck out behind the tent as it was, it received almost no attention, just the occasional passing chuckle. With only a week of November worms left, business was down to zero, excepting of course Jedediah O'Dell, who felt the Cultural Center was irrelevant. The demise of the worm store would have passed unnoticed had it not been for Dave Roper, who absorbed each new day of no business like a blow to the head with a battle-axe. Once again he was the butt of jokes as he lobbied for more publicity, a better location, and even a booth inside the main tent. This time the abuse Dave took was so obvious that even he was aware that something was not right. And so he sought help from Simon Irving, because he was such a "well-respected, level-headed guy."

"Simon, is there something wrong with me?" Dave asked, while Simon wondered why this was happening again. "I mean, I'm the only guy out of the whole school who cares about the worm store. Now, you're a person whose opinion I can really go by. Tell me the truth — is it stupid to love the worm store?"

Simon squirmed. What could he say? Of course it was stupid to love the worm store. "Well — uh, you can love anything you want. This is a free country."

"I know that. But is it stupid if it's a worm store you love?"

Simon sighed. "Look, Dave, I don't know what to tell you." There it was again. If painting didn't pan out, Simon might still be able to avoid a career in Interflux by opening a plush office on Central Park West, and charging people $100 an hour to hear him say "I don't know what to tell you." If he was going to be the public access guru, he might as well turn a profit.

* * *

With "Subway Breakdown" ready and bound for greatness, the Cultural Center practically running itself, and worries about women all a thing of the past (until next time), Simon was able to turn his attention to his other classes. Things were looking up on the academic scene. Even in art history class, where it had once looked as though he were about to take the fall with Mr. Monagle's "Don't worry. No problem," still ringing in his ears, he was staying afloat. His D average wasn't pretty, but it was a pass, and with T.C.'s help, he'd be able to shake off probation and put Mr. Monagle and his soil erosion behind him. On the other end of the spectrum, he was running three A's. This was no surprise in design and composition, but in English it was totally unexpected. With the energy-obstructing furniture gone from the classroom, the psychic growth was flying all over the place, and Xerxes "Buzz" Durham seemed to think that some of it had settled on Simon. Luckily, psychic growth had many of the same characteristics as aggravation, which put Simon at the top of his class, head and shoulders above the rest. The third A, however, was a stunner. He and Johnny Zull were the top pair in biology. Naturally, this was impossible, since the only experiment they'd completed all year was the one that proved that Simon's shoes performed photosynthesis more efficiently than any of the plant samples. Apparently, Miss Glandfield was so devoted to the attack on Interflux that, as top pair, she picked the only two names she recognized. Certainly, there was no time to grade lab work, as she now spent most of her time at home with a bad back, which she had acquired doing her bit trying to dig worms. From there, she launched a massive letter-writing campaign against the enemy.

This left only math, which was going to be a nuisance again for, that week, the homework pool succumbed to slow decay and simply ceased to be. At seventeen members, it comprised more than half the class, and the sheer confusion of the morning copy session was more than the whole business was worth. On Monday morning, a brawl nearly erupted, after which every single ex-member told Phil what he could do with his pool as the fifteen of them filed out the study-hall door.

"What a lousy break!" Phil muttered. "And just when I need the extra time for innovative arts, too. I could be in for some trouble there."

"But, Phil, I thought you said you were doing really well," Simon protested.

Phil shrugged. "I may have been kind of premature on that one. You see, I'm really great at 'innovative,' but I'm kind of short on 'arts.' Copadrick said

'Banana Surprise' was a good try, but I don't think he was too crazy about 'Technicolor Wheat.' If I can really blow him away with my next project, I should be cool. If not — " He shrugged again.

* * *

Interflux said nothing on the subject of the Antiflux Cultural Center. Company officials would not speak to reporters regarding it, nor would Cyril Irving mention it to his son as the two snuck hamburgers behind Mrs. Irving's back. It was as though the new conflict didn't exist. Even more perplexing to Simon was that his father had quite suddenly become the world's most considerate dad. No longer was he argumentative or resentful, and at the club, his killer instinct seemed to have cooled. Simon could have sworn that his father let him win their last one-on-one basketball game. Also, Mr. Irving had taken to slipping Simon a little extra spending money, backsliding on his own rule that "youngsters must learn to budget." Most disconcerting of all, his father was suddenly taking a keen interest in the Vishnik Prize and in Simon's work, and Abercrombie Prep was virtually dropped from conversation. Simon couldn't help thinking that all this new treatment was in some way connected to Antiflux and the Cultural Center. But how? Surely it couldn't be that Interflux was admitting defeat over Lot 1346B. Or could it? Certainly the press stated in no uncertain terms that the Cultural Center was a major triumph. Still, Interflux — losing — it just didn't compute.

* * *

He found the summons taped to his locker on Tuesday morning.

NATHAN KRUPPMAN REQUIRES YOUR PARTICIPATION IN
HIS NASSAU ARTS FILM PROJECT, *OMNI*,
TONIGHT AT SIX P.M.

It gave an address in a remote section of Brooklyn, and instructed everyone to ignore the towaway zone signs, as they were enforced "very rarely."

Simon smiled. Well, here it was. Finally, he had gotten a part in Nathan's movie. Now he would be able to see what everyone else was so excited about. And it had to be a good part, too, since Nathan himself said that he'd been saving it just for Simon. But — he looked into the envelope — where were his lines? Nathan had forgotten to include his lines. He frowned. If his role was as important as Nathan said it was going to be, there would be an awful lot of lines — too many for him to learn without at least a few hours of practice.

He found T.C. in his office in front of locker #0750, and briefed him on the emergency.

The agent was unperturbed. "Don't worry, Simon. Nathan never forgets anything. If he didn't provide a script, it means it wasn't necessary, and there are probably just a couple of lines that you can learn on the spot."

"But Nathan personally assured me that this was going to be a major part," Simon pointed out.

T.C. shrugged. "If he said so, then it is. There just

aren't very many lines, that's all."

Faint indications of that gnawing feeling which signified that something was not quite right began to bud in Simon's stomach. He fought them down. The shoot was probably going to be a high action-low dialogue scene, and he was playing the part of a grim but able hero, the strong silent type. After all, it was well-known that Nathan Kruppman always lived up to his word.

Sam Stavrinidis also had a part in tonight's shoot. Sam had lines.

"I have a high action part," Simon explained as the gnawing feeling returned.

Phil needed the wreck that night, so Simon and Sam drove to Brooklyn in the Mustang. The rush-hour traffic was bumper to bumper, but finally they pulled into the towaway zone in front of the address indicated in the summons. It was a partially burnt out multi-level warehouse bearing a faded sign which read: CALVIN FIHZGART & CO. WHOLESALE CORSETS.

The shoot was taking place in the main storage area where, abruptly, the dilapidated warehouse ended and deep space began. All around were placed various sets depicting the surface of planets, the interiors of space ships and stations, and an enormous communications tower that shot up three quarters of the way to the huge storeroom's hundred-foot ceiling, gleaming against the star-speckled void of intergalactic space.

Everywhere, organized chaos reigned, with Nathan at the center, radiating competence. He darted around, giving directions and talking at a mile a minute, but his expression was calm and collected, and it was obvious that he had everything under control.

Simon was anxious to talk to Nathan to clear up this whole lines issue, but on the bustling set, Nathan was completely inaccessible. Soon Simon was whisked off to wardrobe and makeup.

There, a large group of students was being outfitted in dashing spacesuits, and being issued futuristic-looking laser guns, communicators, and other equipment. Simon was in a spacesuit, too, but his was mutilated, charred, bloodstained, and dirty.

"Your life pod was just hit by an antiproton plutonium torpedo," explained Bob Lawrence, who was in charge of costumes for the shoot. "You're lucky to be alive. Okay, makeup. He needs severe radiation burns."

Bob's girlfriend, Grace, hustled Simon into a chair, and made his face and hands match his suit. When he viewed his finished self in the mirror, Simon was profoundly shocked. Maybe this was Nathan's idea of the after-effects of an antiproton plutonium torpedo, but in his own eyes, he looked like he'd been run over by a train. His face was scarred and bloody, and his hair was matted with filth and mud. His eyes peered bleakly out of this arrangement, like the headlights of a Jeep in a sandstorm. He reflected in some annoyance that he would never get any glory for this major part in *Omni*, since the person in the film was going to be totally unrecognizable as Simon Irving.

A freshman girl serving as chief production assistant told Simon to follow her, so he presumed he'd finally get his chance to meet with Nathan. But instead she led him to a small bare room, and told him to wait until he was called.

"But I have to see Nathan," Simon protested. "There's a problem with my li— "

"Nathan's very busy. Your scene doesn't come up until much later. Don't worry. I'll come for you when it's time. Just make sure you don't leave this room." She walked out and shut the door, leaving Simon seething and sweating in his space suit.

He examined his surroundings. He was sitting in a white box with a wooden table and chair, and a bare light bulb hanging from the ceiling. On the table was a large fruit bowl which contained a single sickly pear. His stomach growled. He had missed dinner in order to make it here on time for this wonderful shoot. He seated himself and wolfed down the pear. Half an hour went by as Simon did a slow burn. The nerve of that Nathan Kruppman! Who did he think he was, playing around with the valuable time of the head of Antiflux?

A horrible thought occurred to him. This was all a practical joke, and he had no part in *Omni*. Everyone had gone home, leaving him waiting in a deserted warehouse in Brooklyn. They'd taken his clothes, too, and his wallet, and his car, so he'd have to present himself at the nearest police station, looking like he'd just been hit by an antiproton plutonium torpedo. In a panic, he left the room, went through the deserted makeup area, opened the studio door a crack, and peered out. There was a full-fledged planetary war going on, involving no fewer than sixty or seventy space-suited troops, as Nathan's five portable cameras panned around, recording the action. Suddenly, he heard Nathan's voice shout,

"Cut! Cut! Hold it! Where's that light coming from?"

Quickly, Simon ducked back inside and shut the door. But even from makeup, he could hear Nathan yelling, "*Don't open that door!* Come on, Simon! We're trying to make a movie here!"

Simon slunk back to his box, muttering, "Yes, Mr. Director, sir; whatever you say, Mr. Director, sir; drop dead, Mr. Director, sir."

The temperature inside Calvin Fihzgart & Company was in the high seventies, leading to a temperature inside Simon's space suit of ninety-five. The shoot was delayed another forty-five minutes because of his unfortunate intrusion into the last scene, so by the time the freshman girl showed up to fetch the star, Simon was close to collapse. Bathed in sweat, he sat gnawing on the denuded core of the pear.

"Okay," Nathan was announcing as Simon was led onto the main set. "This is the big one, people, the very last scene, and it's absolutely important that we get it in one take. Here comes our star. How are you holding up, Simon?"

"Nathan, I never got a copy of my lines."

"You've got no lines, Simon. We're doing the last

scene with nothing but the music Johnny Zull's writing for us. So I'll be able to talk you through this and tell you exactly what to do."

"But — "

"Now, pay attention — you're the last man left alive in the universe, which is going to end in a few minutes. Everywhere, planets and whole solar systems are blowing up, and here you are, half dead, on this isolated planetoid at the edge of the galaxy, waiting for the end. Now, I've got fifteen special effects people on this, so there's going to be a lot of fireworks out there. I mean, the universe is ending, right? There's no script, Simon. Just do exactly what I say. And never look in my direction or at any of the cameras. Okay. Stage crew, put him in the destroyed life pod."

Too tired to argue, Simon allowed himself to be stuffed into a large pile of rubble right near the base of the big tower on the central set. The scene was cleared, the lights adjusted, and Nathan called, "Action!" The cameras started rolling.

"Okay, slowly lift yourself out of the life pod. That's it. Now stand up. Not too fast. That's the way."

As Simon rose, there was a blinding quadruple-flash explosion coming from space over his right shoulder. Involuntarily, he threw himself flat on the ground.

"Good reaction!" called Nathan. "I hadn't thought of it, but it looked great. That was a nearby solar system exploding. Now, you get up, you see the crashed spaceship over by the meteorite crater, and you recognize it. You're shocked! It belongs to the woman you love, who's been separated from you for the last seven years. You rush over to the ship and open the door."

Simon tried to run, but found himelf stumbling because of the bulky space suit, his own hunger and dehydration, and the roughness of the terrain. Explosions were going off all over as the universe approached its end, and he realized with a shudder that if one of Nathan's special effects people made a slight miscalculation, more than just a few little planets could get blown up here.

"Great acting!" Nathan encouraged. "The stumbling seemed so real! Now, don't fall in the crater. Open the hatch of the ship, where you find the woman you love still alive. Come on, Simon! Put some muscle into it! My grandmother could open that door!"

Finally, Simon succeeded in wrenching the door open, and there she was, the woman he loved. She was made up to look almost as disheveled as he was, but there was no mistaking it; he was looking at Wendy Orr.

"Love it!" crowed Nathan as Simon stared. "Cameras two and five — move in! Simon — gently lift her out of the ship!"

Simon's mind raced. This was Wendy! If he touched her, she'd slaughter him! He stared into her eyes, but her expression was inscrutable. Experimentally, he grasped her shoulders, and when she didn't hit him, he lifted her out of the ship and laid her carefully on the ground.

"Oh, beautiful!" Nathan shrieked. "You really look like you feel it! Okay, she's going to die, and you both know it! So take her in your arms and tell her you love her! Come on, Simon! Do it now! She's going to die any minute!"

For art, thought Simon, but as he held her close, he had a great surge of feeling. About how this was Wendy, and how much he liked her, and how stupid he'd been to kick her out of his car. Even an idiot would have the brains not to throw away a *third* chance. She'd said she wouldn't have anything to do with him if he were the last man in the universe! Well, now he was! Surely she could make an exception!

"I'm *really* sorry about what happened Friday night!" he whispered into her ear as Nathan screamed at his cameramen for more close-ups.

"Simon — not here!" she whispered back.

"I don't know what came over me! We were having such a good time! The movie was lousy, but everything else was so good! I'm so sorry!"

"Stop it!" she hissed. "You're ruining Nathan's movie!"

Nathan was standing up on his director's chair, howling like a madman. "Great! *Great!* Okay, Simon, kiss her!"

It was the cardinal rule of Nassau Arts: you always did what Nathan told you. He kissed her as planets, solar systems, and galaxies vaporized all around them. And Simon knew that the force of the antiproton plutonium torpedo that had leveled his life pod was a wet Roman candle by comparison.

Suddenly, Nathan's voice reached him. "Okay, Wendy — die!" And she went limp in his arms.

Involuntarily, Simon sprang up to make an angry gesture at Nathan, but he lost his footing and tumbled backward down the crater.

"Beautiful, Simon! Now when you climb back out, I want to see the pain and anger of your loss! Camera five — get ready for an extreme close-up!"

Simon hoisted himself out of the crater, completely shaken.

"Okay, Simon, here's the hard part. Forget Wendy — she's history. And you're about to be history, too. I want you to run over to the tower and climb up the ladder to the very top. There you stand, the last survivor of the human race, defiant to the end! And you shake your fist in anger at the whole universe!"

In a daze, Simon staggered to the base of the tower, and looked up. In his present condition, there was no way he was going to make it to the top. Well, he'd followed Nathan this far, and he wasn't turning back now. He climbed. As the explosions and flashes went on all around him, and the starry sky turned into a huge fireball, he climbed, hanging on for dear life, giddy images of Wendy spinning in his head. All the way to the top, he fought fatigue, hunger, emotional upheaval, and the discomfort of his suit, until finally, weak with exhaustion, he pulled himself onto the small platform at the pinnacle.

Here it was — the end of *Omni*, the climax, the key scene to the whole business. And a stupid movie it was, too, if Simon Irving was any judge. But even so, no one would ever say that the head of Antiflux hadn't done his bit for Almighty Nathan. He was going to give Nathan an ending that would bring the house down. Rearing back, he raised both arms to the exploding heavens, and bellowed with all the rage and defiance he could muster.

"All right!" cried Nathan, far below. "Blow it!" A blinding flash sliced through the blackness, and sixteen columns of flame rose up around the tower. In horrified disbelief, Simon felt the platform give way beneath him.

"Naaaaa-thaaan!!!"

Simon hurtled through the air toward certain death, his whole life flashing before his eyes in disjointed lightning visions. Seventy feet he fell, his one thought that Nathan was so crazy that he'd kill to get an ending for his movie. He hit the net ten feet from the floor, and bounced sickeningly for a few agonized moments. The whole set was covered with smoke, and he began choking as he floundered in a vain attempt to get out of the net.

"Cut! That's a wrap! Clean-up crew!"

In a matter of seconds, the smoke was fanned away and the lights turned on, revealing the cast and crew of *Omni*, cheering and congratulating their director. Instead of killing the little — !

"Hey, Simon," Nathan called from amidst his admirers, "are you all right over there?"

Simon saw red, and before he knew it, he was out of the net, and had Nathan by the collar up against the nearest wall. "Why, you homicidal *maniac* — !!"

* * *

"Think about it! I could be dead right now! He could have killed me!" Simon babbled, trembling against his cracked cup with a combination of shock and rage. Anxious to get Simon away from the set, Sam had led him to the nearest coffee, which was available in a dingy diner across the street from the Calvin Fihzgart building. "He's a lunatic! He should be locked up! He's so obsessed with that dumb movie of his that he's lost his regard for human life! What he did to me was attempted murder! You can't get away with that in America, can you?"

"Hey, pal," called the counterman, a lumberjack type with a beer belly and a tattoo on his right arm that said BROOKLYN. "Calm down. Everything's going to be okay."

Simon lowered his voice, which did nothing to reduce his agitation. "He dynamited me off a building! That's not movie-making! That's guerilla warfare! Sam, are you listening to me?"

Sam had become distant, lost in his own thoughts. "Simon," he said seriously, "I have to talk to you. About Barbara."

"Barbara? *Barbara?*" That was another sore point. Simon never wanted to think about women again as long as he lived, which was going to be a long time, since he had also resolved to steer clear of Nathan Kruppman. After he'd calmed down from his attempt to strangle the director, he'd ransacked the set in search of Wendy. But she had left right after the shoot, possibly without even bothering to find out whether he was dead or alive. "I've just been hit with guerilla warfare, and you want to talk about Barbara?"

"I've got to get rid of her."

Simon was instantly distracted. "Get rid of Barbara?"

"Why don't you dynamite her off a building?" wisecracked the counterman.

They ignored him.

"She's a nice enough girl, Simon, but I'm dying of loneliness with her, because when you go out with Barbara, that's all you do. You don't go out yourself, you don't go out with friends, you don't even think on your own. It's driving me crazy."

"I thought everything was working out great between you two."

"That's another thing about going out with Barbara. Everything has to be working out great, even if it isn't. I don't like it that much, Simon. Having a girl-friend is — overrated. It's not very good."

"Women," said the counterman philosophically. "You can't live with 'em and you can't live without 'em."

Sam shook his head. "I'm so out of everything, I feel like I've been on a desert island. I hardly ever see you guys anymore, and when I do, it's just 'hi/bye.' And I know I complained a lot, but I liked being in on all the Antiflux things. Do you realize that I never even saw the worm store?"

"Must have got by me, too," said the counterman thoughtfully. "But I don't get out of Brooklyn much."

"We were in Burger King the other day," Sam went on, "and Dino and Bill were a few booths down. Bill was going to try to sink an onion ring in a hanging flower pot across the room, and I knew they had at least a couple of hundred thou on the line. I was dying to be in on it, but I was with Barbara, and she wouldn't have understood. It's gotten to the point where I never have any fun anymore. And on top of it all, I'm not enjoying my painting, either. You saw my Vishnik entry. It's a zero. I've just got to get out of this relationship. It's making me feel — uh — "

"Strangled?" The counterman was refilling their cups, and also one for himself as he pulled up a chair.

"Yeah. Strangled."

"Well, Sam, I — uh — don't know what to tell you," said Simon lamely.

"I do," the counterman put in eagerly. "You go to Barbara and you tell her like this: 'Nothing against you; I just don't like the life.' End it nicely, but end it."

Simon snapped his fingers. "Yeah! I agree with — "

"Jake," said the counterman.

"Jake's right," agreed Sam, nodding slowly.

"Would I steer you wrong?" said Jake, beaming into both their faces. "And if that don't work, you can always use guerilla warfare. Hey, you guys feel like a couple of doughnuts?"

* * *

"I think Sotirios is seeing a psychiatrist," Phil said the next morning.

Simon stared at him. "Why?"

"He came over last night really late, and he was a

lot like his old self again. But he kept mentioning this guy named Jake, who's been helping him with his problems. From what I can see, our man is well on his way to being cured of boyfriend syndrome."

Simon laughed. "Jake isn't a psychiatrist exactly. He's more like a — sage."

"Well, anyway, it was the real Sotirios. He dumped on my innovative arts projects pretty bad — you should have heard some of the things he said about 'Technicolor Wheat.' You know, Simon, I never realized just how much I missed that big, dumb, overly good-looking fool. Even the wreck ran better this morning."

Simon looked up and down the hall. "Where *is* Sam today?"

"He's at home, redoing his Vishnik entry, painting around the clock. He had this great inspiration last night, and he's going to cut school today and tomorrow. He says for you to cover for him."

"Aw, no!" moaned Simon. "He's going to paint himself a camel, and this time Querada's going to set fire to *him*! Why does he *do* this?"

Phil grinned. "He's the old Sotirios, and he's back."

Simon prowled the halls of Nassau Arts in search of Wendy, but the Student Council president was nowhere to be found. He did see Barbara, hanging out with a few of her friends from the Dance Department, and from her face he could tell that Sam had had a chance to drop by last night to carry out Jake's advice. She made a point of ignoring him, so Simon abandoned the idea of asking her where he could find Wendy. Chance number three was slipping through his fingers.

Just before first class, Simon was approached by T.C., acting in his official capacity as Nathan's agent. "Nathan got the idea that you might be a little irritated with him. He wants me to tell you he's got no hard feelings over the segment you fluffed."

Simon was still touchy. "Me? I didn't fluff the segment! The segment practically fluffed me!"

T.C. grinned. "My information is that, when the universe ended, the last man alive looked straight into the cameras and screamed 'Nathan.' Well, it's not really that bad. There was one camera that wasn't directly on your face at the time, so hardly anyone will know what you're yelling."

Simon flushed. "Yeah, okay. That's great. Tell Nathan I'm sorry I roughed him up."

T.C. lowered his voice and cupped a hand to his mouth. "Confidentially, you should be congratulated for this. When Nathan ran back the tape and saw you, he laughed till he cried. I've never seen him get a really good laugh like that before. Nice going, Simon."

* * *

The last days before the Vishnik deadline just seemed to fly by. Querada was a mass of tingling nerve endings as the most important day of his year drew closer. He accepted the students' final entries with all the philosophy of a man facing a firing squad.

"Mr. Ashley, what happened? This is your picture? *No! No! No!* Miss Chernik, Mr. Lawrence, you reworked this from a *kindergarten project*, yes? Oh,

Querada can't bear to look at it! It will give the Vishnik judges heart attacks! Miss Dixon, Querada hates your sister and her new baby! This is not a winner! This is a cure for insomnia!" He turned his face to the ceiling. "Oh, great organizing principle of the universe, why have you done this to Querada? What offense, what crime has he committed that he should suffer so? What has he done that he should have to take the bus to Albany to visit the shrine of Vishnik winners? Oh, the pain! Garbage from Miss Dixon! Garbage from Mr. Ashley! And from Mr. Simon — from Mr. Simon — *nothing!*" Clutching at his heart, he staggered backward, his head thumping against the blackboard. "Congratulations, Mr. Simon! You have killed Querada!"

"No!" exclaimed Simon, jumping up and rushing to the front with his canvas. "It's called 'Subway Breakdown,'" he said breathlessly, placing it on the front easel. "Really — it's okay. I've got an entry."

As Simon watched expectantly, the teacher sat down on the small stool in front of the easel and stared at the painting. He was still staring some forty-five minutes later when the first of the students began to tiptoe out of the room. Simon was up there with him for the whole time, still awaiting some sort of comment as the artist sat in stony silence, not even moving a muscle. Cautiously, Peter Ashley crept to the front of the room and waved a hand in front of Querada's eyes. There was no reaction. Even long after the class had gone, and Simon had removed "Subway Breakdown" to frame it for submission,

Querada still sat, his long legs tucked up under his chin, staring.

"It's going to be a showdown between 'Subway Breakdown' and 'Mother and Child,'" Peter Ashley later commented, and there was general agreement. The painting seminar was split over who would win, and the news spread through the halls that the Antiflux boss and one of the school's top artists were going head-to-head for the state's most coveted art prize. Simon knew it was big stuff when he heard that Bill and Dino had a $400,000 bet on the outcome.

Throughout the excitement, the Antiflux Cultural Center continued to reach new heights of unpredicted success. In addition to the regular programming, the Center now ran special morning events for bussed-in groups of junior- and middle-school students. Prominent among these morning sessions was Bill McIntosh giving public readings from *The Legend of the Glass Caves*. Bill had decided to fight his writer's block by boosting his confidence, and it was working, since the audience seemed to hang on his every word.

Money continued to pour in in the form of donations stuffed into the ancient Greek urn. Some of it was used to pay the rental on the tent, and the balance was deposited in the Program Board bank account, which now stood at $2,300. Phil wanted to add a second tent and make several other improvements, but The Dungeon was now carefully monitoring the running of the Cultural Center, and they said no. As it stood, though, the Cultural Center seemed solid for a while, so as long as the weather held out, Simon couldn't see that there was anything Interflux could do about it.

* * *

Thursday afternoon, Simon lovingly crated up "Subway Breakdown" and placed it in the back of the Mustang. It was time to go to Manhattan and make the Vishnik submission in person. But first he had to pick up Sam and his entry. At the last minute, Phil had begged the use of the wreck for an innovative arts emergency. Mr. Copadrick had demanded his third project tomorrow, and Phil needed wheels.

Sam was already outside, engaged in a loud shouting match with Phil. In an instant, Simon could see why. The wreck was parked in Phil's driveway, and on its rusting roof was a gleaming white five-tier wedding cake. It was tied down with every means at Phil's disposal, trussed up with cord, anchored with twine, firmed up with thread, and completely encased in fine white netting. All this was attached to the strong ropes which fastened the whole arrangement to the roof of the orange Beetle.

"I don't get it," said Simon. "Why the cake?"

"It's his project!" raged Sam.

"It's time to go for broke," said Phil solemnly, "undo the safety catches and throw all caution to the wind. I'm going to take this cake and run it through the car wash. It'll either blow Copadrick's mind or land me out on my butt."

Sam turned earnest eyes on Simon. "Has there ever been such an idiot? Talk to him!"

"Look, Phil," Simon pleaded. "We've got to get our pictures into the city, but we'll be back in a couple of hours, and then the three of us can work all night on a project for you! Don't do anything stupid!"

"No." Phil was adamant. "I got into this school my way, and if I make it here, it's going to be my way, and if I bomb out, it's going to be my way, too."

"But they're going to burn you on this one, Phil! Really they are!" Simon moaned.

"Maybe. And maybe it'll be great."

"But it won't, Phil! Trust me!"

Phil got into the wreck and started the engine. "We'll know soon enough," he said cheerfully, and drove off.

Simon and Sam watched as the cake eased around the corner and out of sight. Simon sighed. "All right, Sam, let's get going. Where's your picture?"

Sam's entry, unwrapped and uncrated, was sitting out in the backyard. He had finished it not two hours earlier, framed it wet, and left it to dry in the late afternoon air. The two boys scooted to the yard, and Sam paused for a moment before lifting the picture up to show to Simon.

"Presenting the all-new 'Traffic Jam.'"

Simon gaped. It was exactly the same painting as before, with the elevated highway in the foreground and Manhattan in the background, only the stopped vehicles and angry motorists were gone from the Brooklyn-Queens Expressway. The roadway was now packed with camels, hundreds — possibly thousands — of them, jammed hump to hump, nose to tail. The motorists had all become Bedouin nomads, walking, riding, and leading the beasts. Even the billboard by the side of the freeway was for Camel cigarettes. It was amazing, and it had the spark that was all Sam Stavrinidis.

"It's beautiful, Sam! But you can't hand it in! You'll be killed!"

"It's a symbol of my rebellion against stifled creativity," Sam announced with satisfaction.

"Yeah, but you promised Querada no more camels!"

"I told him that I wouldn't bring another camel into his classroom." He grinned. "But these are going straight to the Vishnik gallery. I hope I get a chance to explain that before he hits me."

Simon sighed. "My two closest friends, on the same day, are committing suicide by art!"

* * *

According to Emile Querada, the space of time between one's official submission for the Vishnik Prize and the actual announcement of the results is known as "the period of oblivion." During this time, the artist should do absolutely nothing for fear of offending the great organizing principle of the universe, thereby causing him to take the Vishnik Prize away from the artist and his teacher (especially his teacher).

Simon thought this was as good advice as any, and spent Friday drifting from class to class, walking softly, breathing lightly, and doing nothing that might upset the equilibrium of the system.

At lunch, he decided to risk a trip to the Cultural

Center, where "Tavern Scene" and "Assembly Line" had just been put on display. At the Center, most of the visitors were seated outside, listening to the Nassau Arts Woodwind Ensemble, a group which featured Dave Roper on bassoon. This had to be a step in the right direction, Simon thought. Less than a week ago, Dave would have refused to join the group and leave the worm store unattended.

There were only a few visitors browsing around the tent, but one of them was standing right in front of Simon's two exhibits, studying them with great interest. Simon looked at the man curiously. He was wearing a full-length raincoat with the collar turned up, and a soft fedora with the brim pulled down. And sunglasses.

Simon smiled and sauntered over. "You'll be able to see those a lot better, Dad, if you take off the shades."

Cyril Irving started. "Oh, hello, son." He removed the glasses in some embarrassment. "How are things?"

A couple of students came near, so Simon dropped his voice to a whisper. "What are you doing here?"

"What kind of question is that?" his father asked defensively. "This is a public exhibition, and I'm a member of the public. Listen, Simon, have you had lunch yet?"

"Not yet. Somewhere in my locker there's a bean sprout sandwich with my name on it."

His father made a face. "Ditch that. Let's go out for some real food. I'd like to talk to you."

They went to lunch at Gavin's, a Fosterville restaurant where Interflux held most of its luncheon business meetings. There were Interflux people all around, and Simon felt a little outnumbered, but a small sirloin beat a bean sprout sandwich any time, any place.

The conversation was light until the entrees had disappeared, and then Mr. Irving got right to business.

"Simon, I was going to talk to you tonight at home, but when I saw you, I couldn't hold off, because I think it's very important that you hear this first from me. Son, this whole Antiflux thing — it's over. You put up one heck of a fight. You can all be proud of yourselves. But it's finished. We've got to start building now, so we need your land."

Simon stuck his chin out in defiance. "I've got one cultural center and one worm store that says you can't have it."

"Hear me out," Mr. Irving said calmly. "Yesterday we informed the Town of Greenbush that, if we're not able to commence full construction shortly, we will build elsewhere and eventually close up our Greenbush installation. Early next week, you'll receive notification that the land is to be expropriated — no technicalities, no conditions. You'll get your sixty-seven hundred dollars back, but you've lost. You see, son, there never really was any contest. We played by your rules for a while, and you matched us blow for blow. But this week we switched to our rules."

"Your rules mean blackmailing the town," Simon observed.

His father nodded. "Yes. And whether it's right or wrong is not our argument. I just wanted you to hear it from me before it came in the mail, and I wanted to give you some time to work out a way to pass the word around your school. I don't want there to be any problems for you, especially if someone knows who I am."

Through his disappointment, Simon had a strange sense of all things being right with the world. There was no balance in a universe where Interflux didn't always get its way. As soon as his father had announced the winning strike, Simon had wondered where his anger and frustration were. Instead, he had thought: yes, of course. How could I have expected it to be any different? Throughout all the Antiflux excitement, enthusiasm, and triumph, Interflux had always held the winning cards, and he had known that and forgotten it somewhere along the way. The fact was that, in real life, the tortoise would never beat the hare. The hare would always wake up at the last minute and pull it off in the final stretch.

Mr. Irving cleared his throat carefully. "Are you very upset, son? No, that's a silly question — of course you're very upset. But are you *really* very upset?" He added, "Huh, Simon?"

Simon smiled in spite of himself. "Mom was right," he said. "It's business. Thanks for the early warning." He sighed. Now he had to break the news to the co-owners, all fifteen hundred of them.

Fourteen

"Mother and Child" by Laura Dixon won the 2005 New York State Vishnik Prize. "Subway Breakdown" finished a disappointing fifth. Peter Ashley came second, Lawrence and Chernik came third, and fourth place went to an underdog entry from a small school in Buffalo. Sam Stavrinidis's "Traffic Jam" received a special award, created on the spot, in recognition of its wit and style. The head judge commented, "It didn't deserve the top prize, but it was by far the pet entry of this year's competition, and too good to be ignored."

Querada was so delighted by this special honor that Sam received instant forgiveness for changing his entry without the teacher's approval. "Yes, I suppose it does have — a few camels — "

"But, Mr. Querada," Sam baited, "there are over four hundred of them."

"All right — *several* camels. But it also has a prize ribbon, and this is saving your life."

The teacher was even more pleased to note that last year's winner from Albany failed to make the top ten.

It was Querada's best finish ever, and he was so

jubilant that his style of celebration would have looked more in place in the center-field bleachers at the World Series. Soon gallery security asked him to leave, which was an annual event. In the history of the competition, Emile Querada had never seen a judging through to the end. As was the tradition, his students left with him, and the teacher resumed his festivities in the middle of West Broadway. This continued until the residents of nearby buildings began to shout obscenities at this six-foot-eight-inch disturber of the peace. Then Querada kissed each of his glorious dozen fondly on both cheeks, and sent them home.

Of the twelve, Simon alone went home unhappy. He tried to tell himself that to make the top five out of over three hundred entries should be enough for him, but it just wouldn't wash. He'd been so sure that he'd take this year's prize, just as he was sure to this very moment that "Subway Breakdown" was better than the four pictures that had come ahead of it. Naturally, he was happy for Sam. And he didn't grudge Laura, Peter, Bob, and Grace their success. And placing fifth wasn't *that* bad. But coming on the heels of the news that Antiflux was finished, it just didn't seem right. He thought things like this were supposed to balance out — A goes wrong, so B goes right. You blow it with Wendy, but you're a resounding success in Nathan's movie. Antiflux goes sour, but they give you the Vishnik Prize. That was equitable, reasonable, fair, and also the pipe dream of an idiot.

Sam and Phil called to say they were coming over to cheer him out of his Vishnik blues, then called a half hour later to report that the intermittent defect had stranded them at a busy intersection halfway between Greenbush and Fosterville. Simon went out to the rescue, and the three finally ended up at their usual hangout, the DeWitt Burger King.

"This is your fault," Sam accused Phil. "We're dealing with a vehicle that works on a shoestring as it is, and you have to take it through a car wash with a wedding cake!"

"We think there may be some icing sugar in the engine," Phil explained to Simon.

"How did the project come out?" Simon asked.

"Sickening!" said Sam. "Disgusting!"

"Oh, I don't know about that, Sotirios. I kind of like it. Sure, most of the cake got washed away, but the metal parts are bent into some pretty interesting shapes. And the little bride and groom look kind of funky half-melted like that. I think it's got a shot."

"How'd Copadrick respond when you brought it in?"

"Hard to tell. He said 'Very original,' and went on to the next thing. If I had it to do over again, I'd have passed on the hot wax. But otherwise I'm pretty satisfied. I call it 'Wet Wedding.'"

The subject changed to the Vishnik results, and Sam talked about how everyone, even Peter and Laura, was surprised that "Subway Breakdown" hadn't fared better. Simon sat through this sympathy session until he was good and depressed, and then he decided it was time to get everyone else good and depressed, too. So he told them about the upcoming expropriation of Lot 1346B, and how there was nothing at all Antiflux could do about it.

The hardest part was convincing Phil that Antiflux had, in fact, run out of options. On the spot, he came up with seven different defenses, all of them crazy enough to give Sam palpitations. "Well, can't we at least get ourselves a lawyer and tie the whole thing up in the courts? That could drag for years!"

"We can't do anything," Simon insisted. "No one would ever let us make a move that could risk having Interflux leave Greenbush. The town's just going to grab our land and hand it over. That's it."

Phil scowled. "Well, if that's the way it is, then my faith is suffering a severe blow."

"The weather's still nice," Sam pointed out.

"Big deal! We may as well have hurricanes twice a day if we're going to have to close up the Cultural Center anyway! What a downer!"

"I suppose you and your old man are kind of on the outs," said Sam to Simon.

"Not really. You see, I was brought up on Interflux. I knew something like this was going to happen sooner or later, but somewhere between weed-cutting and the worm store, we all kind of lost touch with reality. When we stood up on that platform and looked down on all those cheering enthusiastic Antiflux supporters, and we'd already pulled off half a dozen minor miracles before, and our minds were balled up with women and school and art prizes and a lot of other things, we started thinking that maybe the impossible might be possible. But in the end, hundreds of kids are no match for zillions of dollars. Like my dad said, it was never a contest."

"You know," Phil mused, a distant gleam in his eye, "they can take away our land and everything on it; they can force us into submission and slap our wrists from here to Mongolia; they can blow us off the face of the earth if they want to. But no matter how rich and powerful they are, they can't wipe out the moments we've had, the odds we've beaten, *the memory of six hundred kids marching out to cut weeds!*" Phil was on his feet for this last statement.

"Sit down, idiot," Sam intoned.

"Phil, that was beautiful," said Simon.

"Beautiful, but useless," Sam agreed grudgingly.

Phil sat down, nodding sadly. "Yeah."

They drove back to the wreck, which started perfectly, and Simon followed Phil and Sam back to Greenbush. Sam went home to catch up on some sleep, but Simon and Phil weren't tired, and elected to take a walk.

They walked in silence for a while, then Phil stopped suddenly. "Where are we, Simon?"

"About three blocks from your house."

"No, I mean where are we *really*? You know, 'Wet Wedding' wasn't the first title for that project. I originally called it 'Farewell Nassau Arts.' And all that stuff about it having a shot — just air. I'm not going to be at Nassau Arts that much longer, you know."

"I know. So does Sam. That's why he's so cranky." They began to walk again.

"I talked to T.C.," Phil went on, "and there's no way I'm going to get into another department. I already hold the record with four. It's burn-out time."

"Then why did you try that lunatic stunt with the cake? You knew it wouldn't work."

"Why? Who knows why? Because I'm a crazy person. It's impossible to explain to a guy who's got talent, but if I'd have tried to do something serious, it wouldn't have come out any better. No matter which department I was in, the best I could have been was a guy who tried. I told you the first time we met. I show potential, and that's all. Me being at Nassau Arts was a lot like our whole Antiflux thing — temporary. I could keep my head above water on any given day, but the long-term result was never in doubt."

The words were out before Simon could think. "I don't know what to tell you, Phil."

"And that's why tonight it's getting to me more than it ever has. I mean, what have we accomplished in these three months? Antiflux is going down the drain, you lost the Vishnik Prize, and I'm marking time waiting for someone to hand me a one-way ticket to Greenbush High. Wendy was a disaster, Barbara was a bigger disaster, and I didn't even have anyone to have a disaster with. Even Sam, who won himself a prize, isn't that happy about it because he's still got a serious hang-up about painting camels. We didn't do so hot, Simon."

Now Simon was genuinely depressed, as he wracked his brain for something positive to say and found nothing. If the irrepressible Phil Baldwin, who could be depended on to find a silver lining to the blackest cloud, was down and out, what could neurotic Simon Irving do but throw in the towel?

Phil stopped walking again. "I mean, think about it, Simon. What have we accomplished? Really!"

Simon shuffled uncomfortably. "Not much, I guess."

Phil looked at him. "Then why was it so *good*?"

* * *

The notice of the expropriation was waiting for Simon first thing Monday morning. It came, opened as usual, through Wendy. It was the first time he'd seen her since the last shoot of *Omni*, and he studied her face anxiously for a clue as to her mood.

"It's bad news, Simon."

Simon nodded. "I've had some advance warning."

Wendy shrugged. "What can I say? I'm sorry. You guys did a great job."

There was a long awkward silence, during which time Simon ransacked his mind. He'd been searching for her all week. What had he been planning to say? Why couldn't he say it now? As she looked as though she were about to walk away, he blurted, "I thought you were really terrific in Nathan's movie the other day."

She smiled, and for one fraction of a second, Simon was at least forty percent positive that he saw a flush in her cheeks. Suddenly she said, "I've got to go to class. See you later."

She hurried off, leaving him in no position to ponder the symbolic meaning of their meeting. The town letter was in his hands, and it took priority over everything.

Well, here it was, the divine word of Interflux, via the Town of Greenbush, all in black and white. At noon Friday, Lot 1346B once again became town property. And at 12:05, Simon knew, the Interflux bulldozers would be rolling over the spot where the Antiflux Cultural Center and Worm Shop had once been. Good old Cyril Irving never reneged on a promise. Four short months ago it had brought Simon a new car; now it was bringing him possibly the biggest problem of his life — how to break the news to Antiflux's fifteen hundred-odd faithful that it was all over. One look at Dave Roper, heading dutifully out to his worm store, served to drive home the message that there were a lot of students who weren't going to take this well.

A meeting would be the only way. Otherwise, it would spread through the school like gossip and end up blown all out of proportion. At a big assembly, he could let everyone know at the same time. The question remained: would he be able to find the right words to soften the blow of what was bound to be a major disappointment? And would there be any trouble?

He sat through a couple of classes with the result that it only clogged up his brain with too much input, threatening an overload. This was no time for education. He had to think. Maybe he'd go out to the Cultural Center and think there.

* * *

There was a play in progress outside behind the big tent, an all-Nassau Arts production, written by one of the school's top playwrights and performed by the Acting Department. The audience consisted of three classes of bussed-in seventh graders, and a sprinkling of adults, some of them teachers. Reaction seemed very positive. There was laughter and some applause from the students, and the adults were chuckling at some of the better one-liners. But the best response of all was coming from one man in the back row, doubled over with mirth, clapping wildly and cheering between guffaws. He was a handsome young fellow, with a touch of the dashing hero look, very stylishly dressed. Simon's breath caught in his throat. It was Kyle Montrose. What was The Flake doing at the Antiflux Cultural Center?

Simon rushed over. "Mr. Montrose — hello. What brings you here?"

"Simon!" Montrose exclaimed in sudden recognition. "How are you? You've grown up into quite a lad!" Simon noticed a hint of champagne on the billionaire's breath.

"I'm fine, Mr. Montrose. How are you?"

"Never better. I'll be with you in a minute. I must see the end of this absolutely brilliant piece of satire."

Later, when the play was, over, and he had "Bravo'd" himself hoarse and congratulated all the cast, Montrose walked with Simon back to the school building.

"Does my father know you're here?" Simon asked.

"Certainly not. If he'd known I was coming, he would have done his utmost to prevent it. Quite a bully, your father. I came because I received a call from someone here that Interflux was having trouble with a group called Antiflux. So about a month later, I caught the first plane out of Auckland to New York, and told the cab driver to take me to Antiflux in Greenbush, and he dropped me here. I didn't find Antiflux, but there was this terrific play going on. Then you came along, and here I am."

Simon held the large fire door open for the Interflux president. "I think we should alert — I mean, tell my father the good news that you're here."

Mr. Irving had to be called out of a meeting, so while Simon waited on the phone, Montrose lost interest in the call and began to browse around the halls, viewing exhibits of the students' work, and peering inside open doors.

"Son? What's the emergency?"

Simon grinned. "Hi, Dad. You'll never guess who's here with me at school right now."

"Simon, I don't have time for guessing games. My secretary said this was urgent. What's going on?"

"Mr. Montrose is here."

There was a pause on the other end of the line. "You mean The Flake? Oh my God! How? Never mind. I know how. One of my ninnies must have panicked and phoned him about your Antiflux. I knew this was going to happen! I'm surprised he didn't show up a month ago!"

"Do you want me to bring him over to Interflux, Dad?"

"Good God, no! Under no circumstances is The Flake to come anywhere near this office!"

Simon chuckled. "If you let me keep my land, I'll consider not bringing Mr. Montrose over right now."

"That's not funny, Simon. Don't be an idiot. Now, ease him out of there before he starts something. Has he been drinking at all?"

"I think it was a champagne flight."

"Terrific. Bring him home to our place. Under no circumstances are you to allow him to check into a hotel or to go anywhere except our house. I'll phone your mother and tell her to be ready with the coffee, and I'll be home myself as soon as I can get away. Hold the fort, son."

"What about my classes?"

"Tell them you've got a terrible disease! It'll be the truth! Tell them your father's out on the ledge of his office window! That'll be the truth, too! Tell them anything, but get him out of there!"

"Okay, Dad. I'll do my best." Simon hung up and hurried out into the hall. Montrose was gone. In alarm, Simon ran up and down the long corridor, looking desperately in the window of each classroom door. He did not know Mr. Montrose very well, but if he went by his father's evaluation, having the man loose in Nassau Arts was a catastrophe beyond anyone's wildest nightmares.

Just when Simon was about to panic completely, he caught sight of Montrose in one of the studios, conducting a dance class.

"So, as I was saying, ladies, your instructor is ill today, and I am taking over your session. You may call me Kyle. Now, I thought we'd start off with a few warm-up exercises and then get right to business."

Simon burst into the studio like a bomb, grabbed Montrose by the arm, and began hauling him bodily out the door. There was some booing from the girls, and a few of them threw slippers at Simon.

"Same time tomorrow," Montrose called to his class. "Remember to practice what we've learned." To Simon he said in a vaguely reproachful tone, "I was having a good time."

"I'm sorry, Mr. Montrose, but my father says we have to go home."

"Well, yes, of course he does, but what Cyril doesn't know won't hurt him." He turned glum. "The only problem is there's nothing Cyril doesn't know. That's why I spend so much time in places like Europe and Asia. You see, Cyril doesn't approve of my lifestyle. He thinks I'm a bum. He's right, you know, but naturally, that doesn't mean anything."

"He's going to come home early to see you, Mr. Montrose."

"All right, Simon. But first, couldn't you maybe show me around this wonderful school of yours? I'd forgotten that you were a painter. And some of the work around here is really first-rate."

Simon gave him a brief tour of the school and the Cultural Center before loading him into the Mustang and heading home, where Mrs. Irving was stationed with the coffee.

* * *

"Ah," announced Kyle Montrose with satisfaction, "that was a wonderful dinner. Thank you, Mary."

Mr. Irving leaned over to his son. "For us, beans and greens. For The Flake, beef Wellington."

"Lovely to have you, Kyle," Mrs. Irving beamed. "We don't see enough of you."

A strangled sound escaped Mr. Irving as he applied himself to his peach Melba.

All through the meal, the Interflux president had spoken on no other subject besides how impressed he was by Simon's school. Obviously, dessert was going to be no different.

"The talent," he raved. "The magnificence, the maturity is inconceivable for kids that age. Cyril, you must be enormously proud to have a son with the ability to be accepted by this wonderful school."

"Simon has done a lot since he came to Nassau Arts," said Mr. Irving with a crooked grin.

"That school has better artwork sitting in the back corners collecting dust," Montrose went on, "than I've seen in some of the great museums of the world. Why, this one storeroom had, hidden away in a cupboard, the most creative and insightful piece of work it's ever been my privilege to see. I think I'm going to have to speak to someone about getting to meet the talented young person who produced 'Technicolor Wheat.'"

Simon choked on his peach Melba.

Montrose was still warming to his subject. "And that Cultural Center is a stroke of genius. I really enjoyed myself there. It has everything — culture *and* entertainment. You may be seeing more of me, because I think I'm going to stay around for a couple of weeks and drink in all the Cultural Center has to offer."

Simon looked at his father as though to say, "It's *your* expropriation — *you* tell him."

"Kyle, that Cultural Center will be closing up within the next three days," Mr. Irving said irritably.

"What? Why?"

"Because of the complex."

Montrose looked puzzled. "What complex?"

Mr. Irving blew his stack. In exasperaton, he recited the whole history of the Greenbush complex, leading up into the entire episode with Antiflux. Simon held his breath, determined not to interfere, but he noted that his father was fair to both sides, and never once mentioned who the leader of Antiflux might be. ". . . and it's all because you wanted a complex with a monorail, just like Hypertech."

Montrose looked thoroughly chastened. It was obvious he didn't remember wanting anything. He sat quietly for a moment, then said, "I think it's a shame to bully these poor kids after they've made such a strong stand."

"Whether or not it was going to be a shame was never part of the decision," Mr. Irving replied readily.

"Aw, but Cyril, why can't we, let's say, build the new complex and leave out the warehouses so the kids can have their woods? I never did like warehouses. They're boring."

"The whole point of a complex," said Mr. Irving under tight control, "is to have the offices, manufacturing, and warehousing all together. Without the warehouses, you don't have a complex; you have a pile of manufactured goods sitting on the street."

Montrose frowned. "Well, how about this, then? We scale down the warehouses just a touch and leave some of the woods, so the kids can still have some natural setting, and there'll be a buffer between their property and ours. If we need extra storage room, we can use those empty warehouses in New Jersey. You see, Cyril, you may assume that I know nothing about the state of our company, but I keep up better than you think. I happen to know that we have a lot of empty warehouses in New Jersey."

"Because they wrote about it in *Business Day*, and you read it on the plane."

"Well — yes. But couldn't we do it that way, Cyril? Please? I know I don't exactly pull my weight in the company. But I do own a lot of stock, and that should count for something."

Simon could keep silent no longer. "Mr. Montrose, it would be wonderful if you could work it out that way, because that's all Nassau Arts ever wanted in the first place — to keep — "

"All right!" Cyril Irving bellowed. "If the plan can be changed without problems, then we'll let them keep some of the woods! We can even deed it over to them so they don't have to worry about us changing our minds! *But* — " He looked Montrose right in the eye. "No monorail!"

"No monorail?"

"No monorail! Shuttlebus or nothing!"

Take the shuttlebus, Simon prayed silently. If you want a monorail, go to Disneyland! Take the shuttlebus!

The president nodded. "Okay."

Simon leaped to his feet. "That's just great! I've got to go make some calls!"

"No!" his father thundered. "You're not going anywhere until you admit that Interflux is the *best* neighbor any school could have, much better than a certain other Flux I could mention!"

Simon grinned. "You've got it, Dad!"

* * *

The final Antiflux meeting was held Tuesday at three-thirty in the gym, with a record attendance of over fourteen hundred. Student Council program director Simon Irving was at his dramatic best as he told the crowd how, just when all seemed lost and the land was a few short days from expropriation, a near-miracle had saved them. In the darkest hour, last-minute negotiations had been convened with none other than the president of Interflux himself, who had flown in especially from Auckland, New Zealand. He was sympathetic to the Antiflux cause, and a compromise had been worked out in hard bargaining.

"We've got the woods!" howled Phil in summary of Simon's fifteen-minute speech, and the celebration began.

No one, not even Dave Roper, was unhappy about dismantling the Cultural Center and worm shop or vacating Lot 1346B. There was nostalgia, but there were no regrets.

"They're just the tools that shaped our great victory," Phil analyzed.

"Our great compromise," Sam amended.

"Our lucky fluke," Simon added.

"Gee, I'm sure going to miss that worm store, though," was Dave's comment.

A small ceremony was arranged for noon Saturday, at which land deeds would be exchanged between Antiflux and Interflux, and the whole quarrel would be officially ended. Simon couldn't suppress a grin when he heard that Wendy was going to get her party money back.

Kyle Montrose insisted absolutely on staying in town for the ceremony, and Cyril Irving insisted even more absolutely that he stay with the family in Fosterville. This was not through any great hospitality, but so that Montrose's behavior could be monitored and, if possible, controlled. It didn't work, though, because on Friday night after the family had gone to sleep, the irrepressible billionaire tiptoed out of the house and headed for the bright lights of New York City. His absence was not discovered until the morning, when the family was waking itself up for breakfast. Mrs. Irving was quite distraught, but still much calmer than her husband, who was creating a scene worthy of Querada.

Luckily, at that very moment the doorbell rang, and all three Irvings rushed to answer it. There on the front step stood two uniformed police officers. Between them hung a bleary-eyed Kyle Montrose, wrapped in a large police blanket.

"Hi, gang," he greeted the family.

"He's been a very busy boy," Officer O'Hara said with a big grin. "Let's just say that the people who went to see the big Christmas tree at Rockefeller Center got more than they bargained for last night. "

"And somebody got a free tuxedo," the second policeman added.

"I didn't know whether to arrest this guy or thank him," O'Hara went on. "He put smiles on a lot of faces, and isn't that what the holiday spirit is all about?"

Mr. Irving hustled his boss in the door. "Thanks a lot, officers. I'm terribly sorry about all this. Simon, go get a bathrobe so we can give the officers back their blanket."

"Yeah, well, so long, Mr. Montrose. Nice meeting you. Don't forget to read about yourself in the *Post* tomorrow."

When the police had gone, Simon and his mother withdrew discreetly. It was not suitable for them to witness the president and chairman of the board of Interflux being raked over the coals by his subordinate.

* * *

The ceremony was held out on Land Lot 1346B, which, courtesy of Antiflux, had been cleared of Cultural Center, worm store, and fence. Representing Interflux were Mr. Irving, four of his top people, and Kyle Montrose. Montrose looked much under the weather, and at first Mr. Irving had refused to allow him to attend on the grounds that he was a disgrace. On second thought, however, it was decided that leaving him alone where he could escape again was far more of a risk than bringing him among humans. So he was there, pale and dazed, under the strict warning from his senior executive vice-president that if he tried to make a speech, he would be throttled.

Representing Antiflux were the Program Board, Student Council president Wendy Orr, and the entire student body of Nassau Arts, some fifteen hundred strong. They swarmed in front of the platform in a great show of support for their Program Board. Even Nathan Kruppman, who was putting in twenty-hour days editing *Omni*, was right there at the front of the crowd, T.C. at his side, the two flashing Simon the thumbs-up signal.

Also in the audience Simon could see Johnny Zull, beaming with pride for his lab partner in spite of his depression at having no band to play with. Near him was Dave Roper, a little misty-eyed, but otherwise bearing up well. He could also see Barbara, who was now casting her intoxicating green eyes over at T.C. Serrette. And Laura, and Peter, and all the other students from painting class. Bill McIntosh was there, shepherding the quarter-ton couple. Bill and Dino had a bet on the duration of Mayor Van Doren's speech. If the mayor, who was known to be long-winded, spoke more than twelve minutes, Bill stood to win three quarters of a million dollars.

Bill only lost his bet by eight seconds, and probably would have won had not the scowls of Cyril Irving, the snores of Kyle Montrose, and the boos of the students finally penetrated the mayor's thick skull. He turned the microphone over to Wendy Orr, whose task it was to introduce the program director. This she did with such glowing praise that Simon was beginning to think the next speaker was going to be Albert Schweitzer. But no. It was Simon Irving, and when his name was announced, the air rang with applause and cheers loud enough and long enough to make the Interflux delegation squirm, and even to wake up Kyle Montrose temporarily.

When the ovation died down, it was a perfectly poised Simon Irving who spoke to the group. He thanked Antiflux for all their support, and told them they could be proud of what they had accomplished. Then he thanked Interflux for altering their plans and leaving some of the woods, and for being in the end a good neighbor after all. He finished with, "Now I'd like to turn things over to Mr. Cyril Irving, who is the senior executive vice-president of Interflux. And — this may seem a little strange, but he also happens to be my dad."

Dead silence hung in the air, to be replaced a few seconds later by confused murmuring as the students absorbed this new piece of information. Phil and Sam started the applause, soon to be joined by a few members of the inner circle out in the crowd. And by the time Cyril Irving stepped forward to shake hands with his son and exchange land deeds, the crowd approval was a hundred percent, and the cheering was tumultuous for the father-and-son All-Flux team.

Mr. Irving was just about to pronounce the whole affair joyfully over when three shrill blasts on a referee's whistle brought the audience back to silence. Suddenly, Miss Glandfield burst through the crowd and leaped up onto the stage. Simon was just about to make the observation that she seemed a touch bulkier than usual when she ripped open her ski jacket to reveal that she was wearing a thick vest studded with several dozen sticks of dynamite, all wired to a small remote control button in her hand. The crowd froze in shock. Everyone on the platform leaped to his feet.

"All right, you Interflux bullies! You ignored my phone calls, and you wouldn't answer my letters! And now I'm going to show you that you're not invincible!" She poised her rigid index finger above the detonator button.

Pandemonium broke loose. The spectators all flattened to the ground, and those on the platform threw themselves off, hoping that the side of the stage would serve as cover from the blast.

Mr. Irving grabbed Simon under the arms and hurled him bodily off the platform to safety. Dazed, Simon looked up, unable to believe what his biology teacher was doing. "Hey — " he started to shout, but

his protest was cut off by the flying figure of Cyril Irving, who dove on top of Simon in a selfless attempt to shield his son from the explosion with his own body. He landed with a tremendous crunch just as Miss Glandfield depressed the detonator button.

There was a click, and a spring-loaded pole popped out of a small door in the front of the vest. At the end of the pole, a red flag unfurled. It read: *BOOM*. Tinny recorded music played "Happy Birthday to You."

The scene was as comical as it was bizarre. More than fifteen hundred people lay in various flattened attitudes on the ground, Miss Glandfield stood alone on the platform with a *BOOM* flag sticking out of her stomach, and on the horizon bobbed the running figure of Kyle Montrose, dashing at top speed in a desperate flight from Ground Zero. (He would not surface again for six weeks.)

"There!" shrilled Miss Glandfield in evident satisfaction. "Now you see how vulnerable you are! If this had been a real bomb, there would be no Interflux board of directors! So don't be so smug! Next time it could be someone who's really crazy!"

Cyril Irving stood up, his face redder than Simon had ever seen it. "It *was* someone who's really crazy! *You!*" He wheeled to Mayor Van Doren, who was on all fours. "Arrest that lunatic!"

It was later agreed among the fifteen hundred students of Nassau Arts that Miss Glandfield had rewritten all the record books with this one. And, as always happened in a Glandfield episode, ultimately some

degree of calm was restored. Even Mr. Irving was eventually convinced that there was no such criminal offense as "impersonating a deadly weapon."

Only when the crowd dispersed, and Simon was walking with Sam and Phil to the parking lot, did he have a chance to notice that there were snowflakes in the slightly nippy air.

"Now, what have I been telling you guys all along?" Phil crowed. "Faith! When we owned the land and needed good weather, we had good weather. How long has Interflux had it? Half an hour? A blizzard!"

"I wouldn't exactly call a few flurries a blizzard," Sam pointed out.

Phil opened the door of the wreck and climbed inside. "Give it time. It'll blizz. The point is — faith." He turned the key in the ignition. No response. He tried again. Nothing. "Aw, man — it's the intermittent defect! We could be stuck here for an hour. Maybe two."

By nightfall, it was painfully clear that the intermittent defect had become permanent. The wreck would never start again.

Fifteen

The next week, word came from The Dungeon that Phil Baldwin had officially failed to live up to his potential in everything, and was no longer welcome to study at Nassau Arts.

"I'm allowed to finish out the semester in my academics," he said to Simon and Sam, "but if I come within thirty feet of an art class, they're going to shoot me down like a dog. Coming on top of my wreck, this is a real drag. Thanks a lot, Mr. Copadrick. I hope I get a chance to do something for you some day."

There were a lot of smiles, though, in the halls of Nassau Arts, including Johnny Zull, who had hooked up with a new, "really classy" band called Doofus, and Dave Roper, who had secured himself a part-time job in a bait shop and was back in the worm game. There was even a smile on the highest face in the school. Bill McIntosh had shaken his writer's block and was now working furiously on a sequel, even as publishers continued to turn down *The Legend of the Glass Caves*. He had taken a healthy attitude

toward rejection, commenting, "Stupidity is a disease; I pity them."

The biggest news was that Nathan Kruppman had completed the editing of *Omni*, and had already won the Northeastern Student Film Prize. Scheduled for future student competitions in Chicago, Seattle, San Francisco, Montreal, and Cannes, *Omni* was almost definitely going to clean up across the board, proving that Nathan Kruppman was almost as big a genius as he thought he was.

* * *

The following Monday after school, Simon was dismayed to find a note taped to his locker, asking him to report to Querada's office immediately. His first impulse was to seek out T.C. But then he remembered Sam's experience when Querada set his office on fire. No. No T.C. He would face this on his own.

"Mr. Irving Simon," the artist delivered, along with his intimidating gaze. "Querada has been observing you in class lately, and I get the impression that you are a very unhappy person. It is, of course, finishing fifth in the Vishnik competition which upsets you."

Simon shuffled uncomfortably. "Well, sir, I was kind of expecting to do better. I'm sorry. Maybe next year I can — "

"I have some news for you, Mr. Simon," the artist interrupted. "Next year you will not win the Vishnik Prize either. You will never win the Vishnik Prize."

Simon bit at his lower lip. "But why?"

"Let me tell you a story. When I was a student in Lisbon, there was a very important painting prize.

Year after year, Querada would try for this prize. But I always lost."

"And you learned to live with it?" Simon asked.

"No. To this very day I still curse the names of those who won in my place, especially those who are still alive. You are entirely missing the point. Your Vishnik entry had two ways to go. The judges would see that it was very good, award it the prize, and I would know that you are a good painter. Or the judges would not have the depth to appreciate its subtlety, place it fifth or sixth, and I would know that you are a *great* painter. Mr. Simon, you will never win a Vishnik Prize because you are far too good."

Simon glowed.

"Miss Dixon won by starting with a very ordinary idea and doing exactly what Querada told her to. You, on the other hand, lost because every time I told you how to improve your painting, your mind was already planning the next experiment. And Mr. Stavrinidis — " The teacher raised a huge hand. "Querada does not pretend to understand Mr. Stavrinidis. He has talent, but where it is going is a mystery. But you, Mr. Simon, you I understand, and I will tell you why. I suspected it at first, and now I am positive. You remind me of — of — " Suddenly, great tears rolled down his cheeks to be absorbed by his beard. "You remind me of *Querada!*"

Simon felt that, were he to die at that very moment, he would have no complaints. "Mr. Querada, I really — "

"*Silence!*" The tears were gone without a trace, and

the artist was on his feet, holding a long bony finger an inch and a half from Simon's right eye. "Someday we will work together, but for now, I am Querada, and you are *not!* And if you speak a word of this meeting to anyone, I will kill you as you sleep! So when I see you in class again, you will not sulk. Now go away. Querada has already said too much."

Simon fled the office, hugging the meeting to him like a security blanket. He drove home, but he was sure that he could have covered the distance by floating on the sheer energy of the supreme compliment he had received from Querada.

He let himself in the front door, and was about to call out a greeting when he heard his parents talking upstairs. On his way up to join them, he paused as he realized that the conversation was about him.

"I'm telling you, that kid is something amazing," his father was saying. "He was running Antiflux like a pro."

"And don't forget that he's a wonderful painter," Mrs. Irving put in.

"Everything we threw at him, he threw right back in our faces. And the leadership potential — those kids at school all worship him. He's going to be the best executive Interflux ever had."

"But what about his paintings?"

"He can hang them in his office."

With a smile, Simon tiptoed back downstairs, reflecting that he and his father had covered a lot of ground and had still ended up at progress point zero on the career question. Well, Cyril Irving, there were

still a lot of battles ahead before this war would be decided, but at least now the combatants were identified — on one side, the world's richest and most powerful corporation; on the other, a little talent, a lot of guts, and a six-foot-eight-inch maniac who thought destruction was all a matter of energy levels. It was going to be interesting.

Interesting was the word for it because, for the first time in months, he was actually looking forward to seeing what was going to happen tomorrow instead of worrying about the many problems of today. It even looked like Wendy Orr might not be a dead issue. Her glowing introduction at the ceremony and her friendly greetings in the hall now made him at least seventy percent sure that that had, in fact, been a flush in her cheeks the time he'd mentioned the scene in Nathan's movie. And even though he'd proved it possible to bungle a third chance, passing up number four was right out of the question. Yes, he was definitely going to ask her out again. It was nice to be in the driver's seat for a change, especially for a guy who spent so much time tied up and locked in the trunk. As for the events of the last three months, Simon felt strangely removed from it all, as though he had merely watched the whole business on TV. But it had worked out well for everyone. Everyone except Phil.

At that precise moment, the loud roar of a defective muffler sounded outside. This was followed by the squeal of brakes, and the insistent honking of a car horn. Simon rushed out to see Phil and Sam beaming

at him from the front seat of an ancient Dodge Dart. He beamed back, pleased because they were pleased.

"Now *this* is transportation!" Phil declared proudly as they took Simon out for a spin.

"It's a rust bucket par excellence," Sam corrected, "but my cousin's cat's former owner was selling it for only eight hundred bucks."

"I thought you guys were broke," Simon said.

"That's another thing we came to tell you," Phil said smugly. "I am a man of means. I, who they threw out of Nassau Arts, happen to have just sold a piece of art."

Simon goggled. "Not the cake!"

"Of course not. That was terrible. But a highly prominent citizen of the world has made an offer for 'Technicolor Wheat.' Simon, you'll never guess who."

"Mr. Montrose," said Simon instantly.

Phil seemed annoyed. "How did you know? Never mind. I accepted his offer of a thousand dollars, and put 'Technicolor Wheat' first-class air mail registered to his address in Zaire. I hope it doesn't bust. Where's Zaire?"

"Africa, stupid," said Sam.

"Oh, that's far. It's going to bust. I should have added more toilet paper."

"No great loss," muttered Sam.

Phil was indignant. "You're just jealous, Sotirios, because I'm a professional artist and you're not. Who bought 'Traffic Jam,' huh? What did you get for it? A plaque! With that and fifty cents, you can buy a cup of coffee! I talked to Mr. Montrose on long distance,

and he seems like a totally cool guy. He couldn't believe that I got booted out of innovative arts, so he commissioned me to do a new major project. Man, when it's finished, he's going to pay me twenty-five hundred dollars!"

"You know, Phil," said Simon carefully, "Mr. Montrose can be kind of flaky at times. He's been known to disappear for months. You might not even know where to send the work when it's done."

"Sure I will. Interflux. It's a surprise present for your dad to hang in his new office. So don't say anything to your old man. The contract came in the mail yesterday. I'm considering something along the lines of pumpkins and high-voltage electricity. What do you think?"

Simon swallowed hard. "I haven't seen the new color scheme yet. Uh — so you're over your depression at leaving Nassau Arts?"

Phil shrugged. "In all my experience bombing out, I've made one rule: never look back. Besides, I'm on a roll. You see, I've figured out that if I stink at things I show potential for, I should be great at stuff I stink at. Get it?"

Sam groaned. "Here we go again."

"So last night I was leafing through my mother's *Cosmo*, and I came across this 'test yourself' thing called 'Do You Have What It Takes to Be a Woman Psychiatrist?' And I flubbed that test completely. So now I know exactly what I should be."

"A woman psychiatrist?" Simon asked.

"No! Just a psychiatrist! Don't you see how perfect

it is? No? Well, think about it for a while. It'll come to you."

"Don't think about it," Sam advised. "You'll go crazy."

"See?" said Phil. "I've got patients already."

"Philip, leave poor Simon alone with your lunatic ideas. We're supposed to be showing him the new car."

"Mind your own business, Sotirios! Simon is interested in my career planning, and if you were a real friend, you would be, too!"

"This isn't career planning! This is more stuff you cooked up just to be annoying!"

"Oh yeah?"

"Yeah!"

The car backfired, and suddenly Simon realized that everything was as it should be. When life was bad, it was still better than nothing, and when it was good, a guy might just get lucky enough to end up taking a spin in a 1971 Dodge Dart with two crazy people fighting in the front seat.

Sometimes the great organizing principle of the universe wasn't such a bad guy after all.